Raves for Margaret Fortune's *Nova*:

"There is much to praise about this novel, including its clever rethinking of an SF standby, the interstellar war, and its carefully drawn characters. . . . There are some very nice plot surprises, too, best left unrevealed here, that should give readers some thrills and chills. A super start to what looks like a fine series; readers will be eager for the next installment." —*Booklist* (starred review)

"*Nova* grabbed me from the first chapter, and never let go. What a ride! Unforgettable, fast-paced and original, this book kept me guessing to the end." —Amie Kaufman, *New York Times* bestselling co-author of *These Broken Stars*

"This book definitely scratched my kick-ass teen heroine itch, and it did it in SPACE. That's a perfect combo if I've seen one." —Book Riot

"*Nova*, by Margaret Fortune, is a story of interstellar war taking place in a future that may be distant, but does not feel so far away. Though the locations may be different from what we know, the message and themes of the story are familiar to us all." —Bibliofiend

"I loved the originality of this story and the huge character arc Lia goes through between the first and last pages of the book. I loved the world-building and the details Fortune included to give clues to readers as the book progresses. . . . *Nova* was such a unique and memorable read that I have no doubt I'll jump at the sequel." —The Daily Quirk

"This is an excellent debut. . . . The teenage characters are well developed and avoid cliché. As such, though marketed as adult fare, young readers would enjoy *Nova*, too." —*RT Book Reviews*

"Like a thriller in space . . . extremely accessible to readers who prefer the fiction to the science in the science-fiction genre. We get a good sense of the political tensions without being overloaded . . . And I loved the ending." —The Infinite Curio

NOVA

MARGARET FORTUNE

DAW BOOKS, INC.

DONALD A. WOLLHEIM, FOUNDER

375 Hudson Street, New York, NY 10014

ELIZABETH R. WOLLHEIM

SHEILA E. GILBERT

PUBLISHERS

www.dawbooks.com

Mississippi Mills
Public Library

First paperback printing, June 2016
1 2 3 4 5 6 7 8 9

For my family—Mom, Dad, & Wendy.
Thanks for always believing, even when I didn't.

1 **MY NAME IS LIA JOHANSEN,** and I was a prisoner of war. Taken when Aurora Colony fell, I lived in an internment camp for two years along with ten thousand other civilian colonists. My parents died in front of me from starvation and sickness. And I wept for them.

Or did I?

The memories are fuzzy most days; disjointed and piecemeal, they skitter out from under my grasp, leaving my mind empty-handed and blank. Today it is all I can do to remember my own name, to keep repeating my story over and over again in my head, the way they taught me to.

My name is Lia Johansen, and I was a prisoner of war . . .

Until today.

Standing at the viewport on the forward deck of the *Xenia Anneli*, I watch as the New Sol Space Station slowly draws into view. It's even bigger than I imagined, with two concentric rings connected by spokes to an inner hub shaped like a top. The station spins like a top, too, its lights flashing by like strings of holiday lights in blue and yellow and red. It's magnificent.

Magnificent . . . and frightening.

I reach out and lightly touch the viewport, slowly tracing my index finger along the curve of the upper ring, over the top of the hub. They tell me this place is my freedom. My first step to starting a new life now that a ceasefire has been reached with the Tellurian Alliance and us prisoners released. But how do I start a new life when I can barely remember my old one?

A loud whooshing sound catches me off guard, and I yank my hand back from the viewport in alarm before realizing it's just one of the ship's thrusters guiding us toward the gap between the rings. I glance around, slightly embarrassed by my reaction, though I have reason to be nervous. A door control malfunctioned just a week into the journey and gave me a nasty electric shock. I wasn't badly harmed—a burn on the end of my finger was the extent of my external injuries—but the jolt was enough to make me momentarily black out. Though I came to within seconds, I spent the next day and a half feeling dizzy and out of sorts. It's an experience I'd rather not repeat.

I step back to the viewport again, taking care not to touch anything this time. We are passing between the rings now, and I can see the docking ports straight ahead, positioned in the middle of the hub. The ship begins to turn, moving to align itself with the station's docking bay, and I find myself staring between the rings, at that long spill of ebony space painted with stars.

It's a view I've been staring at for three weeks now, ever since the transport left Tiersten Internment Colony. While the other ex-prisoners quickly grew tired of it, preferring to talk about what life would be like when we reached the station and were repatriated back into the Celestial Expanse, I've remained here at the viewport, watching. Though usually it's the aft deck I stand on, looking back as though there is something on Tiersten I can't let go of, no matter how much I may try. Not that I can remember what that might be.

The ship judders as we lock into place against the station, and the passengers' excited chatter only increases, never mind the captain's piped-in voice exhorting us to stay calm and quiet until the officers come to de-board us. I can't blame them; many of these captives lived in the camp for far longer than I. They have families to find, homes to return to. Not that New Sol is home for most of them. It is only a waystation, a stepping stone into the Celestial Expanse. From here, they will all board transports to every corner of the Expanse, every colony and planet not lost in the war. Everyone but me, that is.

For me, New Sol is the last stop.

I blink, uncertain where the thought came from. A memory tickles at the back of my mind, and I scrabble for it, instinctively sensing its importance . . .

My name is Lia Johansen, and I was a prisoner of war.

The memory is gone, slipped through my mental fingers, and I shake my head. Perhaps New Sol will be my last stop, perhaps not. With Aurora gone and my parents dead, I suppose I will go wherever they tell me to go.

"Attention! Attention, please!"

I swivel my head to the entranceway, craning to see between the two middle-aged ladies behind me. An officer in the crisp black-and-golds of the fleet is giving instructions for our debarkation, and everyone starts forming up into a ragged queue to the door. I fall in line behind the two ladies, my legs aching from an eternity of standing in one place until finally the back of the line begins to move. Following the others through the corridors and into the ship's docking bay, I hesitate as I look through the security scanners and into the station beyond. With a glance back into the transport, I frown. I have the nagging feeling I was supposed to do something. An officer urges me forward, and I shrug. Whatever it was, it's too late now. I step through the docking ring and take my first breath as a free citizen of the Celestial Expanse.

Matte gray walls, metal floor tiling, soft white light. These are the only things I have time to take in before the jostling of the prisoners behind me presses me forward and down the corridor. I glance around to either side as I walk, letting the crowd in front lead me as much as the smiling officers standing at intervals along the passageway. There's little to see in this monotonous hallway, though I do notice two strips of flat blue lights sunk into the floor on either side of the passage, running down the hall as far as I can see. Emergency lights, I wonder, or do they have another purpose?

At the end of the hall, they wave us into what looks like a large cargo bay. They managed to empty or relocate most of the contents before we arrived, and the remaining barrels, bins, and crates have been pushed up against the walls to accommodate us. Despite this, it's still a tight squeeze, long lines of people queued up behind makeshift checkpoints manned by a handful of officers. Many have already sat down on the floor to wait, while others pace in place, the space inadequate to do anything more.

As I join the back of a line to wait, I check out a large screen posted by the other bay entrance. A name and picture flash on the screen. The name and picture of a former prisoner, I realize, its purpose suddenly becoming clear when I catch sight of the crowd waiting behind a tapeline on the other side of the door. I understand now. The screen isn't for us; it's for them. For the stationers who have come to see if their loved ones are part of the lucky few that have been returned. I marvel at how long some of them must have stood there, will stand there, waiting anxiously for that *one* special name to appear. I picture my face and name on the screen.

Lia Johansen.

No family, no relatives; no one will be waiting to claim her.

To pass the time, I listen to the conversations around me. A few feet to my left, a father is telling his children about his family's old house back on Devora Colony. They look so young, I'm sure they don't remember it, even if they have seen it. Ahead of me, the two middle-aged ladies hold hands, unspeaking though they occasionally exchange looks brimming with equal parts hope and disbelief. Perhaps they are listening to the grandmother not far behind us as she sings an old Earth lullaby to the little one on her lap.

Everyone seems to have someone, even if only a friend they made after months, even years of captivity. Everyone except me. After two years on Tiersten, it seems like I should know at least a few of them, but if I do, I don't remember. Of course, there were thousands of prisoners in my camp alone, so I could hardly have known them all. I kept to myself on the transport, turning away from any who spoke to me. No sense getting attached to people I don't remember anyway, and will just lose in the end.

The line inches forward, and I with it. My attention drifts to a pair of soldiers standing along the wall not far from my new position. They appear relaxed as they scan the crowd, but their hands rest on their hips, within easy reach of their weapons. I strain my ears to catch their conversation.

". . . know anyone from the Tiersten Colony?" the first is asking.

The other shakes her head as her gaze takes another pass through the crowd. "Not me. You?"

"My cousin knew someone," the first soldier replies. "Old sweetheart who moved to Aurora just a few years ago."

"Talk about bad timing."

"No kidding. She thinks she's going to start a new life after her divorce, only to end up interned on a prison planet for two years. Assuming she survived the initial invasion, that is. I keep looking for her, but I haven't seen her yet. Of course, this is only a small percentage of the prisoners on Tiersten. What are the chances she'd be one of the lucky five hundred?"

The female snorts. "I'm just surprised the Tellurians are letting any prisoners go at all, with the future of New Earth still up in the air."

"They're probably hoping a few released prisoners will soften us up, make us more open to bargaining. What was it they called it? A goodwill gesture?"

"Goodwill? That'll be the day! One hundred milicreds says the ceasefire doesn't last more than a four-square."

"You're on," the first soldier agrees. "I give it six weeks at least. So did you catch the game two nights ago?"

"No, missed it. Why? Was it good?"

"You'd better believe it. By the end of the first quarter . . ."

The line moves up and the soldiers move down, their conversation lost to my ears. I've been waiting for two hours now, and I'm starting to understand the pacers, so restless that even pivoting in place is better than simply waiting.

To distract myself, I peer around to the head of the line. I'm close enough now to see the officer in charge of my checkpoint. A young man with sandy hair, the insignia on his uniform marks him a lieutenant. And not just a lieutenant, but a member of the Celestial PsyCorp.

A psychic!

I instinctively stumble back a step, narrowly missing the elderly man behind me. My heart speeds up, though I'm not sure why. I'm old enough to know that all the stories about PsyCorp being the boogeyman are just that—stories. Everyone knows that most psychics need direct contact to pick anything up, and even a brief touch won't garner them much more than a sense of your emotions and intentions, and maybe a stray surface thought. Besides, it's not as if I haven't seen a psychic before. I saw one just three weeks ago while boarding the transport off Tiersten. Still, my uneasiness only continues to grow the longer I stare at him, and all I know is that I want to avoid him at all costs.

I'll just switch lines, I decide, slipping out of place and moving toward the next queue. It will mean more waiting, but then, it's not like I have anywhere to go.

Except the officer at the next checkpoint bears the same patterned half-star on her tunic, as does the one at every other checkpoint in the bay. Is that why there are so few checkpoints for so many people? Because they're only using psychics to process the refugees? But why?

The elderly man is kind enough to let me back into line, no doubt assuming I stepped out to use the hygiene facilities at the other end of the bay. Wiping my sweaty hands on my jumpsuit, I reluctantly slide back into my original place. Minute by minute, the line pulls me inexorably forward, closer and closer to the checkpoint just ahead. I'm finding it hard to breathe now. The psychics, the soldiers, the crowds, the walls. This place suddenly feels like a trap, as much of a prison as the one I just left. By the time I reach the front of the line, I'm starting to feel lightheaded, like my head will detach from my body and float away any minute.

"Name, please."

I look down, mouth too dry to speak. He wears no weapon, and yet every nerve in my body is screaming that this man is *dangerous*.

"Miss? Your name?" the officer asks again, fingers hovering impatiently over his tip-pad.

I clear my throat and finally manage to force out the words. "Lia. Lia Johansen."

"Okay, Lia. I need you to lift your head, lean forward, and open your eyes wide."

He's holding a retinal scanner in his hand, a short metal tube about the size of a stylus with a circular scanner on top. Retinal scans are standard practice, a fast and painless way of ascertaining identity, but for some reason the device only heightens my anxiety, as though it is a weapon rather than a tool. I should do as he says, but somehow I can't seem to make myself move.

Cool fingers nudge my chin up. A spark of light bursts in my head and I jerk back, twisting my head away from the touch with a gasp. Fear shoots through me, cold and icy down my back, and even through the din of the bay I can hear my breaths grow ragged and short. I struggle to find the reason, to pinpoint the danger, but a fog rolls over me, pressing down through the cracks in my mind, shrouding my thoughts, smothering my memories, forcing every rational notion into oblivion. My mind goes blank, and for a moment I am gone, lost and adrift without a name, without a memory, without anything to call myself. I scrabble frantically in the fog, searching for something, *anything*, to anchor myself to . . .

"Lia?"

My name is Lia Johansen, and I was a prisoner of war. And I am back.

My heart slows, and finally I turn my gaze back to the officer.

His impatience is gone, his face creased with concern, and I wonder what he saw in my mind in that brief touch to engender such sympathy. For the first time, I look beyond the lieutenant's bars and the half-star on his chest. Though only in his twenties, he looks weary, like a man who has looked into the eyes of too many and seen too much in those depths. His own eyes, a startling shade of blue, shine clear and deep and surprisingly gentle. My gaze flicks to the name spelled out across his breast pocket. *Rowan.*

"Lia, it won't hurt. I promise."

My fear is still there, frothing beneath the surface in frantic eddies, but I have it in check now. Leaning forward, I allow him to pass the scanner slowly in front of my right eye. The device hums, then beeps, and Psy-Lieutenant Rowan glances at the data readout on his tip-pad. He frowns. "Where are you from, Lia? Before you were taken prisoner?"

"Aurora Colony."

He nods, expecting the answer. Aurora's central records were destroyed when the colony was taken, which means anyone born on the colony wouldn't have a ret scan on file or any other personal information. He types some data into his tip-pad, possibly opening a new file for me.

"And your family? Do you have any living relatives here with you from the camp?"

I shake my head. "I only had my parents, and they died at Tiersten."

"I'm sorry," he says, and again I hear that gentle tone, so unexpected. "What about off-planet? Do you have any friends or relatives that weren't on Aurora? Anyone that might take you in?"

"No," I whisper, and again I think of that board of names, those people waiting behind the tapeline.

PsyLt. Rowan pauses for a second, regarding me silently, then finally nods. "Can you tell me your birth date, Lia? Your age?" he adds when I don't immediately answer.

My age? The answer eludes me, and I experience a momentary stab of panic at being put on the spot with a question I should know the answer to, but don't. I force myself to remain calm, breathing a sigh of relief when the number flashes in my head. He smiles when I tell him the date.

"Sixteen? I thought so. You look so much like—" He stops suddenly, a faraway look in his eyes, and shakes his head. "Never mind."

He asks me a few more questions, and I answer as best as I can, watching as he rapidly types the information into his tip-pad, his fingertips as precise as a surgeon's scalpels. He saves the file and codes it into an identity chit the size of my pinky. Loading it into a small insertion gun, he holds out his left hand, palm up. A silent request for my hand, I realize after a second.

Touching him is the last thing I want to do, but I give him my hand anyway, this time prepared for the rush of fear and adrenaline the contact brings. Taking my hand, he turns it over and staples the chit into my palm, right into the fleshy part at the base of my thumb. The metal spikes sink into my skin, and I jump as the chit's biometal filaments unfurl and spread up through my palm to twine themselves into the nerves of my fingers.

"Did that hurt?" Rowan asks with a frown, releasing my hand and absently fingering his own chit.

I cock my head at the question, thinking. *Did* it hurt? The sensation was so brief, I can't place it. Finally, I shake my head. "You just surprised me."

"Sorry," he apologizes. "All right, Lia. You've been temporarily assigned a cot in Cargo Bay 8A. You can use your ID chit to get food in the cafeteria, and here's your sleeping kit. We hope to get everyone a change of clothes within the next couple days, but for now you'll have to make do with what you have from the transport." He shrugs apologetically at my plain gray jumpsuit, then hands me a bedroll wrapped around a towel and toiletry kit. Gesturing toward the entranceway, he offers a few final tips. "The nearest cafeteria is in the main hub, that's here, along the yellow ring on Level Five, and the cargo bay where you're assigned is along the red ring on Level Eight. We've posted a map right outside the bay so it shouldn't be hard to find. For now, we're asking that you stay . . ."

36:00:00

The clock activates so suddenly in my mind, my head involuntarily jerks a bit to the side. The fog vanishes, dissipated in an instant as though it never was. Memories come slotting into place, their edges sharp enough to leave furrows in my mind, and suddenly I know. I know exactly who I am.

My name is Lia Johansen, and I was named for a prisoner of war. She lived in the Tiersten Internment Colony for two years, and when they negotiated the return of the prisoners, I was given her memories and sent back in her place.

And I am a genetically engineered human bomb.

2 RELIEF POURS THROUGH ME AS the last crystal-clear memory clinks into place. After weeks of being enslaved under a cloud of confusion, of second-guessing every thought and double-checking every memory, I am free. My mind clear and my identity assured; my purpose—unquestionable. Even my fears are not so powerful now that I understand them. I stand in the enemy's camp, a genetically engineered human bomb created from some scientist's DNA. All around me are people who would destroy me if only they knew they should, while in front of me stands the man who could reveal me with a touch. No wonder the sight of him was enough to make me panic.

"... can be confusing at first," PsyLt. Rowan is saying, his voice sounding far away to my negligent ear, "but remember that the levels—"

35:59:59

"—have been coded into four sectors—red, yellow, green, and blue—"

35:59:58

"—which each correspond to one of the quadrants of the hub. So if—"

35:59:57

"—you get lost, just look at the floor. Do you under-stand, Lia? Lia?" He reaches out a hand toward me.

Don't let him touch you, don't let him touch you, don't let him touch you!

Attention snapping back to the world around me, I jump back just in time to avoid his hand. "I've got it," I quickly affirm. "Thanks. For everything. I think I can manage."

Even as his brow furrows in concern, I am already nod-ding and stepping away toward the bay entrance. I shiver, recognizing just how close I came to being discovered. With the memory overlay shattered and my true memory restored, all it would take is one touch for him to realize I'm no longer the confused refugee he read before. If I'd let him touch me, or if my clock had started just minutes earlier, before they processed me in . . .

I rub the chit in my palm, remembering the way Rowan took my hand, held my chin. They had orders to touch everyone who came in, I realize. They were look-ing for enemy agents. It is the only explanation for every post being manned by a member of PsyCorp.

"Oh, and Lia?"

My feet freeze only steps away from the entrance. *Did I give myself away somehow?* Every instinct bids me to flee, but I force myself to look back.

Rowan smiles. "Welcome to New Sol Station."

In just under thirty-six hours, this man will die by my hand. He'll perish in a blaze of fire, blown apart in his prime by the very hand he touched, his young life ended after it barely began. This man who showed kindness to an abused refugee who was not what she seemed. Should I feel bad for my part in his demise?

Perhaps Lia would. But I am not Lia.

———

I pause just outside of the cargo bay to get my bearings. I'm standing in a huge circular room at the center of the hub. Sections have been cordoned off for the crowd, leaving makeshift corridors running along the wall and out to the lift station at the center of the room. A few crowd members glance at me hopefully, their faces falling as they realize I'm not their daughter, sister, cousin, friend, but I ignore them. Instead I concentrate on the map posted on the wall.

Thirteen levels make up the Central Hub, all connected by the lift station running down the center. The level I'm currently on, Level Seven, is made up of docking ports, hangars, and cargo bays, as are Levels Six and Eight. The station is a military outpost as well as a colony, and from what I can tell, the hub is primarily for military and transport use. I zero in on the top three levels—Station Control—and file the location away for future reference.

Levels Five and Nine are public levels. They contain the spokes leading out to the two habitat rings, and the space has been devoted to shops, bars, restaurants— places where visitors can eat, relax, and resupply. My stomach rumbles as I notice that both also contain the two hub cafeterias. I check my internal clock, still ticking down one second at a time. Thirty-five hours, forty-six minutes, three seconds. Plenty of time to get something to eat.

Feeling confident of my direction, I head down the roped-off corridor toward the lift station. People call out to me as I pass, wanting to know if I've seen this loved one or that. I keep my eyes forward, not responding to their queries.

"Lia? Lia!"

I keep going, certain the voice is addressing someone else. Lia's parents are dead. She has no family now; no one who would come looking for her.

"Lia Johansen!"

This time I have to stop. There is no mistake; someone is calling *me*. Well, not me, but the person they think I am. Even though I know better, my eyes begin involuntarily scanning the crowd.

"Lia!"

The voice sounds practically in my ear, and I whirl around to find its owner standing right behind me. I step back so quickly I trip over my own feet. Warm hands grab my wrists and right me. Dark eyes, so brown they're almost black, stare back into mine.

I forget to breathe.

It's not that I haven't been touched before, looked at, spoken to. I spent three weeks in the company of five hundred prisoners, after all. Only the contact was always impersonal, that of stranger to stranger. I was no one to them. Not one of them ever looked at me like I was *someone*. Until now.

His hands relax, but don't let go. "It is you," he says softly. "When I saw your name on the list, I didn't really think it would be."

The smart thing would be to tell him I'm not. To deny being who he thinks I am, to push him away and forget about him. I have only one mission, and it doesn't include him. Whoever he is. It's just . . . I don't want him to let go of my wrists. I don't want him to stop looking at me.

I stall for time. "Who did you think I'd be?"

"I don't know. Some other Lia Johansen from Aurora Colony, I suppose."

"Were there that many of us?"

"If there were, none of them mattered but you." He ducks his head, looking embarrassed, and adds, "It's good to see you again, Lia."

"It's good to see you too, Michael."

Michael? The name popped out without thought, but it must be right or he wouldn't be smiling at me. When the overlay shattered, Lia's memories scattered and fell away, disappearing from my conscious mind. I'd thought they were gone for good, but apparently they're still in there, crouching somewhere within the pockets of my mind.

I plumb the depths of my memory, trying to place this Michael. He looks about my age—or rather, Lia's age—but with his skin dark and mine pale, it seems unlikely that we're related. Besides, Lia has no living relatives. A friend, then?

"It's been a long time since those summer days in the park, hasn't it?" he continues. "Seven years now?"

The park.

A playground, grass, white flowers everywhere.

"Higher, Michael! Push me higher!"

"How high, Li-Li?"

"To the sky!"

I blink, surprised by the memory. Now where did *that* come from? In my three weeks aboard the *Xenia Anneli*, I never recalled that. "You used to push L—me on the swings."

He grins. "You always wanted to go higher."

"To the sky," I agree. It's starting to come back now. Michael, from Aurora Colony. Childhood playmates, he and Lia lived next door all their lives until his family left the colony when he was nine. I cried for days after he left.

She, I correct myself. *Lia* cried for days after he left. I have never met Michael, and he has never met me. For the first time, I suddenly feel like the imposter I am. Not because I'm an enemy agent, not because I'm a bomb, but because I'm basking in the warm glow of a gaze meant for someone else. Someone special. Someone who is not me.

In its way, that's even worse than being looked at like I'm no one.

I pull my wrists from his grasp and look away, suddenly all too aware that they aren't my hands Michael is holding but Lia's. "I should go," I say, careful to avoid his eyes as I begin edging around him. "Thanks for coming to see me."

He doesn't take the hint, falling into step beside me as I head for the lift station. "Where are you going? Maybe I can show you the way."

"The cafeteria, but I can fi—"

"Oh, sure. You must be hungry after traveling all day. Come on, we'll go up to the one on Five."

We? "That's okay, you don't—"

"There's one on Nine, too," he continues, reaching out to take my sleeping kit before I even realize what he's about, "but Five always has better desserts."

Somehow our positions have gotten reversed, and now instead of Michael following me to the lift, I'm following him. I trail behind him, uncertain how to detach myself from him now that he's so neatly taken charge.

The lift station is essentially a giant metal pulley that is continually in motion, one side always going up while the other goes down. I watch as the man in front of us steps onto a platform sliding up a track in the pulley as it comes level with the floor, briefly touching the metal pole to steady himself as the lift continues up. Glancing down the hole, I hesitate as the next platform comes into view. As if sensing my uncertainty, Michael grabs my hand and steps on, pulling me with him.

On instinct, I latch onto the metal pulley only to find that I don't really need it. The lift isn't moving particularly fast, and besides, the platform is surrounded on three sides by waist-high glass walls. The crowd shrinks as the lift bears us up and away. We pass the thick metal divider that serves as both floor and ceiling, and then we're gliding into Level Six, which looks similar to Seven, but without the crowd or roped-off areas. I barely have time to take it in before we're passing the next divider into Five. I'm so intrigued by the ride, I would have forgotten to get off if not for Michael's hand tugging me along.

I pause next to the lift, watching as the platform disappears through the hole in the ceiling. "What happens if you don't get off at the top floor?" I ask nervously.

"I guess we'll have to try it sometime," Michael answers with a shrug.

My eyes widen, visions of being smashed into the ceiling or pitched off at the top abounding in my head. Michael suddenly grins.

"Don't worry, we won't go splat. I promise."

No, not splat. Just *boom.*

I mentally check my internal clock. Thirty-five hours, twenty-eight minutes, three seconds, and then . . .

Nova.

They told me what it would be like, when I finally go. It will begin with a stretchy feeling in my mind, as if my brain is being thinned out, flattened and pulled taut like skin over a drum. My vision will go next, the world around me blurring as sparkles of silver and gold begin dancing in my eyes. Then my heart will begin pounding— it will have to, to force the chemicals through my bloodstream and into my chest where they will meet and ignite. The chemicals come from my arms, one from a sac engineered into my left forearm, the other from my right. Separate, they are completely benign, undetectable by any security system, but together they have the power to take down this entire station.

I'll know that the chemicals have been released into my bloodstream when I feel a burning sensation in each arm. It won't be long then. My eyes will go completely blind, vision obscured by a million glittering sparkles as the chemicals combine under the furious pumping of my heart, and then it will all go white. Brilliant, dazzling white the likes of which no one has ever seen before. It will be glorious.

So they tell me, anyway. Of course I have never experienced it for myself. Yet.

I give Michael a sideways glance. It's a shame he'll never get to feel what I'll feel, to see what I'll see, to experience what I'll experience. To know the awe-inspiring power of going Nova. At least, he'll still get to be a part of it like everyone else on the station, I remind myself. Just not the way I will.

Michael is waiting for me, lips quirked in an expression I can't fathom as he studies me. Does he know I'm not Lia? If anyone could tell, surely it would be her childhood friend. But he only waves a hand at the area around us and asks, "Shall we?"

I nod and follow Michael away from the lift station and into Level Five. Compared to the relative quiet of Six, Five is a veritable hive of activity. The area is divided by four wide concourses marked by floor lights in red, yellow, green, and blue. They jut out from the lift station in the shape of a cross, each one leading to a spoke that connects the habitat ring to the hub. Between the concourses, shops and eating establishments vie for space with pop-up kiosks and traders with the odd grav-sled of merchandise to sell. Military officers in black and gold mix with colonists and station visitors, and I even see some refugees wandering around the floor, their origin easily denoted by their gray jumpsuits. It's a good thing I have Michael to guide me, for I would be lost within the shuffle in a second without him.

He leads me through the bustle with unerring direction, skirting a couple kiosks and drawing me down a corridor between an Ionian restaurant and a clothing store. As we move away from the kiosks at the center of the level, the din quiets a bit, the outer reaches of the circle filled with more sedate lounges and bars. I glance at the floor and spy yellow emergency lights set into the decking. Yellow Quadrant.

The cafeteria is tucked into the back arc, its patrons a mix of military personnel and refugees. Apparently I wasn't the only one who was thinking of food after being processed in. Tucking my sleeping kit under his arm, Michael grabs a tray for me.

"So what do you like?"

I take the tray and look around at the dizzying array of food, not entirely sure how to answer. I was engineered without a true sense of taste, or smell for that matter. To me everything gives off the same odor: a pale sour-and-sweet tang that tickles around the edges of my nostrils and lays lightly across my tongue. Only the intensity varies. The odor was persistent on the transport. Here in the cafeteria, it is hardly noticeable.

The lack of smell or taste hardly mattered on the transport. The soldiers offered us no choice, and it was either eat what they gave us or go hungry. While I recognize most of the dishes, I have little preference for one over the next.

Food holds no pleasure for me. It is a means to survive, nothing else. I suppose I could choose based on nutritional content, but there seems little point when I have less than thirty-six hours of existence left. I try to think back to what I ate before the transport ship, but for some reason I can't call to mind a single meal I had before boarding.

Shrugging, I choose a medley of items: a piece of chicken, a stalk of celery, an orange, some fries. Michael raises his eyebrow when he catches sight of my plate.

"I thought you hated celery."

I do? I struggle for an answer. "They gave us lots of celery on Tiersten. I guess I got used to it."

"They did? Celery? Glitchy." Michael shakes his head, then shrugs and helps himself to a piece of cake from the bakery corner.

After swiping our chits for the cashier, we find a place at a small table in the corner. I concentrate on my food, using it as an excuse to stay silent. With Lia's memories submerged firmly beneath the surface, I don't dare talk any more than I have to. It would be too easy to say something Lia would not.

To my surprise, Michael seems just as uneasy, his earlier confidence somehow diminished now that we are sitting face-to-face with nothing to do but talk. He drums his fingers on the table.

"You're so quiet," he finally says.

"I am?"

"When we were kids, you never stopped talking. My mom used to say you were a regular little chatterbug."

Just by staying silent I have erred. I search my mind for Lia, hoping to find the words she might say, but she's not there. I shrug uncomfortably. "Things change."

It's not a great answer by any means, but he seems to accept it.

"I noticed your parents' names weren't on the list," he adds carefully. "Are they . . . ?"

My parents died in front of me from starvation and sickness.

His eyes widen, and I realize I spoke the words aloud, the catchphrase automatically tumbling from my mouth before my brain could even process it. "I'm sorry," Michael says. "I really liked your parents. You must miss them a lot."

"I wept for them."

Another manufactured answer, for I have no other. I have no sentiments of my own; no words besides the ones they put in my head. Even my name is not my name, but another girl's treasured possession, now taken and bestowed on me. And like any piece of stolen property, it has been worn in by the original owner, and I know it will never fit me quite as well as it did her.

We eat in silence, or at least attempt to eat, Michael poking at his cake with his fork and me absently swirling a slice of orange in my ketchup before I catch myself and surreptitiously stick it in my mouth. Would the real Lia be this tongue-tied if it were she meeting Michael again for the first time in seven years?

Michael glances around, as if hoping a topic will condense out of thin air, and his eyes fall on my tray. "You never got dessert," he exclaims.

"Oh, well—"

"That was the whole point of coming up to Five, remember? The desserts. Here, try some of mine," he offers, stabbing his fork into the uneaten side and holding it out at me.

"I really don't—"

I duck my head at the same time he jabs the fork forward, and instead of the cake going in my mouth, it ends up all over my nose. Michael starts apologizing, and for a moment I freeze, unsure what the protocol is for a situation like this. I only know that I don't want him to feel bad.

I tentatively reach up and catch a daub of frosting on my finger, then stick it in my mouth. Michael's stricken look slowly dissolves into a grin, a chuckle coming out of his mouth as he asks, "How is it?"

It tastes exactly like the ketchup. Which is to say, it doesn't taste like anything at all.

"It's really good," I tell him, accepting the napkin he offers and wiping off my nose.

Somehow I did the right thing, because as Michael starts telling me a story about his first time at the station cafeteria, his easygoing manner suddenly returns. He eats some of my fries, and I nibble on his cake, content to just listen and nod.

After a while he stops, shaking his head in self-deprecation. "Listen to me. Now I've become the chatterbug."

I shrug. "I don't mind."

He gives me a look I can't read, then busies himself gathering up our trays and plates. I grab my sleeping kit, and together we bus our table and head out of the cafeteria. We wander along the outer edge of the level until we reach the concourse at the edge of the quadrant, one side bordered with yellow lights, the other green. Sliding doors at the end of the concourse periodically open to let people come and go from spoke to hub and vice versa. Michael jerks his head toward the doors.

"I should probably go before Gran starts to worry." He hesitates. "I'm really glad to see you again, Lia. Maybe I could come by tomorrow? Where are you staying?"

I think back to PsyLt. Rowan's directives. Cargo Bay 8A.

"With the refugees in Cargo Bay 7C," I tell him.

"Okay, great." He raises one hand in a wave as he takes a couple backward steps down the concourse. "See you later, Lia."

34:17:02

No, Michael, I think as he strolls through the doors and disappears, *you won't.*

3 **MY CONFIDENCE RETURNS** the moment Michael walks out the door. The last hour was difficult, confusing, me trying to put on a performance without knowing the lines. Now that he's gone, everything is clear again. My identity, my purpose, my existence. They are all one and the same.

I take the concourse back to the lift station, drifting along among all the others coming and going. No one pays any attention to me, a pale, sixteen-year-old refugee who is small for her age, but I pay attention to them, examining their clothes, analyzing their movements, listening to their conversations.

"... have those reports to the colonel by eighteen-hundred ..."

"... afford to get behind schedule, what with the *Santa Maria*'s arrival in a few weeks ..."

"Our docking pass expires in three hours. We have to secure that shipment ..."

"... so I told him, not on my milicred, he's not ..."

A woman in a flowing red dress, its hues rippling in time with her movements, sweeps past me complaining of a produce sickness in hydroponics, and the white-haired man with her mentions Chinese cabbage. Their words hold no meaning for me, all part and parcel of lives I have never lived and could never comprehend. Perhaps that is why they intrigue me so.

I reach the lift station, but instead of joining the busy line to go down, I step on a platform going up. No one else is headed in this direction, the platforms above and below me all empty as far as I can see. I pass the divider and Four comes into view, an administrative level with offices and conference rooms. It holds no interest for me, and I crane my head up, watching as the lift comes even with the ceiling and then slides into Three. Station Control.

Getting off, I find myself in a small vestibule created by four metal walls completely enclosing the lift. Aside from a bench, an artificial plant, and a piece of framed artwork, the room is empty. A keypad and retinal scanner are mounted by each of the two doors. Clearly not just anybody can enter this level.

Climbing back on the lift, I ride up to Two, which is an exact match for Three, except for the artwork. I let my fingers drift over the keypad, wondering if it will spark a memory, an instruction of some kind, but it doesn't. Dropping my hand, I turn back toward the lift just as the door slides open and an officer comes striding through. He collides with me before I can avoid him, and I jump back from the contact, nose wrinkling as the sour-and-sweet odor sharpens. He must be wearing a pungent cologne.

"What are you doing up here? This level is for technicians and military personnel only." He narrows his eyes, taking in my jumpsuit with a suspicious look.

My mind flips back to my conversation with Michael. *Don't worry, we won't go splat. I promise.*

"I just wanted to see if it was true," I answer.

"True?"

"That if you forget to get off the lift at Level One, you'll go splat into the ceiling."

He lets out a bark of laughter. "Who told you that?"

I shrug. "Some boy on Level Five. He dared me to come up and try it, but I got scared, so I got off at the last minute."

His suspicion is gone, replaced with reluctant amusement. "Kids," he grunts. "If I had a milicred for every time I've heard that."

I tense up as he puts a hand on my shoulder and gives me a gentle shove toward the lift, but my quick search reveals no half-star on his uniform. I let him guide me around to the down side.

"Go back to your friends, kid, and try to stay out of trouble. Remember, we can always find you if you stray," he says, tapping meaningfully on his palm chit. I look at my own. So it's not just an identity and credit device, but a tracker as well. Of course.

The officer watches me while I wait for the next down platform. As I'm getting on, he grudgingly calls out, "If you really want to explore, you could try Level Thirteen. There's an ob—"

His words are cut off as the platform descends below the floor. Not that it matters. I have no interest in poking around the station like some curious child away from home for the first time. Not unless it will aid my mission in some way. I search my mind for instruction; surely my makers left me with some sort of direction for carrying out my assignment.

Nothing surfaces.

Uneasiness fills me, but I shrug it off. I'm sure if there was something I needed to know, I would remember it. Again, that nagging sensation flits through me that there was something I was supposed to do on the transport.

I let the thought go. It doesn't matter now. Thirty-three hours, fifty-five minutes, forty-nine seconds. In mere hours, nothing will matter anymore.

The levels float by, one after another, and I think about my next move. With so much time at my disposal, I might as well find my quarters and set down my sleeping kit.

Getting off the lift on Eight, I thread my way through a group of refugees and set off in search of Cargo Bay 8A. By some luck, I manage to find it without too much trouble. The bay looks similar to the one where PsyLt. Rowan processed me a couple short hours ago, with cargo pushed up against the walls to make way for rows of cots laid out in the middle of the floor. Well, rows more or less. With the arrival of the refugees, bunches of cots have been pulled together in clusters, blankets propped up with makeshift supports to create small bits of privacy within the vast space.

An officer peels away from the wall as I step farther into the bay. "Chit, please?"

I hold out my palm, and he scans it with his tip-pad. "Johansen, Lia. Yes, Cargo Bay 8A is correct. Hygiene units are in those corners there"—he points—"and there. Take any bunk you want."

"They're not assigned?"

"Well, that was the original plan, but . . ." He grimaces and waves a hand at the chaos.

Ah. With an understanding nod, I locate an empty cot in the corner near an elderly couple. By some miracle they are asleep, harsh light and the noise of the crowd notwithstanding, their cots pushed together and their hands entwined. In the grip of sleep, they don't look like refugees sacking out in a cargo bay teeming with people, but a couple at home in their own bed, each secure in the knowledge that they are not alone. Feeling strangely like I'm somehow intruding, I push my cot up against the wall as far as I can.

My sleeping kit contains bedding—a thin mattress, sheets, and a blanket—which I lay out on my cot. I look at my new bed a bit longingly, exhausted though it's only midday by station time, but knowing I have no chance of finding rest in this noisy maze. Too bad I'm no longer Lia. Lia could curl up in this nest and be asleep within a minute. She could sleep anywhere. I'm sure she wouldn't feel the sharp edge of unease dogging her steps every moment since the memory overlay shattered.

Since I can't sleep, I join the line for the hygiene units. The wait for the showers is long, but it's worth it even though all I have to put on afterward is my spare change of clothes from the transport, which aren't much cleaner than what I already have on. At least my hair is clean again, the once-filthy ponytail now falling in damp strands over my back.

For the next several hours, I pass the time as best I can. After combing out my hair as slowly as possible, I take a turn around the bay, scouting my temporary home. I find nothing of particular interest, though by late evening the stationers have set up a makeshift laundry service, collecting dirty jumpsuits and passing out the first batch of clean clothes some of us have seen in weeks. Their supply is exhausted by the time I reach the front of the line, but they take my other jumpsuit with a scan of my chit and a promise of a clean replacement by the following morning. Afterward, I catch a second meal in the hub cafeteria, this time going down to the one on Nine just for a change of scene. Michael was right; the selection of desserts on Five is far superior to that on Nine. Not that it matters to me, of course. It's simply an observation.

To my surprise, the bay is quiet when I return from my meal. The lights are dimmed and a feeling that could

almost be described as restful has descended over the
room. Most of the refugees are sleeping, or at least pretending to, and the ones who aren't keep their voices low
in deference to the others. A screen on the wall shows
the time: 2349. Almost midnight. No wonder everyone
has finally settled down.

I lie down on my cot and pull my blanket over me.
The past few hours have been about marking time until
the end, nothing more. I check my internal clock.

26:22:13

Just a little over a day to go; the station will be sleeping when I make my final exit.

I like that—the station quiet and still, my final moments a meditation before I go up in a blaze of sound.
The idea feels peaceful, serene. Safe. I close my eyes and
let the thought slowly lull me to sleep. And when I
dream, I dream of white.

Pure, brilliant, dazzling white.

————

When I wake the following morning, I'm pleased to see
I've slept almost ten hours. Lines are long for both the
laundry and hygiene units, but I don't mind. Every minute that passes is another minute drawing my wait
nearer to a close. Perhaps I should feel differently. Perhaps I should cling to every second I have, dig my fingernails into each moment until the pressure of time's
passing rips it from my hands. This is what Lia would
do—fight for her life with every breath.

Of course, Lia's purpose was to live. Mine is to die.

Mindful of Michael's promise to come see me today,

I keep an eye out for him as I emerge from the bay, ready to melt back into the crowds should I see him. I do not want to meet Michael again. His presence only complicates things, confuses them when they would otherwise be clear. In his way, I can't help sensing he's almost as dangerous as PsyLt. Rowan, though I don't understand how.

It doesn't matter, for I never see him. Not when I slip down to Nine for some breakfast, or later, as I wander aimlessly through the levels, my itchy feet unable to stay still. My misdirection was successful, or else he didn't care enough to come find me again. The reason isn't important.

Despite my disinterest in exploring, my restlessness is enough to make me look around anyway. With One through Three blocked off, Four nothing besides offices, and Five and Nine already known quantities, I spend a good deal of my time on Six, Seven, and Eight. The three levels are mainly taken up with docking rings, landing bays, and more cargo holds. A customs office at the center of the hub does a brisk business processing in new arrivals and issuing various station permits, their dealings mostly with the array of freighters and passenger liners stopping off to deliver their goods and take on new ones. No one seems to notice me in the bustle, everyone in a hurry to get where they're going, whether they're returning home after a long trip or dropping off cargo or just looking to kick back in a good bar for a much-deserved rest. It's no wonder my creators thought a sixteen-year-old girl would be the ideal operative.

It is only mid-afternoon—eleven hours, ten minutes, fifty-nine seconds to go—so I take the lift down to the lower levels. A cursory glance shows Ten to be a barracks for select military personnel, so I head down another floor. My heart practically stops when I see the half-star emblazoned on the doors leading from the glass vestibule into Eleven. PsyCorp.

I don't even bother to get off the lift, but let myself continue riding down.

Twelve and Thirteen are the bowels of the hub, the facilities that keep the rest of the place going. Not power, which I presume is on one of the top levels, but everything else. Waste management, in particular, seems to be the staple of Thirteen, though I don't get very far before a worker in coveralls and a face mask stops me. He makes a face when I tell him that an officer suggested I might find the level interesting. His expression suddenly clears.

"Oh, he must have meant downstairs." He stares at me for a moment and finally nods. "Okay, come on. Just don't be telling all of your little friends about this place, huh? We can't have an influx of refugees coming down here and making a mess of things."

The worker leads me down a corridor to the outer edge of the level and opens a door in the wall. A staircase on the other side descends to a space just below. I immediately understand why they didn't bother to designate it a level. The area is small, the ceiling barely high enough for a grown man to stand without bending over. Pipes run along the ceiling and crates are stashed in erratic stacks throughout the area—unofficial storage for the personnel that work down here, I would guess.

The worker leads me through the labyrinth to a trap door in the middle of the floor. With a twist of a handle, he throws back the hatch and unrolls a rope ladder down into the hole.

"Have at it, sweetheart. Just make sure to roll up the ladder and close the hatch when you're done, okay?"

I watch his retreating back, my forehead furrowing in

a frown as I wonder just what's down there. There don't seem to be any lights inside the long, narrow tunnel; nothing to show what's below. For a moment I hesitate. Then sitting at the edge of the opening, I grasp the ladder and carefully inch my way down. My feet hit the decking below, and I gasp.

Space. I am hanging in the middle of space.

It surrounds me in every direction, blackness punctuated only by a million points of lights with nothing to stand between me and it.

I instinctively grasp for the ladder, heart thudding in panic before I realize there must be walls around me or I would have already been frozen by the vacuum of space. Letting go of the ropes, I move forward until my hands encounter glass, curved and round and impossibly clear. Even the floor is glass, or at least a substance remarkably like glass, for I can see the stars beneath my feet. It is the ultimate observation deck, this little room no more than five feet in diameter. A window into the heavens themselves.

I stare out into the abyss, and I instinctively know this view is Lia's. That if she were standing here right now, her memories in my head and her past in my heart, my soul would be bursting with wonder and joy and awe and amazement.

It would, except Lia is no longer here. I am, and I feel nothing. Nothing at all.

———

00:30:00

I sit on my cot and watch the minutes count down toward the end.

00:29:59

00:29:58

00:29:57

Not quite a half hour left, and I can't think of a single thing I want to say, a single thing I want to do.

00:25:34

00:25:33

00:25:32

If I have a specific target, I do not know it. If there's somewhere else I'm supposed to be, I am not there.

00:21:12

00:21:11

00:21:10

In all likelihood, it doesn't matter where I am when I go Nova. The chemicals in my arms, when properly mixed, have more than enough power to take down the hub, and the rings with it.

00:18:56

00:18:55

00:18:54

This cargo bay is as good a place to go as any, and perhaps better than most, with the darkness breathing softly around me, its thick arms enfolding me in its tender shroud. It's as close to a grave as I will have.

It is enough.

00:15:03

00:15:02

00:15:01

At the fifteen minute mark, it begins.

My mind suddenly goes lax, as though my brain has been wrapped taut around a spool and only now is loosed. I let it reel out within my head, expanding, stretching, lengthening. The sensation is curiously pleasurable, and I let myself sink into the moment. If anything, the spool only seems to unwind faster with my acquiescence.

00:12:52

I feel a shivering sensation in my left eye and then a gleam of light—so impossibly bright!—pops into my vision. For a second it is alone, one tiny speck dancing across my vision. Then a second one sparks, gold and twisting, across the corner of my eye, and then another, and another. Gold spots are flickering across my right eye now, and the cot across from me begins to blur, skewing and sliding within the metallic froth. *So beautiful, so brilliant!* Like holding a star before your eyes and looking into it until your retinas burst.

00:10:03

My heart is racing now. It pulses within my chest, squeezing like a fist pumping rhythmically open and closed, open and closed. I struggle to breathe, my lungs heaving with the effort, but it is a good struggle, like the sprint at the end of a long race, when your mind is fixed only on covering those last few hundred meters and making it to the finish. I can barely see, barely think, barely breathe, and yet I feel like I could fly.

00:06:53

I look down at my forearms, not that I can see much of anything anymore. Just like they said, heat begins to warm the inside of my skin. It is happening; my sacs are opening, the chemicals are releasing! My destiny is here, my fate come to—

A sharp pain clubs my head so hard I almost fall off the cot.

I gasp and grab my temple, twisting my head and searching wildly for the source of the blow.

A second strike lashes me behind the eyes, and it's only now that I realize the pain came from the inside, not the outside. My arms are hot now; more than hot, they are burning with the heat of an open flame licking across my skin. I cry out, pain forcing me from my silence.

This isn't right! It's not supposed to feel like this!

The sparkles in my left eye suddenly go out, the silver stars turned to dark embers roiling about in the black field of my vision. Fear courses through me, pulsing erratically out of sync with my pounding heart.

Something is wrong. Something is very, very wrong.

Fire rages across my arms, the pain so great only my clenched teeth are keeping me from screaming. I tear at my sleeves.

Water!

I roll off my bed, stumbling blindly toward the hygiene units, my only thought to find relief for the searing heat under my skin. My feet hit half a dozen cots on my way, tripping me up and nearly spilling me onto more than one sleeper. A chorus of annoyed murmurings mark my passage, but I ignore them, concentrating only on my destination. I reach the first unit and wrench open the door.

00:03:22

I fumble for the taps, but my hands don't seem to want to work anymore. Little growls issue from my mouth, rising in pitch and volume with each passing second. Even in my agony I can't help remembering—*I must not be heard.*

In desperation, I turn my face and sink my teeth into my shoulder, letting the cloth of my jumpsuit muffle the sounds. If it hurts, I do not notice.

A gray fluid, filthy and heavy, begins pooling over my right cornea like a spilled slick of oil—*white, where is my promised white?*—and I feel my legs give out, dumping me to the floor in a tangle of useless limbs. And that's when I finally realize the truth.

I'm a *dud.*

The last thing I know before everything falls silent is a voice, singsong and high, echoing in my mind.

"Cross your heart and hope to die, stick a needle in your eye."

Then everything goes black.

4 *MY NAME IS LIA JOHANSEN, and sky roisters seven larynx beta nine 0001001110000 01110001 0111111100111001*

Error: Sequence Code 248903489
Re-sequencing initiated

My name is Lia Johansen, and I was umbrella avalanching mirrored park lambda eighteen 0111000000 1011111 10001 1100 11000000111

Error: Sequence Code 248903489
Re-sequencing initiated

My name is Lia Johansen, and I steady steady making over upon above camp 00000001 11101100 11000000 101010

Error: Sequence Code 248903489
Re-sequencing initiated

My name is Lia ssfft gibbets size quark 00000000110011 111111110001 010001000 11

Error: Sequence Code 248903489

Re-sequencing initiated

My name is &*###*&^^^^^ 000111011111 1101 11100000001 1000000100000 00001111

Error: Sequence Code 248903489
Re-sequencing initiated

Error: failure to re-sequence

Re-sequencing initiated
Error: failure to re-sequence

Initiating Emergency Shut-down

Shut-down initiated
Shutting down . . .
Shutting down . . .
*Shutting down . . .

*****

5 **MY EYES ARE ALREADY OPEN** when I wake.

One moment I am gone and the next I am here, staring out at a matte gray fog. Not white, not black; just flat, opaque gray. My pupils instinctively try to adjust, but I can see nothing beyond the veil.

It does not matter.

The backs of my eyeballs begin to sting, and I reflexively blink. Fluid gushes down my cheeks, and with its exodus my sight returns in a shock of sensation.

I am sprawled on the floor of the hygiene unit, my shoulder cramped uncomfortably against the toilet, my left leg asleep where it twists awkwardly beneath my right. My body aches and my head pounds, and pain, true pain, radiates from my forearms. I muster up the energy to turn one arm over. It looks normal. So does the other when I examine it. I feel faintly surprised at the observation. The pain was so bad—is still so bad—I expected to find twin burns on both forearms. Something, at least, to mark the agony.

My sacs did not release like they were supposed to, the activated chemicals burning my arms when they found no outlet into my bloodstream. No wonder the pain was so great, with such a defect in my manufacture.

Defective. That is what I am. Flawed. Imperfect. Broken, like a piece of garbage tossed carelessly on the floor until someone gets around to throwing it away. I look in my head for my clock, not even sure if I will find it.

00:02:33

I watch the time, counting the seconds silently in my head. One thousand and one, one thousand and two, one thousand and three, one thousand and four . . .

00:02:33

My lips keep mouthing the counts, but the numbers don't turn. I am stuck. Frozen in time, just two and a half minutes away from nirvana. In my short time on the station as myself, it never once occurred to me that I might be a—

No! I will not say it, I will not even think it—

Dud.

The word doesn't bring the expected pain, only emptiness. A whispered resignation that can't be denied. My identity, my purpose, my existence—they are all one and the same.

Nothing.

I wonder why I even woke again at all.

For a long time, I just lay there, staring at the wall, my eyes caught in some strange trance my mind seems unable to break. Eventually I become aware of voices just outside the door.

". . . busy morning and there are a lot of units. Maybe someone slipped in while you weren't looking."

"I'm telling you, I've been in line for forty-five minutes and *no one* has gone in or out of this unit."

A sigh. Then a soft knock sounds on the door. "Hello? Is anyone in there?"

I have no choice now. I can either come out or they can come in.

"I—I'll be out in a minute," I manage to call after a couple false attempts. My voice sounds rough, my throat raspy after a night exposed to the dry station air, but it's serviceable enough.

"There, you see?" I hear the male voice tell the other. The female's response is muttered, too low for me to hear, but their footsteps do retreat.

Standing is difficult, but doable. I limp the couple steps to the sink, stretching my leg to try to get rid of the pins and needles, and gaze into the mirror. It's a good thing I didn't open the unit door. I am enough of a shock to myself; a casual bystander would find me appalling.

Thick globules of fluid are crusted in the folds around my eyes, the gray gunk echoing the gray of my eyes and congealing in my lashes. Streaks down my cheeks show where the liquid, whatever it was, ran down my face, and when I look down, I see more stains on my jumpsuit and collarbone. It is in dull contrast to the sharper reddish-brown blood coating my lip and chin, and dribbled over the corners of my mouth. I tentatively shift my mouth around and feel clotted remnants inside as well. I must have bitten my tongue sometime last night without even realizing it.

Turning on the taps, I cup my hands under the water and rinse out my mouth, spitting half-dried chunks of red out with each mouthful. I turn my attention to the rest of my face after that, unzipping the top half of my jumpsuit and using the tail of my undershirt to rub at the various stains. Despite some vigorous scrubbing, though, the gray stains around my eyes are still there, faint smudges that make me look dull and exhausted. Even the whites of my eyes have a grayish cast to them. I look haggard by the time I'm finished, with dark circles under my eyes and skin that looks much too pale, but I am decent at least. Not out of place for a traumatized refugee who spent two years in an internment camp.

Or a genetically engineered human bomb who spent the night malfunctioning on the floor of a hygiene unit.

As I smooth my shirt back into place, I notice a nasty bite mark in my shoulder, in the fleshy part just above the armpit. A corresponding tooth hole peeks through the fabric of my jumpsuit. I blink at it. Did I do that? I must have. I don't remember that, though. I wonder what else I did last night that I don't recall.

The showers are located in the other block of hygiene units, but I use the toilet and clean the rest of myself up as best as I can using only the soap and water from the taps. My clothes look presentable enough once I put them in order. Everyone's clothes are so dirty and worn by this point that a few gray stains, a couple drops of blood, and a tooth hole blend right in. My hair, too, looks okay once I pull out my ponytail and tuck the bloody ends into a messy bun.

My ablutions finished as much as they can be, I reluctantly turn toward the door. My fingers hover over the latch. It's locked: another thing I don't remember doing, though it's lucky I did or I would have been found passed out on the floor and hauled to the infirmary—and then to security. There's no way I could pass a medical examination without being discovered for what I am.

For some reason, I expect everyone to be staring at me when I emerge from the unit, as though they will see me and immediately realize what I've been through, but I garner surprisingly little interest. Even the complaining female from earlier doesn't seem to be around, probably already having snagged another unit.

The cots near mine are mercifully empty, their occupants already up and about. I sink down onto my bed and stare dully at the wall. What does a genetically engineered human bomb do once she discovers she's a dud? Will someone come looking for me when they realize the station didn't blow? Or will they simply wash their hands of me, write me off as dead or as good as?

I search my mind, trying to recall what they told me to do if anything went wrong. I find nothing. No troubleshooting techniques, no contingency plans, no instructions on how to reach them. I cannot even remember who "they" are. No names, no faces, no voices. Fear courses through me, and I struggle to recall one—just *one!*—memory from before I boarded the transport here.

I can't think of a single thing.

Impossible! I didn't spring to life on the ship; I must have come from somewhere. The internment camp? No, that's Lia's past, not mine. The few memories I bore of that place were all hers, and now that she's gone from my head I don't even have those. Even my name—Lia. I do not ever remember having another, and yet how could I have passed sixteen years without one? It's as though my past has been completely wiped from my memory. But how? *Why?* Is this a symptom of my malfunction, or have I never known the answers? I'd like to believe it's the former, but in my gut I can't help fearing it's the latter. That they sent me in here with nothing but a mission and a head full of some dead girl's memories, and now that both have failed me, I really am nothing.

I really am no one.

I laugh. Why should I be someone? I was meant to die seven hours ago—dead girls don't need names. Dead girls don't need pasts. Every minute I live now is a min-

ute I was never meant to exist. So many minutes. I have
no idea what I'm supposed to do with them. *Supposed* to
do! I was *supposed* to go Nova! And now that I haven't,
there's nothing I'm meant to do. Nothing at all.

So nothing is what I do.

Lying down on my cot, I curl up in a ball and pull my
blanket up over my head. I stare into the darkness—not
resting, not sleeping, just . . . lying.

Before I close my eyes, I check my clock one last
time.

00:02:33

Still unmoving.
I do not get up again for a long time.

6 EYES OPEN.

00:02:33

Eyes closed.

7 EYES OPEN.

00:02:33

Eyes closed.

8 EYES OPEN.

00:02:33

Eyes closed.

"LIA? ARE YOU AWAKE?"

Eyes open.

00:02:33

Eyes closed.

"Lia?"

I open my eyes again. No, I am not dreaming. Michael really is here, standing over my cot, an uncertain expression on his face.

"I'm sorry. Did I wake you?"

Yes. No. I don't know. Go away.

The words don't seem to make it from my brain to my mouth, for he continues to stand there, staring at me expectantly. Maybe the defect has spread; maybe I can't actually speak anymore. I *am* a dud, after all. For that matter, maybe my entire body is shutting down, piece by piece, and one day I won't be able to move at all.

Can I move?

Reflexively, I try to sit up. My torso swings upright, the muscles stiff but still functional. My voice dribbles out in a croak. "How did you find me?"

Michael immediately plops down on the cot next to my legs, "How did you find me?" apparently translating to "Make yourself at home" in his head.

"Well," he says, "Wednesday I came by the bay on

Seven, just like I promised, only I couldn't find you any-where. I figured I probably just missed you, so I hung around awhile, but you never came back, and then I had to go home. Yesterday was pretty much the same, only instead of waiting I went looking for you in the hub. So then today it occurs to me that maybe they reassigned you to a different bay, only you couldn't tell me because I never gave you my link number. Deficient of me, right?"

I nod uncertainly.

"So I asked one of the officers, and they sent me here. And what do you know? Here you are!"

I blink a couple times, my sluggish brain having to go over his words a couple times before actually latching on to what he said: He thought they reassigned me. So it never occurred to him that I might have misled him on purpose. Well, why would it? He still thinks I'm his friend Lia. I'm tempted to tell him the truth, if only to get him to leave me alone. Of course, knowing Michael, he would probably just laugh it off as one of my wild stories.

Lia's stories. One of *Lia's* wild stories.

"Are you sat?" Michael suddenly puts in. "You don't look so good."

Am I satisfactory? My throat is burning with thirst, my mouth feels like cotton, and my bladder is ready to burst. I haven't eaten in almost two days. Plus, I'm a dud. So no, I'm not sat.

Not that I can say any of that to Michael.

"I'm sat. I'm just really tired," I finally answer, hoping he'll take the hint and leave.

My stomach picks that moment to let out an angry growl, and Michael laughs. "A little hungry too, it sounds like. Come on, get up! I came to invite you to eat with us."

I don't intend to, but somehow I'm standing up, grabbing my toiletry kit, and—at Michael's wrinkle-nosed request—heading for the shower units. I remember to stop at the laundry station on my way over, emerging from the showers in the first clean clothes I've worn in days. Luckily, the lines are short this time of day.

I half-expect Michael to be gone by the time I return—there is something surreal about his presence, about having a friend who is not actually my friend—but he's still here, sprawled over my cot and playing some sort of hologame on his chit. When he sees me approaching, he ends the game with a twitch of his index finger, tapping his chit to turn off the projector. The hologram disappears as if sucked back into his palm. "Ready?" he asks as I stuff my things beneath the cot.

No.

"Yes," I answer anyway, and follow him out.

We grab the lift up to Five, then take the path between Green and Blue Quadrants. Neither of us says much, not until we reach the end of the path and Michael asks, "Have you ridden the SlipStreams yet?"

I shake my head, not really sure what he's talking about but fairly certain the answer is no.

"Well, they're great. You'll love them." He frowns. "You don't still get motion sick, do you?"

Before I can ask what he means, the doors out of the hub slide open, ushering us into a crowded train station. I find myself on a wide platform situated between two sets of empty tracks disappearing into tunnels at the other end of the room. Some benches take up the middle of the platform, but few people bother to sit, instead standing in small groups chatting. The wait must not be particularly long.

As if validating my hypothesis, a low rushing sound penetrates my consciousness. I glance to the tracks on the right, listening as the sound draws closer. With a flash of silver, the SlipStream pulls in, long, sleek, and slender. The doors open and passengers begin to emerge. My eyes are drawn to a set of arrows on the wall above the tracks, one pointing toward the rings and the other toward the hub. As I watch, the arrow pointing toward the hub goes out and the ring-ward arrow lights. I glance over my shoulder at the other track just in time to see the hub-ward arrow light. I nod in understanding. Two trains run on opposing schedules, one at the hub while the other is at the rings. It makes sense.

I follow Michael onto the train and take a seat next to him along the opposite wall. He toys with something small and silver as we wait for the other passengers to board, quickly sticking it back in his pocket when he catches me watching him. I get the weird impression that he's nervous. Strange, since he's the one who sought me out. He couldn't suspect what I am, could he? No, or I would be sitting in a holding cell down in the security station, not on the padded seat of a SlipStream train.

A whistle sounds, and thirty seconds later the doors shut with a hiss. The SlipStream begins to move, slowly at first, then picking up speed. Picking up speed *a lot*.

My stomach lurches at the kick of acceleration, and I gasp slightly. What was it Michael mentioned earlier? Motion sickness? Apparently, Lia and I have something in common, after all. Too bad it's the propensity to get sick on fast-moving vehicles. I grab on to the seat in front of me, tuck my head down, and close my eyes. Perhaps it's a good thing I haven't eaten in two days.

After a minute, my muscles unclench as my body starts to adjust. The ride is fast, but it isn't rough, and the track goes in a straight line. I dare to lift my head.

Without warning, the track drops out from under us. My lungs seize, breath stricken from my body as the SlipStream soars down a steep curve. Fear squeezes my ribs as I struggle to take a breath.

00:02:32

00:02:31

Fear turns to full-blown panic as the numbers in my head suddenly drop without warning. *Oh, slag! Not here! Not now!*

The downward drop gentles and then suddenly we are curving up the other side of the slope. The pressure from the drop abruptly removed, my lungs release. At the same time, the train begins to slow, and just like that, the ride is over. Around me, I hear the others get up, but I continue to sit, frozen as I stare at my inner clock.

00:02:31

Every muscle in my body tenses as I wait for the numbers to turn, but the time remains the same. Only after a good thirty seconds have passed with no movement do I start to relax. Whatever the reason the count started, it is now stopped. I just wish I knew why it started again at all. It's been two days since my ill-fated countdown. I gaze at the numbers in consternation, a petrified realization dawning on me as I grasp their meaning.

All this time I've been so focused on my failure, on

the fact that I didn't fulfill my mission, that I forgot one of the most basic tenets of unexploded ordnance.

Even duds can be dangerous. Even duds can still blow up.

"Lia? It's okay, it's over."

I raise terrified eyes to Michael's face.

He blanches. "Hey, I'm sorry. I knew you got a little motion sick sometimes, but I didn't think it would be this bad." He pats my shoulder awkwardly and glances over his shoulder at the door. "I don't want to rush you, but if we don't want to take another ride . . ."

I lurch to my feet, immediately understanding. Quickly, we slip through the incoming passengers and off the SlipStream. As soon as my feet hit the platform, I feel myself calming. Was that why my time restarted? From the panic of being aboard the SlipStream? I shake my head. I don't know. I just don't know.

The idea terrifies me, this new understanding that I could go off at any time without warning, but I push the fear away. Going Nova is my purpose; I've known that all along. So it's a bit disconcerting not to know when or where it may happen. That doesn't matter. All that matters is that I may not have failed after all. I may still have a mission, a purpose. An identity.

"Are you sat now?" Michael is asking, and I turn my attention back to my surroundings. We are in a train station much like the one in the hub, with twin tracks running along either side of the platform. Sliding doors at the end of the room match the ones on Level Five. The familiar looks help ground me, and I answer his question with an affirmative.

"Shall we go?"

At my nod, he leads the way through the sliding

doors. I follow him, assuming the chamber on the other side will be some sort of residential version of the hub.

I couldn't have been more wrong.

Gone are the cargo bays and corridors, the dull walls and metal deck plating, the lift station and the bustle of military personnel. Gone are any indications that we are on a space station at all, and in their place?

Paradise.

Lawns, sidewalks, streets, buildings—I would think I was planetside if I didn't know better. The manmade structures are neat and well-kept, with greenery of all kinds adorning the area. Ivy and other vines twine in decorative whorls up the building walls, and flower beds create artistic clumps of color in red, violet, yellow, and orange. Trees, too, have been planted along the walks and streets, creating the illusion of the outdoors as well as granting shade from the lights above. When I glance up, I cannot even see the ceiling, just the bright light of late afternoon.

I step slowly along the cobblestone walk, feeling like I'm in some sort of dream. No, not a dream. A memory. A memory of home.

As if guessing my thoughts, Michael speaks. "It's a lot like home, isn't it? Aurora, I mean."

"Aurora," I repeat. Images surface in my mind of a place that looks much like this, a place with a park full of white flowers where a boy named Michael used to push a girl named Lia on the swings. Michael's right—it *is* a lot like home. Just not my home.

I wonder if I even have a home.

"It's beautiful," I tell him, and I mean it. Perhaps underneath the flesh and blood I'm only a machine, but even I can appreciate this place. The open spaces, the greenery, the profusion of color. Even the atmosphere holds a soft quality, the air in here so fresh that the sour-sweet scent permeating the hub has faded into nothingness.

Michael notices me sniffing. "It even smells like home, doesn't it? A fresh, earthy sort of smell. I think it's the nutrient mist they pump into the rings all the time."

"Nutrient mist?"

"It's like pumping fluoride into the water to keep your teeth strong, only through the air instead. It's supposed to keep everyone healthy by supplying vital nutrients that are missing from the artificial station air and food. They don't bother doing it in the hub, though, since everyone lives in the rings. That's why the air in the hub always smells so sterile."

I nod, off-handedly wondering if that's what accounts for the difference in smell between the two places. Craning my neck, I glance between a couple houses to spot what might be a park. I wish I could see more of this place, but the buildings and trees prevent any long-distance views.

"Is there somewhere we can see it all?" I ask.

Michael grins. "Your wish is my command."

He leads me down a couple streets and along a park, the way a slight but steady climb. We are almost to the end of the street when we reach a squat apartment building. We take the stairs all the way up, pushing through a door and out onto the roof. As far as apartment buildings go, it is relatively short, though still tall enough to lift us up over the trees and give us an unrestricted view of the ring.

Huge curving walls enclose the habitat on each side, the upper slopes disappearing into the bright ceiling. Tiers of farms have been built into each wall, like gigantic steps with pathways cut into them to allow workers access to the beds, while the city lies nestled in the lower curve of the ring itself.

I turn away from the walls and look down the length of the city. In the distance, the ring stretches out in one long, sweeping curve, the buildings and farms sloping steadily upward with the ring until they disappear from sight around the bend. The view behind me mirrors it. So the city is situated along the outer edge of the ring, I realize. Which makes sense when I remember the way the rings spin around the hub. It also explains the sudden drop on the SlipStream, the way it curved around down and then up. Well, whatever my impressions on the ground, from here there can be no mistaking the city for what it is—a manmade habitat.

I lean on the short wall surrounding the roof and watch the people down below. They bicycle through the streets and jog along sidewalks, sit in parks and chat on benches. Like dolls constantly in motion, not necessarily hurrying, but . . . *thriving*. Thriving is the word that comes to mind. Without thought, my lips curve in a smile.

"Pretty cosmic, huh?" Michael asks, leaning on the wall next to me, and I nod. "A few years ago, one of the big water mains busted and half the city almost flooded. Luckily, they got it fixed before very much was destroyed."

Destroyed.

The smile slowly fades from my face. If I fulfill my mission, this whole station will be gone. Not just the monotonous slabs of titanium and glass layered one on top of the other, but this mini-world growing within them. Strange. I never really thought about the place I would destroy. For a moment, I'm almost glad I didn't go off. I'm almost glad I didn't go Nova.

Then the moment passes.

My stomach suddenly rumbles, loud enough for Michael to hear. "We'd better get you fed," he says with a wink.

I expect us to head back to the door we came in, but instead Michael takes us down the fire escape on the side of the building. He halts midway down, climbing through an open window then reaching back to help me step over the sill behind him. I glance around what is obviously a kitchen, wondering where we are.

An older woman with thick stripes of white in her hair looks up from the stove. She doesn't seem in the least surprised at our appearance through the window.

"Michael," she greets.

"Gran, this is Lia," he says with a nod in my direction. "Lia, this is my grandmother."

She takes me in for a long moment, eyes scanning down my jumpsuit and back up, and for a split second I panic. Did Lia know her? Does she recognize that I'm not Lia?

"Welcome to our home, Lia," Michael's grandmother says with a quiet smile. "Michael's told me a lot about you. It's nice to finally meet you."

So we—or rather, Lia and his grandmother—haven't met before. I breathe an inward sigh of relief. Michael seems to have accepted my identity as Lia with blithe unconcern, but this woman seems sharper, somehow, and I can't help thinking that if anyone could see through me, it would be her.

"Pleased to meet you, ma'am."

"Please, call me Taylor. 'Ma'am' made me feel old when I was thirty. Now that I'm twice that, it makes me feel positively ancient."

"Aw, Gran! We all know you're only twenty-seven,"

Michael says, throwing an arm around her shoulders and smacking a kiss on her cheek.

She laughs and pats his hand. "My grandson, the charmer. You better be careful around this one, Lia," she warns, but I can tell she's only teasing. I feel a strange pang in my chest as I watch them. The affection between the two is almost tangible. Once again I feel like an intruder, a voyeur, spying on something everyone else takes for granted, but which I will never possess myself.

"Hey, when's sup going to be, Gran?"

I turn as a teenage girl slouches into the room.

"*Teal.*"

"How do you know my name?" she asks, brow creasing in confusion. She glances at Michael, and her face abruptly clears. "Oh, you must be *her.*"

"Not *her*, Space Face. *Lia.*" Michael puts in. "From Aurora? Or are you too oxygen-deprived to remember?"

Teal makes a face. "If anyone here is a deficient, it's *you*, Michael." She gives me a sidelong glance, wariness clear in her gaze. "Sure, I remember Lia. Sort of."

She reluctantly extends her hand for a low five, and I give it a light slap, the universal teen greeting coming without thought. I use the moment to study Teal.

She's younger than Michael by a few years—she's about thirteen, maybe—which means she would have been six the last time she saw Lia. I'm not surprised she hardly remembers me. A memory suddenly flashes in my head—a little girl with scabby knees and frizzy braids flying out in every direction, racing through the playground behind Michael and me.

Her hair is painstakingly straightened now, her legs long and smooth beneath her faux-denim skirt, but I still recognize her as Michael's little sister from so long ago.

Upon closer inspection, I realize she's actually an inch taller than me, and I feel an unreasoning stab of jealousy. No, not my own jealousy. Lia's jealousy. She always hated being short.

"No one in this room is a deficient," Michael's grandmother declares, "and Teal, supper will be in about ten minutes. Please set the table. Lia, you're welcome to join us."

"I'm just going to show Lia around first, 'kay?" Michael says before I can answer.

The apartment is small but comfortable, with two bedrooms, a living room, and bathroom in addition to the kitchen/dining room we initially entered. The décor is an eclectic mix of furnishings tending to blues and greens, and the whole place feels homey and bright. A far cry from the austere cargo bay and transport where I spent my last few weeks.

We end the tour in the back bedroom. Twin beds are set on opposite sides of the room and a sheet is strung up in the middle like a makeshift curtain. I sneak a peek at each side. It's not hard to tell which side is which. Teal's side is done in shades of purple, with makeup and hair accessories cluttered atop the dresser and clothes lying over the bed. Her walls are programmed with digitals of her and her friends. In comparison, Michael's side is surprisingly tidy. The forest-green spread has been pulled up more or less neatly over the bed, and except for a grav-ball vest hanging over a drawer, his clothes are put away. A starscape completely covers his walls.

Michael tosses himself down on his bed. "Teal and I have to share now. Not like on Aurora. It's a serious dissat."

"Try sharing a room with a hundred other refugees," I throw out sardonically. "Then come tell me about it."

He doesn't reply, and I pull my head back from Teal's side. He's staring at me, a slow grin widening his face.

"What?" I ask, suddenly worried I said the wrong thing.

"Nothing. It's just that you sounded more like you than you have since I met you. Here on the station, I mean."

"I did?"

"Well, yeah. You've been so quiet, so withdrawn. Not like you were before." He must sense my dismay, for he quickly adds, "It's okay. I get it, you've been through a lot. It was just nice to see a little of the old Lia for a minute."

He smiles directly at me, and I almost take a step back. They're a punch to the gut, his smiles. Lighting up his entire face, warming his eyes until they glow like embers on a cold night. Just like you could warm your hands by a fire, you could warm your soul by his smiles. Assuming you have a soul, that is.

I look down at Michael's dresser and finger a holo-globe perched there. Do I have a soul? *Can* someone like me have a soul? Maybe if I knew what I was, I could answer that question. A genetically engineered bomb made out of some scientist's DNA, I know that much, but beyond that? Everyone seems to believe I'm Lia — Michael, Teal, their grandmother. Although to be fair, Teal was only six the last time she saw Lia, so it's doubtful she'd be able to tell either way, and Taylor never met Lia at all. Still, Michael believes I'm Lia, so I must bear some resemblance to her, though whether it's through a surgeon's tools, genetic manipulation, or some fluke of nature, I have no idea. Perhaps they chose my DNA from a scientist who resembled Lia in the basics, and then implanted characteristics to make me even more like her. I wish I could remember the scientist whose genes were used to create me. I wish I knew what my creator looked like. For that matter, I don't even know what *Lia* looked like! Suddenly the desire to see her seems far more important than it should. An idea occurs to me.

"Michael, do you have any digitals of us?"

"Digis? Oh, sure. Let me see." He goes to the wall control and types in a few commands. The starscape in the middle section blinks out and a series of images appear. Two kids—running across a lawn, riding bikes, seated at a table in front of a birthday cake. It's the last image, though, that holds me spellbound.

Two kids sprawl across a porch swing caught in midmotion. The swinging must have jarred the girl, for she looks like she's going to fall off at any moment, her feet dangling and her arms flailing, her expression a mix of excitement and surprise. The boy is laughing as he clings to her waist, and I know without a doubt that she didn't fall. He wouldn't have let her.

A strange sensation wells up in my chest, and I find it hard to swallow. I shake it off and force myself to concentrate on the image. The boy is unquestionably Michael; even with the difference of seven years I can see that. So I shift my focus to the girl. Small, with long blonde hair and pale skin—in the basics, at least, we resemble each other. I can't make out her eye color, but my gaze traces over the shape of her face, the length of her nose, the curve of her jaw. Our faces seem similar, but how similar I'm not sure. I wish I could look at myself in the mirror, make the same observations on my own face that I am on hers.

"This one was always my favorite, too."

I glance over in surprise. There is a wistful look in Michael's eyes, the like of which I haven't seen on him before. Is he missing those days on Aurora? Or is he missing the girl in that image, instinctively knowing in his heart that she's gone and will never come back?

"Would you have known me by looks alone?" I ask suddenly. "That first day on Seven, outside the bay. If you hadn't seen my picture on the screen, I mean."

Michael blinks. "I don't know. I never thought about it." He looks at me for a minute and shakes his head. "I'm used to the way you look now. I can't imagine you looking any different. Why? Do you think you've changed that much?"

Outwardly I shrug, but inwardly all I can think is— *Oh, Michael, if only you knew.*

10 WE GATHER IN the dining room at Taylor's call, sitting down at the table just as Teal finishes putting down the last of the silverware.

"I hope you like fettuccine," Michael's grandmother says as she sets a pot in the middle of the table between a bowl of salad and a basket of bread.

"I like everything," I answer. Which isn't exactly true, but isn't exactly a lie either.

Michael snorts. "You don't have to be so polite, Lia."

"What?" I ask, confused.

"You like *everything*?" He raises an eyebrow at me and laughs. "Come on, Lia. I remember when you used to eat at our house on Aurora. You were the pickiest eater ever! My dad always used to say there were only two meals he could serve whenever you came over."

I swallow hard, trying to think of an answer to cover my mistake. A gentle hand suddenly squeezes my shoulder.

"Sometimes people's tastes change as they grow older," Taylor remarks mildly. She squeezes my shoulder once more and lets go. We take our places, and Taylor asks Michael to say grace.

"Sure, Gran." He holds out his hand to me, and surprised, I take it. Teal grabs my other hand and everyone bows their head as Michael begins. I keep my head down, but flick my eyes up to the circle around me as he speaks: Michael to Taylor to Teal to me to Michael. It feels strange to be a part of the circle, a link in the chain rather than a lone ring. Strange, but nice.

Michael finishes grace, and we begin passing food around the table.

"So, Lia," Taylor asks. "How do you like New Sol Station so far?"

Aside from the fact that I failed to blow it up, just fine, thank you. "It's nice."

"You'll have to get Michael to show you around. I swear, he knows every nook and cranny in this place."

I nod, buttering a piece of bread and trying not to let my apprehension show. Taylor asks a few more questions, trivial things, taking care not to touch on my family or my time in the internment camp. Her curiosity seems genuine, and her smile, like Michael's, reaches all the way up through her face and beams out from her eyes. I find myself relaxing a bit, my answers becoming less studied the more I answer.

"Do you know how much time you have left here?"

I drop my fork midway to my mouth, face freezing in shock. *How did she know?* "What?"

"With Aurora still under Tellurian control, I was just wondering if they were planning to keep you all—or the Auroran refugees, at least—on the station or relocate you to one of the colonies," Taylor says gently. "I know Michael would be disappointed to have you leave so soon after seeing you again."

"No slag," Teal interjects. "Ever since you arrived, all it's been is Lia this and Lia that."

"Seal your airlock, Teal!" Michael exclaims, looking a bit embarrassed.

"*You* seal it!"

I breathe a sigh of relief. So Taylor wasn't referring to my clock, stopped inside my head, but to the government's plans for the Auroran refugees. For the first time, I realize I have no idea what they intend for me. I'd never expected to be around long enough for it to matter. I shrug awkwardly in answer to the question.

Michael comes to my rescue. "They're planning to repatriate everyone except the Aurorans back to their home planets or colonies so that the local governments can resettle them. They haven't figured out what's going to happen to the Aurorans yet — maybe divided up and parceled out among the various colonies, or sent to friends and family, if they have any left on other worlds. At least, that's what one of the officers told me," he says when everyone looks at him.

I blink. Michael asked one of the officers about me? He's been talking about me at home with his family? I'm not sure what to think about that.

No, I do know what to think about that. Whoever Lia was to Michael, I'm still a bomb. The last thing I need is someone poking his nose into my business. I should be upset by his attention. I *should* be, but somehow upset is the last feeling I can muster for his presumption.

With the mention of the released prisoners, the conversation drifts to the war. It's impossible to miss talk of the war, not on the transport and not on the station. Even without everything I heard on the journey here, I would still know what they're talking about. I may not know anything about myself, but at least I seem to have a working knowledge of the world around me.

Everyone had always assumed that when we finally went to the stars, we would put all our petty quarrels behind us. That the coldness of space would kindle the warmth of brotherhood among all humankind. And who knows? Maybe if we'd found other life out there, unfriendly life, that's exactly what would have happened. Only we didn't. We were still alone as far as we knew— at least in our own little corner of the universe—and so we brought all of our baggage with us. Intercountry disputes became interplanetary disputes while world wars became galactic wars. No matter how vast space was, we could still find things to fight over—who would settle this planet, who would get the mining rights to that asteroid, who would dictate space lanes and trade agreements.

Out of the initial skirmishes, two superpowers eventually emerged: the Tellurian Alliance, a group of planetary commonwealths allied under the leadership of the original Earth, and the Celestial Expanse, a vast empire of space stations and colonies ruled over by a tight-knit oligarchy known as the Board of Directors. For decades they've slid in and out of war, battling over this dispute or that until finally coming to a truce, only to start right up again the next time some new disagreement comes along.

The current dispute is over a planet, unsurprisingly. However, this planet isn't like any of the previous ones we've discovered. Those were all real fixer-uppers, hard balls of rock with decades of terraforming and generations of tough living standing between them and true habitability. Even Aurora took a good seventy years to become the paradise Michael and I remember. No, this is a planet rich in clean water, fertile soil. A planet with a genuine oxygen-mix atmosphere and, surprisingly, no prior claim by sentient life. I've heard that some people have nicknamed it New Earth, it's so close to the original Earth. The problem is that no one can agree on who has the rightful claim to it.

As usual, both sides took the credit. The Celestians were the first to locate it on the prospecting scans, but the Tellurians managed to arrive at the planet first, slipping a small survey party onto New Earth shortly after its discovery three years ago. By the time the Celestians caught up, Telluria already had a warship in range, ready to blow them out of space if they even attempted to go planetside. Back-up quickly massed for both sides, and the stand-off began. Of course, a battle over the planet itself is out of the question. Can't risk hurting the very merchandise they're fighting over. So both sides kept ships stationed around the planet to keep their rival from sending anyone else down, and took their territorial war back into the inhabited universe, each side trying to inflict enough damage to make the other cry uncle. Just business as usual.

Or perhaps not, I realize as I listen to the conversation around me.

"All I'm saying is, maybe the Tellurians are really serious about peace this time. I mean, if they're willing to free prisoners and open the negotiations over New Earth—"

"Seriously, Michael?" Teal snorts. "That's what you think is going on? Everyone has decided to play nice?"

"Why not? They've made plenty of peace treaties in the past."

"Yeah, and how long have those ever lasted? Besides, those slippery Tellurians wouldn't give up their claim so easily, not after the dirty tactics they used to get ahead of our survey party and cheat us out of our New Earth landing. I heard they deliberately jammed up half a dozen jump paths just to keep us from arriving first. People like that are capable of anything *but* peace. No, the Tellurians are up to something. They have to be."

"Why do you always have to be so neg, Teal? Maybe they're just tired of fighting and figure it's easier to share."

"What are you in, kindergarten? You're just hoping this peace sticks so you don't get drafted next year."

Michael looks over at her sharply, his eyes widening in shock at her rejoinder before darkening in annoyance. He shakes his head, mouth set, and doesn't answer. I glance between the two of them, sensing more to the exchange than meets the eye, but unable to figure out what.

It is Taylor who ends the argument with a decisive, "Only time will tell either way, but I, for one, hope this peace sticks, too. Now, Teal, can you help me clear the table, please? Michael, you can start cutting the cake."

Innocuous as they are, Taylor's words defuse the tension almost instantly. Teal rolls her eyes once at Michael, and he shoots her an irritated look back, then the two go about their assigned tasks as though nothing happened.

I watch this family in bemusement. I barely know them, have only met them for the first time today with the exception of Michael, and yet even I can see that they . . . work. I can't think of any other way to describe it. They work, though they're not the most traditional of families. Everyone has a place, a niche within the framework that makes up their little unit; each is a piece, and together they make up a whole. I wonder if I was ever part of a family like that.

Common sense comes rushing back, and I shake my head. As far as I know, I'm nothing more than some lab experiment, fabricated in a research facility for one purpose alone. As though someone like me ever had parents. As though someone like me ever had a family. What was I thinking?

Yet somehow the idea doesn't feel quite as ridiculous as it should.

———

After dinner, Michael walks me home. He has to, to help me carry all the stuff his grandmother sent with me.

I peek over at Michael, struggling to peer around the big box in his arms, and grin. Taylor only meant to send an extra piece of cake with me. "For later," she'd said with a wink. Only somehow the cake made her think of the extra pillow in the hall closet, and the pillow made her recall the blanket no one was using, and just like that, a small food container morphed into a good-sized packing box. I tried to refuse the items—didn't I have a perfectly good sleeping roll down in the bay?—but Taylor insisted, and I didn't know how to refuse.

We enter the SlipStream station and take a spot on the platform to wait. Michael sets the box on the bench and drums on the top, seemingly content to wait in silence, but all I can think about is the ride here, the way my clock lost seconds, and nervousness tightens my stomach. I cast about for something to say to distract myself from the edginess.

"Your gran's really nice."

Michael's fingers still for a moment. "Yeah, yeah she is. She's been really great to Teal and me."

"Has she always lived on New Sol?"

"Just about. Her family emigrated here when she was only a kid."

"So how long have you been staying with her?"

Michael tenses, a guarded look on his face. Then he takes a breath and releases it with a whoosh. "It's okay, Lia, you can ask. I know you must be wondering what I'm doing here. On New Sol, I mean," he clarifies at my confused look.

I'm not, but I nod anyway.

"It's not what you're probably thinking."

As if he would know what I was thinking any more than I would know what he *thinks* I'm thinking. Which is to say, I have no idea.

"Okay," I answer, not having anything better to say.

"My parents aren't dead. I know you probably didn't want to ask because—" He jerks his head at me, and I realize he's thinking of my parents.

No, not my parents. *Lia's* parents.

"Oh." I duck my head, not sure how to answer, which he takes for a yes.

"It wasn't supposed to be this way," Michael continues. "At least, I don't think so. When Mom got promoted to first officer on Stella Station and we left Aurora, it was still supposed to be the four of us, just like always. Dad's request for reassignment had been accepted, and we were all going to live on the station together."

"What happened?"

Michael shrugs. "Well, we were all together for a while. Then the war happened. They discovered New Earth, and the fighting started up all over again. They needed experienced officers in the field, so they reassigned Mom to a ship of the line. For a while we lived with Dad, going with him whenever he got reassigned. We moved three times in two years, until finally they assigned Dad to the *Victor's Prize* as communications officer. Warship—no civilians allowed. You know what the last thing he said was, before he left? He said his place, *his duty*," Michael spits out the words, "was with the fleet. And off he went."

His fingers toy with something in his pocket. "Of course they wouldn't let Teal and me stay by ourselves, so we were shipped off here to live with Gran. That was a year ago, and we've been here ever since. Not that I mind. It's a lot nicer here than it was on the last station where we lived. More like Aurora. Like home."

He says the words lightly, as though it's no big deal, but I can't help thinking he lost his parents to the war as surely as Lia did hers. Only he has the hope that one day his will come back, and Lia's never will.

I feel a strange lump in my throat at the thought, though I'm not sure why. I clear my throat. "You must really miss them. Your folks, I mean."

Michael slides his gaze toward me, studying me from the corner of his eyes, and shrugs. "No more than you miss yours, I'm sure."

I look away, uncertain how to answer the comment. Mistaking the gesture, Michael hastens to apologize. "I'm sorry! I didn't mean it that way." When I don't respond, he adds, "Hey, you want to see something?"

When I glance over, he pulls out something small and round from his pocket. Curious, I take it, fingering the tiny metal spikes on the bottom of the disc. "It's a chit," I say in surprise, recognizing it as the same communication device Rowan punched into my hand on my first day here.

"It was my dad's," Michael explains. "It got caught on something and yanked out of his hand a few days before he left for the *Prize* and we came here. See the way the spikes are bent there? I was supposed to stick it in the recycler to be melted down when he got a new one, but

I kept it. I don't know, I guess I just thought it was a way to remember him. Pretty stupid, huh?"

"I don't think it's stupid at all," I answer softly. "So do your parents ever come to visit?"

"They come whenever they get leave, but it's been awhile." He shakes his head. "Teal thinks it would be cool to be an officer like Mom, but I never want to join the military. To have people always telling you where to go and what to do? When you can see your family and when you can't? I'd hate it."

All of a sudden Teal's earlier needling makes sense. "Do you really think they might institute the draft?" I ask.

"I don't know. There was talk they might, before the Tellurians suddenly opened negotiations. Maybe if the ceasefire holds . . ."

Maybe, but it won't. If there's one thing I know, it's that. People who want peace don't send human bombs to destroy space stations. I open my mouth to say so, then close it. What, exactly, would I say?

With a silver rush, the SlipStream pulls in on the left, sparing me the need to respond. I spend the ride with teeth clenched, forehead wrinkled in concentration as the train churns down the track. The motion isn't as bad, now that I know what to expect, but I keep my inner eye trained on my clock, certain it will start turning at any moment. It doesn't; the number is fixed in place even after we arrive and disembark into the hub.

00:02:31

Michael drops me at the cargo bay with the box and says goodnight. It got late somehow, without me even noticing. The lights are still on, but people have already lain down to sleep and others are getting ready to. I'm not tired, so instead I sit on my cot and slowly sort through the box Taylor gave me.

On top is a thick pillow stuffed with synthesized down, nothing like the thin headrest provided with my sleeping roll. A blanket comes out next, soft and white and fluffy. I rub the fabric lightly against my cheek, reveling in the texture, a far cry from the stiff gray blanket already covering my cot. The container of cake is on the bottom, along with several other small things Taylor apparently threw in when I wasn't looking. A bag of candy. Half a dozen pairs of clean socks and a new package of underwear. A cheap reader loaded with books. A small basket of toiletries—scented lotion, soap, and shampoo. Frilly, feminine things smelling of lilac, at least according to the package. All I can smell is the usual sour-and-sweet odor pervading the hub.

I finger the items one by one. This boxful is a king's ransom for someone like me, who can carry everything she owns tucked into one small sleeping roll. I wonder: does it make me a thief, to accept things under false pretenses? Would Taylor take it all back if she knew I wasn't Lia? I don't think she would, and it's that understanding, more than anything, that pricks my dormant conscience.

I think back to the evening with Michael's family. I didn't go out of any expectation or desire, but because it was easier to say yes to Michael than no. At times, I felt awkward and out of place, like an extra piece trying to fit into a puzzle that's already been completed. And yet . . . Taylor's hand on my shoulder, the easy way she and Michael came to my rescue when I didn't know the answer to a question, Michael's and Teal's fingers in mine during grace. For a few short moments, there was a place for me in that puzzle, too.

No, I remind myself after a moment. Not for me. For Lia.

Still, as I curl up in the white blanket and lay my head down on the pillow, I can't help wondering for the first time since waking up in the hygiene unit if maybe being alive isn't the worst thing in the world after all.

11 **THOSE LONG HOURS** of lying on my cot doing nothing are over. I know it as soon as I wake the next day. Instead of that dull heaviness pressing me down into my bed, I feel a new energy pushing me up into the day. Michael's coming, his searching me out after all I did to evade him, his folding me into his family for those few short hours—they've changed me somehow. Not in any way I can pinpoint or explain, but they've changed me all the same. The heaviness has been replaced by a restlessness; the will to die by, perhaps, not a true desire to live, but at least by an acceptance that I have.

I see Michael off and on over the next week. School is less formal on the station than it was on Aurora, with students having the option to attend in person or link in either live or after the fact. It explains how Michael was able to come look for me those first few afternoons on the station. However, he still has to attend his classes sometimes—Taylor is too responsible a guardian to let him get behind—and though he doesn't say it, I know Michael must have a life beyond me. Friends, activities, maybe even a girlfriend for all I know.

Still, I can't help feeling a little disappointed the first day he links me to say he won't be coming by. The feeling surprises me. Before, I would have been perfectly content if I never saw him again. Relieved, even. Not anymore. Somehow between our first meeting on Level Seven and that evening in his home on the Upper Habitat Ring, I've gotten used to Michael. Started to like him, even, rather than simply tolerating his presence because he was Lia's friend. Perhaps it's because, even though I'm not *his* friend, he's still mine.

Then again, maybe it's simple boredom that draws me to him, I muse as I step off the lift onto Level Eight. It's my tenth day on the station and already boredom has become second nature to me. As a returned POW, I'm not required to attend classes, nor do I have a job or any assigned chores. Aside from sleeping and eating, there isn't much to do besides walk around the hub—an activity I've done a hundred times now. Too bad Michael's not around. He linked me earlier to say he would be attending classes, so I'm on my own today. As I head for my sleeping quarters, I try to think of something to do. There's always Taylor's reader, I remind myself. Though I've never been much of one for reading, it's better than nothing.

I blink as I walk into the bay. Never much of one for reading? Now was that Lia's preference or my own? Between her hidden memories and my forgotten ones, sometimes it's hard to tell where I begin and she ends.

Pushing past a group of milling refugees, I make my way to my corner only to stop as I catch sight of my cot. My cot which is no longer unoccupied.

My mouth drops open as I spot the intruder. A girl is lounging on top of the blanket, shoveling the last of the candy Taylor gave me into her mouth as she flips through the reader. Over the last week, I'd been careful to pack all my stuff carefully away into the box and stick it back behind a nearby cargo crate whenever I left the bay. I'd thought it was safe enough, but apparently I was wrong. My eyes zoom in on a glob of chocolate carelessly dropped on my blanket, and a hot flash of anger pulses through me.

Words explode from my mouth, and I rush forward. "Hey! Hey, what are you doing? That's mine!"

She jerks at my call, jumping to her feet and searching wildly for the source of the voice. She looks about my age, but she's a lot bigger, topping me by at least six inches and fifty pounds. Her eyes take in my smaller stature with one quick sweep and the nervousness immediately dissolves from her face. She smiles a nasty smile, the sort of mean expression only belonging to the worst of bullies.

Gaze locked on mine, she slides the reader into her jumpsuit. "What's yours?" she asks innocently.

Calm, calm, don't draw attention.

The words whisper through my mind, but that chocolate on Taylor's crisp white blanket stares up at me, overriding everything else. "Give that back!"

"Or what?"

"Or you'll be sorry!"

"Oh, yeah? Who's going to make me? 'Cause it sure in a bloody moon won't be you." She gestures at the box and snorts. "Besides, where would a little frag-nosed refugee like you get all this stuff? I bet you stole it."

"I did not! It was a gift, from *friends.* Something you probably never had in your life."

I hit a nerve; I can immediately see it in her eyes. Her nostrils flare, fingers clenching into fists. Her body tenses, and I realize she's about to charge. So I charge first.

She doesn't expect it, and my weight hits her like a Class II cruiser, toppling her back onto the cot. A leg snaps with a loud *crack!* and then we're rolling across the floor, our arms and hands grappling in each other's clothes, each trying to gain the advantage. She uses her superior weight to push me underneath her. I buck, trying to jerk free, but she's too heavy for me to force her off. She smirks, certain she has me where she wants me.

"Apologize, bitch, and give me your stuff, and *maybe* I'll spare your life."

00:02:30

00:02:29

00:02:28

A spark jumps in my eye and a smile slowly curls over my lips, visions of the two of us going Nova dancing in my head. Quick as lightning, I snake my arms around hers, sinking my fingers into her biceps.

"No, *you* apologize and maybe I'll spare *your* life."

Her grip on me falters slightly, confusion clear on her face. I'm supposed to be scared of her, frightened and begging for mercy at this point. She can't figure out why I'm smiling instead. She doesn't know how to handle prey that fights back.

00:02:23

00:02:22

00:02:21

Two more sparks, so silver they're blinding.
"All right, that's it! Break it up!"
A hand grabs the girl's shoulder and yanks. It takes

three jerks before I cool enough to unlock my grip and let the soldier haul her away. Though finally free, I don't move, heart hammering as I watch the seconds slip away.

00:02:12

00:02:11

The stretchy feeling is starting in my mind now. Is this it? Is my time finally come? I close my eyes, ready to embrace my duty with all my being . . .

00:02:11

. . . and my clock stops.

I don't know whether to gnash my teeth in frustration or sigh in relief. For a minute I was so angry, I was ready to blow the station and everyone in it just as long as I could take that girl with me. Shame rolls through me as that strange bout of temper, so sudden and unexpected, cools as quickly as it fired. My job is to further the war effort, not take revenge against one mean-spirited girl. To go Nova like that, rolling around on the floor with some thief, seems wrong somehow. Unworthy. Maybe it's just as well I didn't.

Then again, isn't it better to go Nova in any way I can than to never go Nova at all? My mission seemed so simple once. How did it ever become so confused?

"Hey! You okay, kid?"

I open my eyes to find an officer staring down at me. She offers a hand to help me up. Pausing only long enough to determine there's no PsyCorp star on her breast, I take it and slowly get to my feet. The big girl is being held by a private a few feet away, the firm hands on her shoulders making it clear she's not still here by choice. Hatred shoots out of her eyes at me.

The officer looks us over, the large-boned girl with the mean eyes and the small blonde wisp who was trapped beneath her, and it's immediately obvious whose side she's on. Still, she scans her tip-pad over both our chits.

"Silverstein, Sharlotte—"

"It's *Shar*."

"—Johansen, Lia. Okay, do either of you ladies want to tell me what happened?"

I open my mouth, ready to explain everything, then close it. While Shar started it all by messing with my stuff, technically *I'm* the one who started the fistfight by hitting her first. I might get in just as much trouble as Shar, if not more, for losing my temper instead of simply going to the officers for help. And if they decide to punish me, who knows what other secrets of mine they might discover in the process? I'm sure whatever punishment they'd mete out for starting a fight would pale in comparison to what they'd do to me for being an enemy bomb come to blow them all up.

My gaze meets Shar's, and for once I see we're in perfect accord. Neither of us wants to tell about the fight. No surprise there. As a bully and a thief, she doesn't come out looking any better than I do.

"It was just a misunderstanding," Shar says.

"Yeah," I back her up. "I thought she was stealing my reader, but she was only looking at it."

The officer glances between the two of us and raises her eyebrows. Shar reluctantly pulls the reader out of her jumpsuit and hands it back. "*Sorry*," she bites out, "for the *misunderstanding*."

I take it, easily reading "sorry for the misunderstanding" as "sorry I didn't pummel you when I had the chance." "Yeah, me too," I say, though I mean my apology no more than she does. The officer is still watching us, clearly not fooled by the exchange, so I reluctantly offer my hand.

Shar scowls at it, but mindful of the officer, gives it a quick slap. A burst of white flashes in my head at the touch, a jolt of pure fear jumpstarting my heart.

I gasp and yank my hand back, but Shar doesn't try to touch me again, the low five more than enough contact for her. I take a shaky breath, trying to regain my equilibrium, but before I can figure out what just happened, the officer speaks.

"All right, you're both free to go." She makes a notation on her tip-pad. "But if there's any more fighting from either of you, you'll both end up down at PsyCorp explaining yourselves. Got it?"

PsyCorp! Visions of being brain-drained dance in my head, and I quickly nod lest she change her mind about sending us down to verify our stories. The officer signals to the private, and he lets Shar go. With a final glare, she slips around him and disappears into the crowd.

The private leaves too, dispersing the onlookers as he goes—"Nothing more to see, folks! Go back to your cots!"—and I try to pick up the wreckage of my stuff. The cot's a loss, with its broken leg, but maybe I can get the chocolate out of my blanket. I look around for something to wipe it off with.

"You sure you're going to be sat?"

It's the officer—Ensign Dern I see from her uniform. She bends down and helps retrieve my things, frowning at the broken cot and linking a quick message through her chit.

"I'm fine," I answer. "I can take care of myself."

She gives me an assessing look and slowly nods. "I'm

sure you can. Where did you get all this stuff, anyway?"
I tense under her scrutiny, but her tone is curious rather
than accusatory.

"Turns out I have an old friend on the station. We
used to live next door to each other on Aurora, before
his family moved away. Michael." His name slips out,
though I didn't mean to say it.

Ensign Dern smiles. "This Michael sounds like a stel-
lar guy. Here, grab your stuff and come with me."

We load my things into the box, and I follow her between some cargo containers and down along the wall.
She stops at a small cargo locker and waves her chit in
front of the lock panel. The drawer pops open. "Give me
your hand."

I do, and she programs the access code into my chit.
She shuts the drawer and signals to me to try. I wave my
hand in front of the panel and the drawer pops open.

She nods. "Good. Keep your extra stuff in there when
you aren't using it. Even the best of people can get
tempted when they have so little and they see someone
else with so much. Got it?"

I nod, and with a pat on the shoulder and the promise
of a new cot before nightfall, the ensign moves off. Shoving the last of my stuff into the locker, I shut the door
and lock it, glad I won't have to deal with the likes of
Shar now that I have a safe place for my things. Or so I
think, until I emerge back into the main bay area to find
her leaning against a barrel, gaze fixed on me, hatred
shooting from her eyes.

I shiver slightly, courage fading without my anger to
back it up, and suddenly know that whatever happened
between us, it's not over.

———

I sit on my new cot later that evening, combing out my hair and thinking about the fight. About the way my clock lost seconds during my tussle with Shar. The first time I lost seconds, it was on the SlipStream when I was afraid. The second time, it was during the fight when I was angry. Is it possible strong emotion restarts my clock? If so, could I go Nova simply by generating enough emotion?

It never occurred to me that I might be able to complete my mission out of sheer willpower, but if there's a possibility I can do it, I have to at least try.

Don't I?

I start to close my eyes, then stop. It is just after the main dinner hour, and most of the refugees are still up, scattered around the bay amusing themselves as best as they can. There should be no outward signs of my going Nova as far as I know, not until it's too late anyway. Still, I hesitate. Going Nova seems somehow like a private event; far too private for such a public place. Maybe I should wait until everyone settles down to sleep.

Glancing down, I catch myself rubbing my forearm. It still hurts, a distant aching deep down in my arm though the surface of my skin is unmarred. I force myself to stop. I'm being a coward.

This time when I close my eyes, I keep them closed. I recall the fight, remember the sight of Shar reclining on my cot, eating my candy and dropping chocolate on my blanket.

Nothing.

I push harder, envisioning the mean look on her face when she slid the reader into her jumpsuit, the way it felt to slam into her, to roll across the floor wanting nothing more than to rip her heart out.

Now something comes, but it is nothing more than a mild indignation, remnants of a fire long gone. I grit my teeth, fists clenching and face scrunching as I reach deep down for that fury I felt earlier.

My breath pours out in an exhale and my eyes open. It's no use. I just don't have anything to be truly angry about anymore. I can no more manufacture it now than I could stifle it earlier. I laugh softly. Maybe I should go seek out Shar. I'm sure five minutes with her would be more than enough to get me good and pissed off. I shake my head, a snort escaping me at the thought of going to her for anything.

Instead, I just lie back on my cot and tell myself that the emotion coursing through me right at this moment isn't relief.

12 **THE NEXT FEW DAYS** pass slowly. I keep an eye out for Shar, but though I catch sight of her several times, she seems content to keep her distance. For now, anyway. Even so, I try to stay out of the bay as much as possible. The sour-and-sweet smell in the hold has gotten stronger over the past couple weeks, no doubt the result of so many people living together in such close quarters. Even with the hygiene units, it's just not feasible to shower every day. The smell never bothered me when it was just a faint aroma, but now I find myself wrinkling my nose in distaste at the oddest times. I wonder how it smells to everyone else.

Probably worse, I realize as I step out of the hygiene unit this morning and spot a beefy man clad in a jumpsuit marred with massive sweat stains. Not that I really have the right to judge. The stains from the gray liquid purged from my eyes the night I malfunctioned still show on my jumpsuit despite two washings now.

Wandering out of the bay, I grab the lift up to Five. Between my reluctant fear of the SlipStreams and my desire to avoid the bay, I have to find a new place in the hub to hang out. The lounge in Blue Quadrant turns out to be the perfect place.

There are two lounges open to the public on Five, quiet rooms where anyone can kick back and relax, both partitioned off from the main roar of the level. A panel on one side of the room holds ports where you can jack in your chit or reader to download the latest zine subscriptions, and viewports on the other side turn the room into an observation deck. It's as good a place as any for a defective human bomb to while away the time.

Walking into the lounge, I ignore both options, instead taking a comfy chair and clicking the controls on the armrest to turn on the wall panel in front of me. A children's show is on, and I click around until I find an independent news station with a reputation for getting into remote places. My mind isn't really on the screen, though. Instead I find myself thinking about Michael.

I look down at my chit and stroke the metal lightly with one finger. I haven't heard from Michael at all for the last three days—not a visit or even a link. I'm sure it's nothing. Knowing Michael, he probably just forgot. He has more to his life than me, after all. Or rather, than *Lia*. Because it's not me Michael is friends with. It's *Lia* he confides in, *Lia* he smiles at, *Lia* he wants to be with. Michael is friends with a dead girl, and though I may look like her and sound like her and carry her name, I'm *not* her.

I feel a slight twinge in my chest and snort at my idiocy. I'm envious of a girl who is more than likely dead. How foolish am I? It's just as well Michael has lost interest.

Turning back to the screen, I gasp as a very familiar-looking image jumps off the screen at me. I hit the armrest to turn up the volume.

". . . can see, the damage is more extensive than the Tellurians have led us to believe. When asked for a comment, they said, quote, 'This was nothing more than an unfortunate accident caused by an overload in the main power relay. We have taken every precaution to prevent any incidents like this from happening in the future, and we feel confident that this will not affect our negotiations with the Celestian government,' end quote. They did not release the total number of casualties, though they did state that the majority of casualties were their own people rather than the prisoners."

The camera zooms in on the wreckage of the hangar, showcasing the billowing smoke and charred debris surrounding it, but not before the wider shot allows me to catch sight of the high fences, the guard towers, the barracks spread out in the background. Even without the words at the bottom of the screen, I would know where this is. Tiersten Internment Colony.

I lean forward, looking for any additional scrap of information about the explosion, but the screen flips back to the reporter. He's clearly in a news shuttle rather than planetside, unsurprising considering the nature of the colony below him. I'm surprised the Tellurians even let them get close enough to film the explosion from space. Of course, with the ceasefire and the recent return of the first group of Tiersten prisoners, perhaps the Tellurians were letting them do a story on the prisoner return.

The reporter continues speaking, but I barely hear him. A million thoughts circle through my mind, but one jumps to the forefront.

So I really did spend time at Tiersten.

It's the obvious explanation for why the images are so familiar. I ponder what this means and finally decide not much. There are any number of reasons I could have been on Tiersten. For one thing, I was sent here with a group of prisoners from the camp. It only makes sense for me to have boarded the transport on Tiersten with the rest of them. Or perhaps Tiersten is where I received the memory transfer disguising me as Lia. For that matter, maybe my memories of the camp aren't mine at all, but hers, still skulking around in my mind only to pop up at the oddest times. Maybe I was never on Tiersten at all. I should not read any more significance into the memories than is warranted.

The camera pops back to the camp again. Image after image of smoking wreckage flashes on the screen, showing the ruin from one angle, then another. A sick feeling starts to bloom in the pit of my stomach. I should look away, change the channel. This explosion, while of interest, means nothing to me. I don't know anyone there; I wasn't even there when it happened. But my eyes are glued to the screen, my head unable to turn away. I press my hand to my midsection, but the sick feeling only intensifies.

Shoving up from my chair, I make a dash for the nearest hygiene unit. My stomach bucks, and I make it just in time to share my breakfast with the toilet. For a minute I stand there, braced against the wall over the bowl. Then the sick feeling starts to subside enough for me to take a deep breath and straighten. Perhaps it wasn't the news program at all, but simply a bit of indigestion from my earlier meal. It would certainly make more sense.

Whatever the cause of my indisposition, it seems to be gone now. I rinse out my mouth and wash my hands at the sink, then exit the unit. Indigestion, I repeat to myself; that must have been it.

But though the sickness is gone, the images still linger, wafting through my mind like the gray smoke billowing in thick waves across the camp.

————

Michael has not forgotten me after all, for he links me later in the morning to invite me over. I don't even have to think about the answer, my head already nodding before he finishes the question.

Michael grins. "You must be really bored over there."

I bite my lip a bit sheepishly and nod again. Signing off, I head up to the SlipStream station. The ride over is less scary the third time around, and I disembark without experiencing any problems. I breathe the fresh air appreciatively and make my way to Michael's.

His apartment building is easy enough to find, but once inside I realize I don't know which one is his. We went in through the window last time, and I didn't bother to look at the number on the way out. I power up my chit and link him back.

"What apartment are you in?" I ask, feeling foolish after having already assured Michael I knew the way.

He laughs. A few seconds later, a door at the end of the hall slides open. My lips curl in an involuntary smile at the sight of Michael, and I go to join him inside.

Taylor is out on an errand, and Teal is closeted in their room with one of her friends. We grab a quick snack, and then Michael suggests a game of checkers.

"Checkers?"

"It's this cool retro game everyone's playing," he explains. "They used to play it, like, a gazillion years ago on Earth. It's not even on the holo; it's an actual physical game. I borrowed a set from a friend of mine."

Michael brings out the board, and I sit carefully on the edge of the sofa while he sets it up on the coffee table. The rules are simple, and it doesn't take us long to get the hang of it. Pretty soon we're into our third game.

Michael jumps another one of my pieces. "Ha, ha, ha, I've got you now," he says in a witchy falsetto, rubbing his hands together. "I'm going to cook you in my oven and eat you!" He grabs the two pieces and mimes the black one eating the red.

Shy chuckles dribble out of my mouth at his antics, and encouraged, Michael throws in some fake chewing noises for good effect.

He starts doing sound effects in the middle of our second game, after managing to take out three of my pieces in one jump, devising wicked ways for my pieces to die and even coming up with a fake trumpet call whenever one of the pieces makes it to the other end of the board and is crowned.

"So is performing sound effects a mandatory part of the game?" I ask as he wins the game with a final flourish.

"Oh, definitely," Michael replies, nodding his head in mock earnest. "Those old Earth folk *never* played a game of checkers without doing sound effects. It's written in all the histories."

I shake my head ruefully at his teasing and begin setting up the board again. We are tied at two games apiece and working on the tiebreaker when Taylor returns.

She smiles at me. "It's nice to see you again, Lia. Are you staying for lunch?"

I glance at Michael uncertainly, but before I can answer Michael puts in, "Sure, she is." He spares a look for me. "Aren't you?"

Taylor laughs. "You might at least ask her first, Michael." She disappears into the kitchen still laughing. Michael shrugs apologetically at me, but I don't mind. There's something about the way he automatically includes me that makes me feel accepted. One of them.

The radio goes on in the kitchen, the end of a news program playing. My mind flashes back to this morning.

Tiersten. The explosion. Numberless casualties.

The cold feeling from earlier returns, niggling within the recesses of my stomach. I swallow hard, resisting the urge to press my fist into my stomach.

"Lia? Lia, it's your turn."

I shake off the memory and return to the game. It was just a news story. Nothing more.

Teal joins us for lunch, her friend having left by the time we eat. She frowns at me as she sits down at the table, and I wonder what I did to offend her. This is only the second time we've met, and both times we exchanged few words. Her gaze makes me slightly uncomfortable. It's not suspicious, exactly—more like distrustful. She hasn't guessed what I am, I'm sure of it, but still I feel a little nervous. Her clothes and room may reflect a typical teenage girl, absorbed with only herself, but I get the feeling her mind is as sharp as they come. While trusting Michael would easily dismiss any small missteps I might make, I bet Teal would notice each and every one. She doesn't say anything, though, and soon enough I forget about it.

This meal is much different from the first meal I ate here. Last time, I was a special guest to be catered to, with Taylor careful to ask me questions and include me in the conversation. This time, I'm just one of the family, free to join in the conversation or stay silent as I please. I listen as Michael and Teal speak of various school projects, and Taylor talks about her work at the Environmental Control Center.

"I just hope they figure out the problem with the misters soon," Taylor is saying. "They've had people look at the system twice now, and they still haven't figured it out." At my puzzled look, she clarifies, "Normally we pump a light but continuous stream of nutrient mist through the rings, but the misters have been acting up lately, pumping way too much on some days—like today—or shutting off altogether on other days."

"Oh. Is it dangerous?"

"Don't worry, a little extra nutrient mist won't hurt anyone. It's more a concern of running over budget if we use too much too quickly."

Michael jumps in then with a funny story about an air filter malfunction when he was on Stella Station, and eager to join the camaraderie, I find myself telling them about an impromptu game of tug-of-war set up in the cargo bay a few nights ago. The only misstep in the meal comes when I accidentally knock over my drink. Even that is smoothed over easily enough, Michael helping me wipe it up while Taylor offers to rinse out my jumpsuit to ensure it doesn't stain.

"Teal, can you loan Lia something to wear?" Taylor asks. "In fact, don't you have some old clothes you were going to donate to charity? Maybe they would fit Lia. I'm sure she could use a few extra outfits."

Before I know it, I'm in Teal's room, changing into one of her skirts and tops. I smooth my hands over the shiny pink material of the skirt, remembering the last time I wore something this nice. It was a blue dress, made out of the same sort of shiny fabric, sleeveless and high-collared. How I loved that dress!

No, wait. That wasn't my dress. That was Lia's dress. It was *Lia* who loved it.

Looking up, I catch Teal staring at me. "I'll get it back to you right away," I promise, thinking she's upset Taylor practically commanded her to give me her clothes. "I have another jumpsuit in the bay."

"It's fine," Teal says with a shrug. "I never wear it anymore. Pink's so un-fash these days. You might as well keep it, and the top, too. Let's see, what else can I get rid of?"

She turns back to her closet and starts pulling stuff out. Skirts, slacks, tops, sweaters; by the time Teal is done, I have a heap of clothes on my lap, all things Teal claims she no longer wants or wears. I gape at the pile in astonishment and shake my head, but Teal isn't any better at taking "no" for an answer than Michael is, and by the time she's through, I've got a bag with two more skirts, three tops, a pair of sweatpants, a sweater, and some tights. Once again I feel a twinge of guilt, like I'm accepting things under false pretenses, but only a twinge. Teal doesn't seem to like me enough to give me anything she's truly fond of. The guilt vanishes altogether the moment Michael walks into the room.

He looks me up and down, a slow smile spreading across his face, and whistles. "Wow! You should borrow Teal's clothes more often, Lia. You look cosmic. Really cosmic."

The look in his eyes echoes his words, and I can feel a blush spreading over my face. "Thanks."

Teal glances between the two of us and rolls her eyes. "Should I leave you two alone now?"

If possible, I only blush harder. Michael just shrugs. "Be my guest! I never wanted a little sister, anyway."

Teal makes a face at him as she leaves—just a typical little sister's taunting, it appears at the outset—but there's something in her eyes, something concerned, almost grave, that speaks of deeper sentiment than simply the typical brother-and-sister exchange. An answering gleam flickers in Michael's eyes, and though I can't quite read either expression, I can sense the strength of their affection.

A pang of envy hits me as I watch Teal go. "You guys really love each other."

Michael glances at me sharply, surprise shining in his eyes along with something else, something I can't quite define. At last he gives me an embarrassed shrug. "Gran, my friends, Mom and Dad—they've come and they've gone. Teal, on the other hand ... Teal is the constant. Teal and I have always been together."

And that pretty much seems to say it all.

It makes sense now, Teal's ongoing animosity toward me. For years it's been just her and Michael. To have his former best friend show up out of the blue, to practically resurrect from the dead and walk back into his life .... No wonder she doesn't like me! She's afraid I'll come between her and Michael. I can't blame her for that. Not at all.

From the minute I walked onto this station, I never wanted anyone. Not a family member, not even a friend. Until now. Now, I can't help wishing with everything in me that I could have what they have.

———

We hang out for a couple more hours until Michael reluctantly admits he has homework to do. Michael accompanies me down to the station, though I'd insisted I could go alone. The whole way he keeps glancing at me, eyes dancing, a smile pushing at his lips though he tries to keep it in check. When I ask him what's going on, he just shakes his head. "Oh, nothing."

Stepping into the station, I am ready to bid Michael goodbye when he suddenly grabs my hand. "Come on!"

Instead of leading me to the platform though, he

drags me past a young couple to a door panel set into the wall. It's no wonder I didn't notice it last time, for with the door painted to match the walls, only its seams give away its presence. Even the access panel has been painted to match the wall. Michael waves his chit in front of it. The door pops open, and with a tug on my hand, he pulls me through.

I look around as the door closes behind us. In front of us stretches a long, metal tunnel.

"Where are we?"

"After your reaction to the SlipStream last time, I thought you might want to walk this time."

"*This* leads back to the hub?" I ask, amazement bubbling up as we begin walking down the corridor.

Michael is practically bouncing up and down beside me. "Yup. Gran knew about it. She mentioned it when you and Teal were doing the clothes thing. She said that when she was a kid, the SlipStreams were always breaking down. The station had only been operational for a year before her family moved here, you know. So whenever they broke down, everyone had to walk. I wasn't sure if her old access code would even work, but I guess it's not that the tunnel is off-limits, just that no one has a reason to use it anymore."

"How long is it?"

He shrugs. "I don't know. Pretty long, I guess. I figured you'd prefer it to the SlipStreams, but if it's too long for you, especially now that you've gone all girly . . ." He motions at my skirt, a challenging gleam in his eyes.

"Girly? I can do anything *you* can do, Michael!" The words shoot from my mouth without conscious thought.

"Oh, yeah? Prove it!"

He suddenly takes off down the tunnel, and without thinking, I launch myself into a run after him. Michael sees me coming and pushes himself faster. I laugh and run harder. Michael may think he's fast, but I'm faster.

Sure enough, as we fly down the path toward the hub, I start gaining on him. Five more meters, and I'll have him.

I bear down on him, my legs pumping harder, my skirt flying out around my knees and a crazy grin spreading across my face. Michael may have been good at sports, but he never *was* much of a runner. No, that was always me.

Me?

I pull up short, legs pinwheeling as I try to maintain my balance after jerking myself out of a sprint. Up ahead, Michael slows when he realizes I stopped my pursuit. He leans again the tunnel wall laughing. "I thought for sure you had me! What's wrong, Li-Li? Lost your touch?"

No. No, what's wrong is that I am not Lia, and never was her, though I borrowed her mind for a short time. Yet for a minute, it was as though this dead girl took possession of my mind. Infused me with her thoughts and personality and made me act as she would act, speak as she would speak, move as she would move. I think back to other times I slipped up, caught myself thinking as though I was her. I know I'm not Lia. So why do I have to keep reminding myself of that?

"Lia? You okay?" Michael walks back down the tunnel toward me.

"Sudden cramp," I lie, grabbing my calf to corroborate my story. "I'll be fine. I just need to walk it off."

"I'm sorry, it was a deficient id—"

"No, it's fine, it was just me. I guess I'm not used to running."

I start down the tunnel at a slower pace this time, Michael beside me. An awkward silence falls. Maybe I'm not really Lia, but I suddenly wish I were. *Lia* would know what to do right now. *Lia* would know what to say.

Beside me, I can feel Michael's gaze on my cheek, as tangible as a touch. I summon up a smile for him, something to smooth over the strangeness. It slips from my face, though, as I catch sight of his expression, pensive and intent. "What?"

He stares at me awhile longer. "It's just . . ." he begins, then shakes his head. "Nothing."

I shouldn't ask, but I do anyway. "What is it?"

"It's just sometimes it's almost like you're two people. At times, you're just Lia, the girl I knew back on Aurora, and then others it becomes clear you're someone completely different."

He knows. My heart freezes at the realization. Somehow he figured it out. He knows I'm not Lia.

"All this time I've been trying to pretend you're just my friend from Aurora," Michael continues, "only you're not her anymore. Or at least, not just her. You're also the Lia who watched her parents die, the one who spent two years in an internment camp. This Lia I don't know at all."

So he didn't figure it out after all. I mentally breathe a sigh of relief until he adds, "You know, you haven't talked about it even once. What it was like living in the internment camp, losing your parents."

My mouth goes dry. This is the part where I'm supposed to bare my soul to Michael. To tell him all my painful memories about the attack on my home and living as a prisoner and losing everyone I ever loved. Only I can't tell him any of this because it's not my past to reveal; it's not my pain to share. You can't tell what you don't know. Even as I make a half-hearted reach for Lia's memories, I already know what I will find.

My name is Lia Johansen, and I was a prisoner of war.

"I can't tell you," I finally say, because I have no other answer.

"Oh." Michael nods and doesn't say anything else, but I can sense his hurt at being so summarily shut out. I remember the way he talked about his parents before, the way he shared his fears about being drafted, and I feel a twinge of shame that I can't return the confidence. That I can't be to him what he is to me. Not that I'm even sure what that is.

We walk in silence for a while longer.

"A power relay blew at Tiersten yesterday," I say suddenly, the words floating up from nowhere. "I saw it on the news. It wrecked the entire spaceport, turned it into a cinder from the inside out."

Michael stops, stunned. "Oh my God, Lia! Was anyone hurt?"

"They said there were casualties, but they didn't say how many."

"Are you okay? You must have known people there."

"No, no one that I—" *Remember*, I was about to say, and settle for, "I mean, not anymore. But if it had blown just weeks earlier, who knows? Maybe I would have been there. Maybe I would have been one of th—"

"Well, it didn't," Michael interrupts fiercely, "and you weren't there."

"Maybe not this time, but what if that's my fate anyway? What if there's nothing more to my life than to die in a fiery blast, no family, no friends, nothing to leave behind?"

I didn't mean to say this. I didn't even know I was thinking it! The words just crawled up on their own from some small, cold place inside of me, and I find I'm no longer speaking for Michael or even Lia. I'm speaking for myself.

His warm hand takes mine. "That's not the way it'll be," Michael says, his words echoing through the passage, confident and secure. "It's not your fate to die friendless and alone."

"How can you know that?"

"Because you have me."

That simple statement, so matter-of-fact and assured, touches something deep within me; and in the quiet world of this tunnel, a world devoid of everything but two people, a boy and a girl walking together, it occurs to me that for once it isn't Lia's hand Michael's holding. It's mine.

And that's almost enough to make me believe him.

Almost.

13

TONIGHT I HAVE MY first dream since coming on the station. At least, the first one I remember afterward. It's not a normal dream, the sort where you never even question that everything is real, only realizing when you wake that it was too nonsensical to be anything but a dream. No, it's the sort of dream that walks the line between sleeping and wakefulness, where you believe you're awake even though you know you're dreaming. Almost a daydream. Except you must have been sleeping, you realize when you wake, because your conscious mind could never have come up with such strangeness.

My eyes open in the half light of the cargo bay, awake though my mind is still half-asleep. The dream wafts on the edge of my consciousness, its images already beginning to flit away as though it knows its time is over. I close my eyes and drift, that I might prolong the dream, trick it into staying another minute.

An exam room in a medical facility. A man is there, a doctor. I watch his hands, large-knuckled and firm, as he turns my arms over one at a time and runs his fingers lightly over the skin of my forearms. Seemingly satisfied, he releases them. I lift my eyes to his face. His lips make no expression, but the look in his eyes is ineffably sad. He opens his mouth and speaks.

I am in the cargo bay again. It is early morning, the lights already lit for the first risers but kept dim in deference to everyone else. Shadows fall against the cargo crate next to my cot, vague and indistinct and unmemorable, not unlike the images of the dream. Even closing my eyes, I cannot picture them anymore. The knowledge of what I dreamed is still there, though. The words the doctor spoke still linger in my mind.

You may be their only hope.

For a long time I lie there on my cot, knowing there was so much more to the dream yet unable to recall the rest. But the dream is gone, and there is no pulling it back this time. With a sigh, I sit up. It was just a dream; it means nothing. And yet there's this lump of misery balled up so tightly in my chest I almost can't breathe. Maybe the dream was false, but the pain is real.

I press my hand to my chest as though I could physically force it out, and after a few minutes it begins to subside on its own.

"Are you all right, dear?"

It's the elderly woman whose cot sits near mine. Her husband is still asleep, but she's half-sitting, watching me with concerned eyes.

I nod, unable to form words. She reaches under her headrest and extends a handkerchief. I stare at it dumbly until she motions toward her eyes with it. My lips part in surprise as my fingertips skim across my cheek and encounter wetness. I must have cried in my sleep.

With a nod of thanks, I take the cloth square and wipe my face with it. The woman turns onto her other side and lies back down, as if to give me privacy with my grief.

Grief? How can I grieve for something when I do not even know what that thing is? It is as though my heart knows something my head does not. Of course, my head knows so little I suppose there must be a lot of things my heart knows that still remain a mystery to me.

My mood brightens when I remember the new clothes I got from Teal. I wait in line to use a shower unit, even breaking open the special lilac soaps Taylor gave me. Afterward, I throw on one of Teal's outfits — skirt, top, and tights — and head out into the hub. While the clothes make me stand out in the bay, they do the opposite on the rest of the station. No longer am I one of the poor refugees in the gray jumpsuit. Now I'm just another teenager living on the station.

I'm on the lift passing into Level Six when a commotion catches my attention. On the spur of the moment, I step off the platform to check it out. The fuss is coming from one of the docking rings. I cautiously creep forward, flattening myself against a bulkhead as a group of medical personnel rush by. The coast temporarily clear, I dare to slip in after them.

Inside the ring, it's chaos. A ship is docked there, ugly gray smoke wafting from the opening. A dozen people in matching shipsuits and various states of disarray fill the ring. A man with a bloody leg is being supported between two women, who look little better off judging by the stains on their uniforms, and another man leans against a crate, barely able to stand. One woman's hands are a bloody, burned pulp, and several people are coughing from the smoke. A medic leans over a stretcher on the floor, the man beneath him more burn than skin. As I watch, the medic looks up and shakes his head at a tall woman with a winged insignia on her shipsuit. A freighter's guild badge; I recognize it from the time I spent exploring the hub.

The tall woman swears angrily, checks herself, then

runs back into the ship. A minute later she reemerges, another shipmate draped over her shoulders. They are followed closely by a med team bearing a woman on a stretcher. The tall woman releases her shipmate into the care of another med team, and before long injured crewmen are being rushed out of the ring. Their exodus is soon followed by the arrival of a pair of military officers. They zero in on the tall woman where she sags against the wall.

"Lieutenant Derrick Ito," the first one introduces himself.

"Marissa Kerr, captain of the freight hauler *Damascus*."

"Is this everyone?" Ito asks, his voice pitched loud to be heard over the din.

I can't quite make out the captain's answer, but I see the nod of her head.

"What happened? Was it the Tellurians? Did they violate the ceasefire?"

"No, yes. I don't know!" She shakes her head. "I don't have time for this right now. The blasts damaged my refrigeration units. If I don't get this cargo moved now, I'm going to have nothing left to show for my run."

She brushes past the officers and barks an order at one of her men. He nods and immediately speaks to the other two crew members remaining in the ring. The three head into the ship. The captain sighs, glancing around the bay as though her dismay could conjure up more manpower. Her eyes land on me.

"You!" I take a step back, startled at being directly addressed. "Yeah, you! You want a job?"

"Captain," the lieutenant begins.

"You want to do something useful?" Kerr barks at him. "Then, help!" She glances back at me. "Well? You in, girl?"

"W-what do I have to do?"

"Come with me."

Without waiting to see if I'll follow, she plunges back into the ship. After only a moment's hesitation, I follow her. My curiosity is piqued too much to leave now. Besides, it's not like I have anything else to do.

As I pass the officers, I hear the second one mutter about uppity freighter captains who don't know their place. However, the force of the captain's personality is enough to get them inside, and soon we're all arrayed in the ship's cargo bay. Kerr quickly arranges us into a makeshift assembly line, some unpacking the units while others transfer the goods to cargo sleds. My job is to truck the full sleds out to the docking ring where I'm met by a crewman who'll bring it to the new storage unit on the station. Another member waits there to pack the cargo into the new unit.

Time passes in a blur as we work, our focus solely on rescuing as much cargo as we can. It soon becomes clear the captain gave me the easiest job. The sleds are self-propelled and only need someone to guide them. Plus, it takes less time for me to take a sled out to the ring and switch it with an empty one than it takes the crewmen to pack them, so I get a respite between each haul. Even so, the work is harder than anything I've done since arriving on the station, and I'm sweating by the time the pace begins to slack.

Wiping my forehead, I lean against a bulkhead for a moment to rest. Before long, another sled is full and I force myself to straighten.

"I got this one, kid," someone says. "We're almost cleared out here. Why don't you take a break?"

It's one of the soldiers the officers called in to help. They slipped in sometime during the whole fiasco, interpolating themselves into the assembly line with ease. I look around for the captain, but not seeing her, turn back to the soldier.

"You sure?"

"Yeah, we only have about one or two loads left. Take a breather. You earned it."

With a nod, I make my way out of the ship. There are no chairs anywhere in the ring, so I sit on the edge of the entrance ramp to rest, watching as the last couple sleds are exchanged. Not long after, the remaining workers begin filtering out, heading for hygiene units or water or both. A couple of them give me a pat on the shoulder as they pass. When the captain returns, I'm the only one visible.

She frowns. "Is that it? Already?"

I nod, and for the first time since seeing her, the stern look on her face relaxes. She starts to speak, only to be cut off as Ito returns.

"Captain Kerr. I trust your cargo has been properly stowed?" At her affirmative, he continues, "Then I'd appreciate hearing your report."

Kerr nods, moving over to join him. "I suppose I owe you that."

I creep quietly down the ramp to listen, ears pricked as the captain begins her story.

"We were doing a run down to Kiva—nothing contraband, mind you. As you know, the Tellurian borders were just opened a few weeks ago. We knew the run was a bit risky, with the ceasefire being so short-lived, but we figured it would be safe enough. No risk, no gain, right? Turns out we were wrong."

"The Tellurians opened fire on you when you tried to cross into their space," Ito guesses.

"No, that's just it. We entered their space without a problem. They fired on us when we tried to leave."

Ito frowns. "Did they refuse to give you departure clearance?"

"No, we *had* clearance. Our cargo had been certified by the docking inspector; everything was in order. We broke orbit without a problem. If anything, they seemed glad to have trade restored. It wasn't until we neared the border into the Celestial Expanse that we were attacked. A Tellurian warship dropped in on us just as we approached the jump path. They told us to turn around and head back the way we came, or else."

"Did they say why?" Ito asks.

Kerr shakes her head. "Nope. They didn't make any charges, didn't try to board us. They weren't even interested in seeing our clearance documents or checking with the port on Kiva. It's like the cargo was the least of their concerns. Just said if we tried to leave Tellurian space they would fire on us." She shrugs. "Well, since we were close to the jump path, we decided to make a run for it. As you can see, we *mostly* made it."

"And this was a warship? A *Tellurian* warship?"

"Yeah, but . . ." The captain hesitates. "There was something off about it. About them."

"Off? In what way?"

"Well, for one thing they didn't demand to board, though that's usually standard military procedure in cases of suspected smuggling. In fact, when I offered to let them check our cargo for themselves, the captain practically bit my head off."

"Strange. So you think they weren't military at all, but pirates or some such who managed to grab a Tellurian vessel?"

"I don't think so. I've met a few pirates in my day, and they didn't have nearly the discipline these people had. No, I'd lay odds they were military." Kerr frowns. "Even now I'm not sure what they really wanted. Not our cargo, not even us. It was as though they were after something or someone else entirely, and we just happened to be in the way. Maybe I was imagining things, but they didn't strike me as a crew in the middle of a ceasefire, alert but at ease."

"No?"

"No, they struck me as a desperate people continuing to fight a war they already knew was lost."

"Maybe the Tellurians took worse losses than we thought. That would explain their offer to open negotiations over New Earth."

The captain's first mate returns to the ring then and the discussion halts. After making arrangements to speak more later, the officer departs, leaving Kerr to take care of her ship and crew. I sit quietly and try to digest the conversation I just heard. Does the Tellurians' behavior have anything to do with my mission here? If it does, I don't see the connection. Not that it matters. My mission failed and nothing their war vessels might do can change that.

"Learn anything useful?"

I glance up. The freighter captain is walking toward me. "I didn't mean to spy—"

Kerr laughs. "Of course you did. As one of my foster brothers used to say, how will you learn anything important if you don't listen in when you have the chance?" She drops onto the ramp beside me. "So what's a nice station girl like you doing down in the freighter bays? Just curious, or are you interested in the business?"

I bite my lip and reluctantly admit, "I live here. In one of the other cargo bays, I mean. I'm one of the Tiersten prisoners."

I've surprised her; it's evident in her tone. "One of the refugees, huh? Where you from originally?"

"Aurora Colony."

Kerr lets out a low whistle. "Tough break, kid. You doing okay?"

Am I doing okay? I've been asked that a few times since I came onboard the station, but this is the first time I don't immediately know the answer. Between my failed attempt at going Nova and my butchered memory, the obvious answer is no. Until I think about Michael, about Taylor's kindness and Teal's generosity, that is. Somehow when the words, "I'm doing okay," come out, I realize I actually mean them.

Kerr nods and activates her chit. She keys in a few things and, grabbing my hand, uplinks to my chit.

Startled, I tug my hand away as soon as she lets go. "What's this?" I ask, checking my chit to see what she's done.

"I hired you for a job, and you did a great one. Never let it be said that Captain Kerr stiffs her people."

She transferred funds to my chit—two hundred mili-creds to be exact. I stare at the balance in surprise. Refugees don't have money. But now I do.

"Don't transfer it all in one place," Kerr says with a wink. Getting up, she heads up the ramp into the ship. She pauses as she reaches the entrance. "I don't know what's going to happen to all of you, but if you ever find yourself in need of a job, look me up. I might be able to help."

Taking my cue from her, I rise and head toward the exit. As I make my way out of the docking ring, I think about Kerr's offer of employment. It was genuinely kind of her to think of me, but somehow I can't manage to conjure up a single circumstance in which I'd want to take a job on a freighter.

———

It's just after lunchtime and I'm finishing up a sandwich in the cafeteria when I get a link. I can't stop the smile spreading over my face as I think of Michael and remember his words from the day before.

Wow! You look cosmic. Really cosmic.

I'm suddenly glad I took the extra grooming time this morning. I activate my chit, expecting to see Michael's smiling face.

A soldier stares back at me.

"Uh, hello," I say, my smile faltering as I take in his stern expression. While I suppose the station controllers must have all the refugees' link numbers, it never occurred to me that they might use them.

"Lia Johansen?" the soldier asks, and I nod. "I'm Corporal Matheson. Please state your current location."

"I'm in the cafeteria. On Level Five," I hasten to add when he continues to stare at me. A bad feeling starts to spread through the pit of my stomach.

"Your presence is required at the entrance to Cargo Bay 8A. Please report here straightaway."

"Okay. I—Is something wrong?"

The soldier's face gives nothing away. "You will be told all you need to know once you report to the cargo bay."

"I'll come right away."

"Good. Matheson out."

The link cuts off, and I'm left staring at the air where his holo used to be. Why would the soldiers want to see me? Have I done something wrong? They couldn't know that I . . . ? They couldn't have figured out I'm a . . . ? Could they?

No, my only recent dealing with the military was with Ensign Dern, and she didn't seem in the least suspicious. If they were going to figure it out, they would have done so a long time ago, I tell myself. Still, my heart is pattering rapidly in my chest, and for a minute I consider not reporting as ordered. I probably have ten minutes before they'll start missing me, and the station is big with plenty of places to hide.

I shake my head, suddenly realizing how deficient I'm being. They can track me by my chit, so unless I find a way to pry it out of my hand first, I'm not hiding anywhere. Besides, hiding would only make me seem guilty. Whatever they want, it's probably nothing.

My appetite gone, I toss the remainder of my lunch in the trash and head down to Level Eight. Corporal Matheson is at the entrance to the bay, waiting for me.

"Lia Johansen?" he asks when I approach, though he just saw my face on the hololink.

"Yes."

"Come with me." He starts striding briskly toward the lift, and I have to trot to keep up with him. It's only as I follow him onto the lift going down that I have a chance to speak.

"What's going on? Where are we going?"

He glances down at me, face expressionless. "Level Eleven."

Level Eleven? I search my brain, trying to remember my long-ago exploration of the hub, back on my second day on the station. Memory clicks into place, and I can feel the blood drain from my face. Level Eleven? But that's . . .

PsyCorp.

14

MY FIRST INSTINCT IS TO run, and I might have, if I wasn't currently stuck on a lift platform with an armed soldier. Instead, all I can do is stand numbly by his side as the lift descends toward my doom.

Level Nine.

Level Ten.

Level Eleven.

Almost as if sensing my reticence, Corporal Matheson ushers me off the lift, and I have no choice but to precede him through those tall glass doors emblazoned with the half-star. I pause just inside the entrance. The office is elegant and understated, its expense subtly insinuated into the room rather than being overtly showy. Like PsyCorp itself.

Ask anyone what PsyCorp does exactly, and you'll never get the same answer. They are part of the military, but not confined to their jurisdiction. Part of the government, but above their laws. Only one in a million humans are born with psychic powers, true psychic powers beyond that modest sixth sense some people carry, and they are all part of PsyCorp in some way. Any child showing psychic abilities must be brought to PsyCorp for testing and registration. Supposedly they have the same rights and freedoms as everyone else, but somehow all of them end up pressed into some sort of military or government service. The Tellurians do the same thing. In this, at least, the Expanse and the Alliance are not dissimilar.

I once heard that only two percent of the personnel on this station belong to PsyCorp. That they have a whole level of the hub devoted to them, despite the space limitations on a station like New Sol, speaks volumes to their power.

The reception desk looms up in front of me, manned by a short guy with the PsyCorp logo on his uniform, and my heart begins hammering in my chest. The last time I felt this terrified, it was my first ride on the Slip-Stream. The SlipStream ride that jumpstarted my clock for the first time.

I imagine my clock suddenly restarting, my final minutes ticking down as I sit before my worst enemies. After all those minutes I spent in the cargo bay trying to re-start the process, and all I needed was a trip to PsyCorp! I almost snort aloud at the irony.

Thankfully, my clock doesn't restart, at least not yet, and any vestiges of humor quickly vanish as the receptionist takes us down a hall and deposits me in a windowless room with a table, a couple chairs, and little else. The receptionist nods me to a chair, and then he and Matheson take their leave. I don't sit, but stare at the door and wonder if the corporal is posted outside or if I could simply walk out that door with none being the wiser.

Before I can test out the theory, the door opens again and another man enters. He looks at me with kind blue eyes. Familiar blue eyes.

"PsyLt. Rowan," I blurt out stupidly. I'm not sure who I expected, but not him. Somehow his presence eases my fear the smallest bit, as though I can't imagine this man ever doing me any harm. *But he can*, I remind myself, *and he will if he finds out who you are.* What *you are.*

Rowan smiles. "So you remember me, Lia. Good. You seemed so frightened that day you came on the station, I wasn't sure you would."

"You remember me?" I ask guardedly, wondering if he recalls his short view into my mind. If he only belatedly realized that something wasn't quite right and called me down here to finish what he started.

"I remember a lot of the people I checked in that day, for one reason or another. Of course, it helps to have a little reminder," he says with a swish of his tip-pad.

A wave of relief courses through me. Of course. He has a file with my name and picture. I suddenly feel deficient for panicking so easily. When Rowan motions to the chair, I take it. He asks a few questions about my time here so far, how I'm settling in, and what I think of the station. I keep my answers short and conservative, unsure what to make of the pleasantries or their purpose. At last he says, "So as I'm sure you already know, we're conducting interviews with all of the Auroran refugees."

I blink. "You are?"

He laughs. "I guess word hasn't *quite* gotten around yet. We've only met with about a third of you so far."

I *hadn't* heard, but then, I hadn't been spending much time in the bay lately.

"As you may know," Rowan continues, "all of the non-Aurorans are being repatriated back to their home planet or colony, where their respective governments will take over arrangements for reintegrating them back into society. We're already in the process of arranging transport, and we should be able to start sending the first refugees home within a matter of weeks. Obviously, we can't do that for the Aurorans. Despite the ceasefire, Aurora is still technically under Telluria's control."

And even if it weren't, it would hardly be fit for anyone to move back to today, I mentally fill in. Least of all a bunch of former prisoners with little more than a set of clothes and a sleeping roll.

"You're trying to figure out what to do with us," I state, understanding coming at last. All this time I spent panicking, and they don't care about me in the least! They have bigger problems, with several cargo bays full of refugees and nowhere to house them all. At least, bigger problems inasmuch as they know.

"You can't all sleep in the cargo bays forever," Rowan agrees. "Now, a few of the Aurorans have ties to other places in the Expanse—friends or relatives who may be willing to take them in. When possible, we're trying to contact those people and make arrangements with them."

"What about those of us who don't have anyone?"

Rowan hesitates. "Let's just say things are still being decided for the rest of you." He glances away, and a bad feeling starts pervading my gut.

"For right now, we're just trying to place as many people as possible," Rowan continues, turning back to me with a smile. "Now, I know you said in your entry interview that you didn't have any non-Auroran ties. However, it was a hectic day and a lot of people were pretty shaken up. Now that you've been here longer, is there anyone you can think of who might be able to claim you?"

For a split second, thoughts of Michael and Taylor and that little apartment in the Upper Habitat Ring flash in my head. I push the thought away and quickly shake my head. After all they've given me, I hardly have the right to ask for more. Besides, just because they gave me a pillow and some clothes doesn't mean they want to adopt me. Or even Lia.

"Are you sure? Even just a friend of your parents who might be able to help you get a job or an apprenticeship?" Rowan pauses as if undecided whether to speak further and then adds in a serious tone, "You're sixteen, Lia. Now if you were fifteen, you would be considered a minor and passed into the hands of social services, to be placed with a foster family on one of our colonies. However, the government has decided to treat all refugees sixteen years old and up as adults. That means if you don't have anywhere to go, you'll be treated the same as all the others."

The bad feeling in my gut turns to full-blown dread. Rowan is warning me, in his oblique way. He has an idea of what's going to happen to the Auroran adults, and it's not good.

I swallow hard. Maybe I should have taken Kerr's offer of a job more seriously. "I-I'll think about it."

"Good. Perhaps something will come to you over the next couple weeks. An old family friend you forgot, a second cousin twice removed or some such."

Come to me? I resist the urge to laugh. Ever since I destructed in the hygiene unit I've been hoping something will come to me, with zero luck. The only things to come back have been the odd memory here and there of Lia's, and they certainly haven't been helpful. And even if something did come back, what would I tell Rowan? *Well, actually I'm a Tellurian, so if you could just arrange to send me back to your enemy so they can fix my detonator . . .*

Yeah, I'm sure the Celestians would be *happy* to do that, assuming they even believed me in the first place!

The Celestians will never believe us.

My mouth drops half-open before I regain my wits enough to close it. Those words, ringing clear as day in my head. Real words, spoken by a real voice. A man's voice. I struggle to identify the owner of that voice, burrowing deeper into the memory as I repeat the words in my head: The Celestians will never believe us.

My name is Lia Johansen, and I was a prisoner of war.

What? I bite my lip and try again: The Celestians will never believe us.

My name is Lia Johansen, and I was a prisoner of war.

With a silent sigh, I let it go. Whatever I had, it's gone now. I resist the urge to growl out loud in frustration. It's as though the memories are *right there*. I just can't seem to reach them.

"... worry if you're not completely up on all your schooling for the past couple years. We understand that education isn't generally considered a high priority in prison camps. This is just to get an idea of everyone's general skills and education."

Huh?

I force my attention back to Rowan, automatically taking the tip-pad and stylus he hands me. I glance down at the pad. It's some sort of evaluation, like the exams you would take at the end of your REQs, or required educational schooling, to receive your diploma.

"Is everyone taking this?" I ask curiously.

Again, the slight hesitation. "No, just the Auroran adults."

That feeling of dread is back. Still, whatever's happening, it's clear Rowan can't talk about it. Leaning over the pad, I begin the test.

The exam is interactive. It starts by asking my age—easy, sixteen!—then going on to ask my last completed schooling year. This question I don't know the answer to, but working off my identity as Lia and assuming I had schooling up until the internment camp, I answer Year 14. From there, it moves to a more traditional test of my intelligence skills, with a variety of math, English, history, and science questions. I do okay on the history and science, struggle on the English, but absolutely ace the math. So I'm good at math. Interesting. Or it would be, if I knew what it meant.

The second part of the evaluation focuses on my technical skills. Do I have any wood or metalworking skills? Architectural or draftsman training? Do I have experience using industrial chemicals? Am I licensed to operate a motor vehicle? Have I ever used a riding lawn mower (or any of a number of other machines)? Do I have any special skills or honors worth noting? A wry smile twitches my lips at that last question. Does being a genetically engineered human bomb with explosive capabilities count? With a slight shake of my head, I answer "no" for everything. It seems safest.

The final portion of the exam focuses on my medical history. Basic questions about whether I suffer from any ailments or conditions, have any disabilities or have ever had a heart attack or stroke, things like that. I put "no" for everything. Though I don't technically know if my answers are true, I feel healthy enough. Rowan nods at the pad when I'm through as though the results are about what he expected.

"That's about it for this time, but there's one more thing before you go," Rowan adds when I get up to leave. "Your file has been flagged. It seems you've gone into the Upper Habitat Ring twice now. We asked everyone to stay in the hub during the initial check-in. Can you tell me what you were doing there?"

They did? I don't remember being told that, but then,

my clock started up in the middle of my check-in. It's very possible I missed the warning. "I'm sorry," I say, feeling a slight squeeze in my insides at the thought of never going back to Michael's again.

"May I ask what you were doing there?"

"I ran into someone I once knew. He invited me over to his house."

"Is that where you got the clothes from?" Rowan asks with a gesture at my outfit. His eyes narrow when I nod. "Why didn't you mention this earlier?"

"I don't know him or his family very well," I admit, "and their apartment is small. Even if they wanted to take me in, they don't have room."

Rowan purses his lips. "We might be able to help with that." He makes a note on his tip-pad. "I'm giving you dispensation to visit the Upper Habitat Ring for now. Renew your acquaintance, Lia. These people may be your best option."

He hits the door switch to let me out, and I leave as quickly as I can without raising suspicion. The interview may have been innocuous enough, but all it would take is one casual touch from a passing psychic to unveil me. As I step onto the lift going up, I think about Rowan's last words to me.

These people may be your best option, he said, as though I have a future worth worrying about. A future worth fighting for.

Do I? I was never intended to live this long, and even now, I can't ignore that clock in my head, silent and waiting:

00:02:11

Maybe it will start up again tomorrow; maybe it will never start up again at all. How can I plan for a future when I have no idea how long I have left? On the other hand, how long can I ignore the fact that I *am* alive? That whatever I was intended to be, I'm now a person with decisions to make and a life to live. A person who could live to be a hundred, to have a home one day, a family, a job. No different from all those other people living and working on the station. No different from Michael and his family.

There is something attractive about that idea, about being a regular person. Could it be that easy? To disappear into the Celestial Expanse and begin a life with no one ever knowing what I am, what I was meant to do?

Only I would know. I was sent to fulfill a mission, and I failed. Staying on this station is my only chance of possibly fulfilling it. Could I really just turn my back on my past simply to make a life of my own? Am I so selfish?

Michael's face flashes in my head, then Teal's, then Taylor's. If I complete my mission and go Nova just like intended, they'll die, too. There was a time when the idea of their deaths didn't bother me one whit. Now, I can't help shivering as I picture them being blown apart by the very girl they thought was their friend.

I'm so confused. If only I knew more about the mission itself! Who I am and why this space station is so important. I've been watching the news regularly on the viewer in the lounge, looking to see if any other Celestian properties have blown up, but found nothing. If they sent any other bombs into Celestian space, they either weren't coordinated to go off with me or they turned out to be duds, too.

Not for the first time, I can't help wondering why no Tellurian has tried to contact me or even come for me. Surely they know by now that their bomb didn't go off. If only I had an instruction, a memory—anything!—that could tell me what to do. But I don't. I have only myself, and if I don't start making decisions for myself soon, someone else will.

I consider that option for a moment. Maybe that would be for the best. Let Rowan and the officers ship me off with all the other Aurorans to who-knows-where. Let them decide my fate. It would certainly be the easiest course of action.

The question is: if I let someone else make my decisions for me, will I be able to live with the consequences?

15

" 'A TELLURIAN WAR CRUISER is flying in quadrant B6 and is currently located at space coordinate (345.6, 9001.4). A Celestian cargo freighter is also flying in quadrant B6 and wants to remain undetected. Tellurian sensor arrays only have a range up to 745,001 space sects. If the cargo freighter is soon to enter space coordinate (589.1, 4999.8), will it be detected by the Tellurians?' What? How am I supposed to figure that out?"

Michael flips back a couple pages on his tip-pad, scans the page, and goes back to the problem. He frowns, clearly no more enlightened than he was before looking back at the lesson, and slumps back against the wall. "I hate math."

From my spot sprawled across the other side of the bed, I laugh. "It's not *that* bad."

"Easy for you to say," Michael grumbles. "You don't have to do it."

Taking pity on him, I put the hologame he loaned me on pause and sit up. Sliding over, I glance over his shoulder at the tip-pad. "This is easy, Michael. Just use the distance formula."

Michael shakes his head at my assessment of "easy," but puts his stylus to the pad. "I don't know how you do it. Even when we were kids you were doing all the advanced math lessons. Mr. Russell was always raving about what a genius you were."

"That wasn't Mr. Russell," I say automatically. "That was Ms. Francis. Mr. Russell was the one I convinced you was an alien for half a day."

"You did not!"

"Did too! You were so gullible back then, Michael."

"I was not. I was just playing along."

I smirk at him. "Sure, and that's why you lined your baseball cap with alumna-seal. Seriously, I could convince you of anything."

Michael gives me a dark look, but I just smile sweetly back. His mouth twists in a wry smile, and then his hand shoots out and grabs my foot. I shriek in surprise as his fingers tickle the bottom of my foot.

"Aah! Stop it, ha ha, oh stop, please! Ha ha, Michael!"

I manage to yank my foot away, and Michael lets me go. "Maybe I was the gullible one," he says, leaning down until his face is right next to mine, "but you were always the ticklish one."

My breath leaves me in a whoosh, and for a second I forget to breathe. Michael's eyes, so deep and brown, are staring into mine with that look he has, the one that says I'm the most important person in the universe. Warmth pours off his skin, warmth and vigor and pulsing life force, so strong they brush across my skin like a physical touch. My stomach flips over, and I'm helpless to look away.

"Get a room, you two! Preferably one I'm *not* in."

Teal's irritated voice breaks the spell, and I drop my gaze. Michael pulls away as well, leaning back against the wall in his original position. "Don't you have homework to do?" he asks her snidely.

"Nope. Finished it hours ago," Teal replies. "It was so easy, it didn't take long at all."

The curtain dividing their room is currently pulled back like it is most afternoons, and she's leaning back in her chair as she scrolls through a fashion zine. Michael scowls at the reminder that, even enrolled in all the advanced courses, Teal still finds school remarkably easy. Far easier than he does.

"Don't you have some sort of science project?"

"That's not due for another three-square. Besides, I'm doing it on the enviro system, so I can't work on it until Gran takes me over and shows me around."

Michael rolls his eyes at Teal's pompous tone and goes back to his math. As I turn back to my hologame, I catch Teal staring at me from across the room. Her lips are pursed and her brow narrowed, a disapproving look on her face. What was once only wariness has morphed into outright disapprobation in the weeks I've spent with Michael, as if the closer I get to Michael the more threatened she feels. I would just tell her I have no intention of coming between her and Michael . . . *if* I actually thought she'd believe me, that is.

With a shrug, I go back to my game. As long as she doesn't suspect what I am, Teal's approval isn't necessary.

It's been three weeks since my meeting with PsyLt. Rowan on Level Eleven, and life has settled into an easy pattern. In the mornings I jog around the hub or along the SlipStream tunnel. Even without Michael to race, the exercise makes me feel exhilarated and alive, as if I could do anything, if only I knew what I needed to do. Afterward, I get breakfast in the cafeteria and watch the news in the Blue Lounge. I haven't seen any more stories about Tiersten. Still, the images of the camp remain burned into my brain, and though I try to explain the memories away as Lia's, more and more I'm convinced I was there. Not that I have any more idea what that means than I did before.

In the afternoons I hang out in the hub. After my encounter with Captain Kerr, I started spending more time in the docking area, managing to pick up another couple of odd jobs. I even ran into Kerr once more before she finished repairs and left to complete her run.

"Hey, kid," she greeted when I poked my head inside the docking ring a week ago.

"How's your ship?" I asked.

The captain shrugged and checked off a couple cartons on her tip-pad. "Banged up, but space-worthy, at least enough for me to finish my run. Luckily, I don't have to go back into Tellurian space anytime soon."

"Did they find out who shot at you?"

"No. When approached, the Tellurian government denied all knowledge of the attack. Said it was a band of pirates, and they would devote all their resources to tracking them down." Kerr snorted, clearly unconvinced by the explanation. "Whatever they said must have been good since the ceasefire is still holding."

I felt a twinge of guilt, as if simply by being Tellurian I was to blame for what happened. The ceasefire is all a ruse; nobody knows that better than me. After all, you don't send a human bomb into an enemy space station if you plan on upholding the ceasefire. Kerr's skepticism was right on the mark, though she didn't know it. Still, I couldn't help hoping that maybe they'd changed their minds. Maybe they took my failure as a sign, and that's why no one came for me.

Then it was my turn to snort. Whatever was going on, I doubted it was that.

Before I left, Kerr gave me her link number. "Good

luck, kid. Maybe I'll see you again when I pass back this way."

"Yeah, maybe."

Assuming the station is still standing at that point. My clock has dropped another eight seconds since seeing Rowan—seven seconds after a slip on the lift led to a near-fall and one second during a nightmare. The latter instance I find particularly disturbing. I never imagined I could lose time in my sleep, but the evidence, boldfaced in my mind when I awoke, was undeniable:

$$*00:02:03*$$

Thirty seconds. That's how much time I've lost since waking up on the floor of the hygiene unit to find I was a dud. If all my time slips away just a few seconds at a time, will I actually go off when my clock finally reaches zero? I wish I knew.

My evenings have been spent in the cargo bay or at Michael's. I visit Michael every chance I get. Even when he's busy with homework, like tonight, there's usually something for me to do. Help Michael with his math, hang out with Taylor in the kitchen, even just play one of Michael's holy games while he works. Last week he even took me to one of his g-ball games, and afterward, to a party with some of his friends. I felt strange, going to a party full of strangers, but Michael stayed by my side all night.

No doubt Rowan would be happy about the amount of time I'm spending with Michael, but that's not why I come see him. I genuinely like being around Michael. Besides, the bay is smelly and crowded, and I much prefer the fresh air and quiet of the rings. Although, even the rings haven't been as pristine as usual, the sweet-and-sour smell creeping in some days in isolated spots, like today. Maybe it's because the misters, still acting up, have shut off again.

I shake my head, not particularly caring about the reason one way or the other, and resume my game. My lapse in concentration has caught up with me, my player suddenly catching on fire in a blaze of holographic flame before I can stop it.

"Stop, drop, and roll," I urge her, but it's too late. She dies writhing in agony on my palm. The game's anguished screams are far too lifelike for my comfort. Even though I know they're holo-generated, I still shiver every time I hear them.

Michael glances at me, having finished the math with my help and moved on to his history. "How many times have you died now?"

"Nine," I admit glumly. "Maybe I should go."

"No, wait. I'm almost done. Just one more question." His chit vibrates to indicate an incoming h-mail, and he stops to check it. "It's Dad!"

Michael's face brightens, and he immediately drops his pad to check the message. A man's face comes up. I can immediately see Michael in the man's strong jaw and brown eyes.

"Hey, Michael," the image says, and it becomes clear that Michael didn't just inherit his dad's eyes and jaw, but his smile. "I hope everything is going well on New Sol, and that you're not giving your gran too hard a time. I got the holo of your last game—watched it twice. I hate to say it, but I'm starting to think you could give me a run for my creds. Maybe you could apply a little more of that enthusiasm to your schoolwork, especially your math?" Michael's dad raises an expectant eyebrow, but I can tell he's still really proud, whatever Michael's math grade was.

The image continues. "We've been on patrol in . . . well, I'm not allowed to say where, but so far everything's been nice and quiet with the ceasefire. We're still on alert, of course. You just never know how these things will work out. Still, your mother and I are hopeful that upcoming negotiations will go well with the Tellurians. We miss you and Teal terribly, and we could all use some R&R.

"Speaking of which," the image sighs, his face creasing with disappointment. "I know I told you it looked like we'd be stopping by New Sol sometime in the next few weeks to take on supplies, but unfortunately plans have changed. We've been reassigned and our new route won't take us anywhere near New Sol. I'm sorry, but it looks like we won't be seeing you anytime soon."

I stifle a gasp and steal a look at Michael. The smile is gone from his eyes, his animated expression now wooden and stiff. Even Teal drops the front legs of her chair back to the floor, a grave look on her face.

"Look, Michael, I'm on duty again shortly, and I want to get a message recorded for Teal before I go. I know this is disappointing, but we'll see each other again. I promise. In the meantime, watch out for Teal. She likes to act tough, but I know the separation is hard on her, too. With me gone, you have to be the man of the house. Remember, your mother and I love you both very much. Bye, son."

Whack!

I jump as Michael's tip-pad hits the wall across the room.

"Geez, Michael!" Teal exclaims, though she doesn't look particularly surprised by the action. Michael doesn't say anything, just grabs his jacket and stalks out of the room. A minute later I hear his and Taylor's voices raised in the living room, followed a few seconds later by the sound of the front door. Silence reigns.

I get off the bed and start hunting for my shoes. "I'll g—"

"It won't do any good," Teal interrupts. "There's no talking to Michael when he vacs out like this."

I abandon the search and sink back on the bed. "Does this happen a lot?"

"It did when Dad first left, though not so much anymore. He just worries a lot. Michael's never been good at sitting home and waiting." She glances down at her chit and waves her hand, a resigned expression on her face. "Here's mine."

Teal's message is similar to the one Michael received. Their dad praises Teal's recent academic honors and tells her she's looking more beautiful with every message. Teal shakes her head as if to say the very idea is silly, but I can tell she's soaking in every word. The bad news following, of course, comes as no surprise.

"Take care of Michael, Teal," the message finishes. "He needs you, even if he won't admit it. Oh, and be nice to that new girlfriend of his—what was her name? Lia? From the sounds of it, she's been really good for him. I love you so much, baby girl. Talk to you again soon."

I gape, shocked to hear my name. Michael's girlfriend? Me? No, that can't be right. Michael's dad must have misinterpreted his last message. Michael doesn't think of me as more than a friend.

Does he?

"Well, that's that," Teal says, turning off her chit and leaning back in her chair. It occurs to me that in her own way, Teal is just as disappointed as Michael at the news, for all that she doesn't show it so dramatically.

"So when do you think Michael will be back?" I ask.

Teal shrugs. "The last time he got like this, he didn't come back for five hours. You should probably go. I'm sure he'll link you once he's over his little snit."

"I'll wait," I say firmly. "I mean, if that's okay with you."

She raises her eyebrows in clear disbelief. "Why would you want to do that?"

"Because . . . it's Michael." Michael, who spent who-knows-how-long searching the lists for me that first day on the station. Michael, who came for me after I malfunctioned in the hygiene unit and forced me to get up. Michael, who held my hand and told me a lonely death would not be my fate.

I don't say any of this, but it must be in my eyes, for after a long moment's pause, Teal nods and hooks Michael's chair out with her foot. "Sit down."

I spend the rest of the evening with Teal. She has a fashion holo that allows the user to upload a digital of themselves and then try out different outfits and hairstyles. It even has an age progression function which extrapolates what you would look like as you grow older. I feel a little awkward with Teal at first, very cognizant of the fact that she doesn't like me, but the earlier disapproval seems to have mellowed somewhat, softened into something harmless and benign. I even start having fun, giggling with Teal as we use her holo to turn a picture of sixteen-year-old Michael in faux-jeans and a T-shirt into a hundred-year-old Michael, stooped and wrinkled and clad in a sparkly ball gown. Then Teal snaps a digital of me with her chit and we try the same thing on me. I'm squinting like a total null in the picture, for she caught me a bit by surprise, but I'm too glad we're getting along to complain. Instead, I watch the age progression and wonder if I'll ever be any of those ages.

Tiring of the game, we're about to put the holo away when I suddenly get an idea.

"Teal, can you do the age thing in reverse? See what someone would look like younger?"

"Sure. Why? Want to see yourself as a baby?" She runs the picture in the opposite direction. I stop her when it hits age nine. For a long moment, all I can do is stare at the holo in front of me.

"Can you make me a digi of that?"

Teal gives me a curious look, but makes the digital and uploads it to my chit. We're about to throw on the viewer when the front door sounds.

Teal checks her watch and whistles. "Only two hours." She gives me a sidelong glance and says grudgingly, "Maybe Dad's right."

Right? My brow furrows in confusion until my mind flashes back to her message.

Oh, and be nice to that new girlfriend of his. From the sounds of it, she's been really good for him.

Me? Good for Michael? I thought it was the other way around. Before I can formulate a response, the door to the bedroom flies open and Michael fills the doorway. "What are you still doing here?" he blurts out.

I stand and fumble for my stuff, suddenly worried that I overstepped some boundary, stayed when I should have gone. I try for a nonchalant shrug. "I had to make sure you were sat, right?"

He blinks, clearly surprised. Then without warning he steps forward and hugs me. "You're a good friend, Lia."

For a second, all I can do is stand there, mouth half-open as the truth hits me like a rogue comet. Michael's right. I may not be Lia Johansen, I may not ever know who I really am, but I'm not nothing.

I am Michael's friend.

Of their own volition my arms rise up, folding around Michael as fiercely as he's holding me. His hug is warm and solid and something I've been craving for an eternity; I just didn't know it. I close my eyes and let myself ache with the most profound anguish I've ever felt. Ache, and be soothed by the balm I find in his arms.

Maybe it's not a name to call my own, but I can't help thinking that I'd take the identity *Michael's Friend* over *Human Bomb* any day.

———

I'm coming back from the hygiene unit after getting ready for bed later tonight when I remember the digital I had Teal make for me. Plunking down on my cot, I activate my chit.

There it is, that blonde nine-year-old, age progressed down from my own image. Hand trembling slightly, I pull up one of the digitals Michael uploaded for me from when we were kids. The two girls look exactly alike.

I gasp, excitement welling up inside of me as I stare at those digis. The clues have been there all along; I just didn't put them together, not until I saw the digital. The way Lia and I both get motion sick, the way we both like to run and hate reading, the way we're ticklish on the bottoms of our feet and are good at math. I'm not just some generic clone cooked up from some scientist's DNA in a lab sent to take her place. I'm *Lia's* clone.

The explanation makes so much sense, I could almost smack myself for not figuring it out before! A clone, grown from Lia's DNA in a lab and rapidly aged to match her age. It explains everything—why we have so many things in common, why I was at Tiersten, even why I have no identity or memories of my own. I'm probably only a matter of weeks old, grown specifically for the purpose of infiltrating New Sol.

Relief pours through me at this new understanding. After all these weeks of wondering about my past, it all makes perfect sense now. Suddenly my friendship with Michael doesn't feel like such a sham. So maybe I'm not the *actual* Lia who grew up with him on Aurora, but I'm pretty darn close. I have her DNA, her natural talents, her personality. I'm not such a fraud, after all!

I pull up a few more digitals from Michael, marveling at how perfectly they match the age-enhanced image. There's the one of Michael and me on the swing, and there's one of us on bikes, and there's another one of just me, sitting on the porch steps in a floral sundress and pigtails. I smile at the image and enlarge it, looking at those chubby cheeks, messy braids, and bright green eyes. The resemblance between us is amazing.

Lying back on my cot, I test out my new identity in my head.

My name is Lia Johansen, and I am the clone of a prisoner of war. Created for the purpose of destroying New Sol Station, I believed myself a failure when my clock stopped and I didn't go Nova. My life changed forever when I met a boy named Michael, and he became my friend.

As stories go, it's not such a bad one, I think, a slight smile curling over my lips. Not so bad at all.

16

THE SWING DANGLES, *limp and drifting, from the bar overhead. I clutch the chains and drag my feet through the dirt below. Around me, the play-ground is abuzz with activity. Children, hanging from the monkey bars and riding the merry-go-round, swishing down the slide and running through the field. White flowers dot the grass at intervals, white flowers with blue centers.*

I pick a blossom near my feet and twirl it around in my fingers. Of all the children on the playground, only I am on the swings. Only I am alone.

No, not quite. There she is, another girl off to my left. My eyes zero in on her. She is blonde, like me, with green eyes and small hands. A jump rope whistles around her head, her feet striking the ground in cadence with her voice. I strain to make out the singsong lyrics.

*"Cross my heart and hope to die
Stick a needle in my eye
My past is gone, my life's a lie
All I have left to do is die."*

I gasp, climbing off the swings and moving toward her, compelled by the sound of her voice. The song continues:

"Wait! Before my time is through
I have one secret left for you
A way to start a ticking clock
A key to loose a stopped-up lock."

A group of boys kicking a soccer ball run in front of me, and I lose sight of the girl. I push against them, straining my head as I try to spot her through the crowd. What secret? What key?

"Cross your heart and hope to die
Stick a needle in your eye
We both know you've earned this pain
And now it's time to die again."

The boys are gone as quickly as they appeared. I take a step forward, and stop. The girl has vanished as well. I turn around, looking for her, but the children have all disappeared, the playground empty and still. "Wait!" I call into the silence. "Who are you? Where did you go?"

No answer.

Something catches at the corner of my eye, and I turn toward the school. The clang of the school bell bursts from the building. Not just the building, but the swings, the bars, all around me, raucous and pulsing, pulsing, pulsing—

The klaxons jerk me from a sound sleep. Strident and shrill, they wail through the cargo bay in high-pitched pulses, and I'm up and staggering off my cot before I even realize what's happening. *What the . . . ?*

Pressing my hands over my ears, I wrench my head left and then right, trying to figure out what's going on.

Are we under attack? Is the ceasefire at an end? Or is this Plan B, the Tellurian's backup plan when I didn't go Nova as intended? I brace myself for weapons fire, for the earthshaking impacts of deton-cannons exploding against the station's hull, but the telltale bangs don't come. Not yet, anyway.

I dare to lower my hands the slightest bit. "What's happening?" I yell at a young woman in sweats a few feet away. She stares at me, eyes glazed in fear, and I scream the question again. Her eyes blink, and this time she manages to shake her head at me. She doesn't know either. In fact, no one seems to, the other prisoners stumbling about in various states of dress, frightened children clinging to bewildered parents with crying infants in their arms, uncertain whether to run, and if so, where to go.

Before I can formulate a plan, soldiers pound into the bay. Their orders are barely audible over the shrieking of the alarm, but I realize from their motions that they want everyone up and following them. I fall in with the mob of refugees stampeding toward the bay entrance, certain that at any moment we'll be annihilated by some terrible weapon of mass destruction.

A terrible weapon of mass destruction. Even in spite of the urgency, the irony of the situation isn't lost on me. I would almost find it humorous, if I wasn't so utterly terrified.

Stumbling over the lip of the bay entrance, I almost fall before a random hand rights me. We are practically jogging now, and I struggle to look around through the dense crowd. From what I can glimpse, the main level is in complete chaos, refugees from two locations being herded through the area while various spacers and station personnel hurry toward their ships or the lifts. Soldiers urge them on their way, quick commands bringing order to the chaos. In fact, for a mass evacuation at seven in the morning, they seem to have things surprisingly well in hand, their sharp eyes watching to make sure no one is trampled in the rush even as they guide us into yet another storage area near the center of the level.

The walls are reinforced—a bunker of some sort, or as near as they have in this part of the station. I take a seat against the wall as directed, smashed up between a large man with a handlebar mustache on one side and a little girl with a red ponytail on the other. The stench is almost overwhelming in here, the sour-and-sweet smell practically burning my nostrils as I sit amid the crush of bodies. I pinch my nostrils together, but it doesn't help. I can still taste them, like a thick film of odor clinging to my tongue. I try to ignore it, again listening for the sounds of attack, but I hear nothing besides the cease-less howling of the klaxons. My hands shake, my palms sweating and slippery despite my best efforts to stay calm. If only Michael was here to hold my hand.

As if some divine presence read my mind, a hand sud-denly slips into mine. I start in surprise and glance down to find the red-haired girl staring up at me. She can't be more than eight, and whether her parents survived Tiersten or not, they don't seem to be with her. She has a death grip on my hand, her palm tiny within my own. My own fear ebbs slightly as I stare at her pale face, and I squeeze her hand back.

"What's your name?" I lean down and ask her, as much to distract myself from the situation as her.

"Kaeti." She has to repeat it three times before I hear her.

"I'm Lia." I take a look around the bay, hoping to find some redheaded adult anxiously searching the crowd for their child, but no one stands out. "Are your parents on the station with you, Kaeti?"

She shakes her head.

"An aunt or uncle maybe?"

Another shake.

"Anyone?"

"There's Lela," she says, and after some more questioning I determine that she's an ex-prisoner who has taken Kaeti under her care along with a couple of the other orphaned children. Against all reason, I feel a sudden sense of kinship with this child. We're nothing alike—not in looks or age or even origin. Not even in experience, for my years at Tiersten are only a fake, the memories someone else's rather than my own. Neither of us has parents, though; neither of us has family. We're both alone, and in that I find a similitude between us that speaks to me.

"I don't have any family either," I admit. "I have a friend, though. His name is Michael. What about you?"

Kaeti blinks at me a few times, and then begins speaking haltingly about one of the other refugee children. It's strange. Here I am, crammed into a reinforced bay while the station's alarms scream bloody murder, somehow having a conversation with a little girl I didn't even know existed ten minutes ago. I'm so absorbed in the experience, it actually takes me a minute to realize the klaxons have stopped sounding.

A murmur sweeps over the crowd, everyone wanting to know what's going on. A voice suddenly booms from the public address system.

"Emergency Drill Beta has now been completed. Station facilities and transit services will be reopening momentarily. All personnel are now free to resume normal activity. Thank you for your cooperation."

Emergency Drill Beta? So these past thirty minutes of terror were nothing more than a test?

Around me, I hear cries of outrage, the other former prisoners no more happy about the ordeal than I. Still, there's nothing to do but collect ourselves and start the shuffle back to our respective holds, to sleep if we can or begin our morning routines if we can't. I'm waiting for the mob in front of me to move when my chit vibrates. I answer the incoming link.

"Morning, Lia."

"Michael! What's going on? Did you go through that too? Was this really all just some sort of test?"

The questions tumble out of my mouth one after another, and Michael laughs. "Hey, power down, Li-Li, everything's sat. It was just a drill."

I raise my eyebrows. "You mean you've done this before?"

"Sure, all the time. We have a drill for every possible scenario that could ever happen—drills in case we come under attack, or there's a hull breach in one of the rings, or there's an overload in the hub's power reactors. That's a fun one—they actually separate the station for that one. I had to watch an informational holo and pass a test on them when I first moved here. Everyone does. I guess they didn't make you guys do it since you aren't permanent residents. They're just to prepare us in case something goes wrong and a real alarm goes off."

"A *real* alarm?" I ask nervously.

"Yeah, there's these small alarm boxes situated around the station, in case there's a fire or a relay explosion or something. Only the officers can set them off, though, so don't get any ideas."

He winks at me, and I find myself doing one of Teal's

signature eye rolls. As though, out of the two of us, it would be *me* who had the ideas.

Michael starts chuckling. "I remember my first drill, about a month after I moved here. I was determined not to look like a null, to play it cool rather than vaccing out like most newcomers, so when the siren went off I took my time moving to the shelter. Trouble was, I forgot that the SlipStreams lock down fifteen minutes after the alarm goes off, so by the time I got there it was closed. I was trapped in the hub! I had no idea what to do."

"What happened?"

"Oh, an officer found me and took me to one of the hub shelters. Gave me a real jawing out, too. The only reason he didn't give me a fine was because I was a minor. You can bet I never missed another SlipStream after that."

Despite my irritation over being woken up so early for a drill, I find myself smiling. Leave it to Michael to get stuck in the hub during an evacuation drill!

"Anyway," Michael continues, going all serious, "I was linking because I just wanted to say I'm sorry. For walking out like that last night. I was a total drone."

"No, you weren't—"

"Yes, I was," Michael interrupts. "Or as Teal put it, 'How could you just walk out on Lia like that? Is your brain *completely* deprived of oxygen, Michael?'"

I can't help laughing. Michael's imitation of Teal's scornful tone is dead on. "Did she really say that?"

"Uh huh. You know Teal. She's never afraid to say what she thinks."

Teal defending *me*? I can hardly believe it. Though her hostility toward me did seem to lessen temporarily when I asked to wait for Michael last night, he and I are only closer now. If anything, I would appear to be even more of a threat to their relationship in her eyes. I wonder what changed her mind.

Then again, maybe she wasn't really defending me, but was just mad at Michael for leaving her to entertain me all night.

"So do you forgive me for acting like a de-oxygenated drone?"

"Of course."

"Teal said you would. You're truly one in a galaxy, Lia."

Well, two in a galaxy, I almost say, thinking of the real Lia and my discovery from the night before about being her clone. Instead, I just thank him for the compliment and wave goodbye as he signs off to go to school. With the hold half-empty now, I find it easy to join in the march back to my cargo bay. As I walk down the corridor, I catch sight of the alarms Michael mentioned, unassuming gray boxes situated at regular intervals along the station walls. Curious, I check one out. It's a simple device, with a scanner for the officers to swipe their chits and a keypad to enter the specific alarm code. Shaking my head, I just hope we never have cause for a *real* alarm to go off.

To my surprise, Kaeti is still beside me even with all my dallying. She follows me the rest of the way to the bay and watches as I pull out clean clothes from my locker. She sits on my cot while I change behind a cargo crate, and even after I return from the hygiene units she's still there, waiting for me. Somehow I made another friend, and I'm not entirely sure what to do with her.

I'm saved from having to figure that out when a tired-eyed matron comes running over. "Kaeti!" she calls, relief evident in her voice.

"Lela?" I hazard as she gathers Kaeti up in her arms and looks at me curiously. She nods, and I tell her my name.

"Thank you for taking care of Kaeti, Lia." She glances around. "Do you have family here?" When I shake my head, she adds, "Neither do I. Kaeti is my family now."

Once again, I feel that sudden sense of connection, that feeling that I'm not so different from everyone around me after all. Even after Lela leaves with Kaeti, I think about them, the orphaned redhead and the lonely matron. Maybe families aren't just born, but made. My mind flicks to Michael, to Teal and Taylor. *Maybe, just maybe . . .* But I don't let my mind finish the thought.

It is only as I'm sitting down to breakfast in the cafeteria on Nine that I remember that strange dream I had this morning, just before the alarms went off. I struggle to recall it, but all I can seem to bring back is this one stanza, repeating over and over in my head.

Cross your heart and hope to die.
Stick a needle in your eye.
Your past is gone, your life's a lie
All you have left to do is die.

———

Afternoon finds me hanging out at the counter of a bar frequented by traders and other assorted spacers. Technically, I'm not old enough to be there, but the proprietor is a friend of Captain Kerr's, and he lets me hang out there so long as I don't try to drink anything I'm not supposed to. It's as good a place as the docking rings to suss out potential odd jobs, with the bonus that I don't have to spend so much time walking around.

I sit at the bar and listen to the patrons as I sip a bubbler. Everyone is keyed up after this morning's drill, their talk focusing less on their usual runs and more on the political situation between the Tellurians and the Celestians. Some think the morning's drill is indicative of a breakdown in negotiations between the two governments, though so far all reports indicate the negotiations—still via viewscreen only—are going well. Others disagree, believing, like Michael, that the drill was nothing more than that—a drill. After all, just because a ceasefire is on doesn't mean the war is over.

A burly spacer with a moustache and stained shipsuit plunks down on the stool next to me. He hails the bartender.

"You just get in?" the barkeep asks as he delivers a beer and scans the man's chit.

The spacer nods. "This morning."

"How long are you here for?"

"A few hours. Just long enough to refuel and get on my way again."

"Heading out or in?" After hearing enough trader talk over the past couple weeks, I know the bartender is asking if the trader intends to head out of the Celestial Expanse or deeper in. With New Sol being the main portal into and out of the Expanse, most traders stop to refuel here when crossing the border.

"Out," the spacer replies taking a pull of his beer.

"That's daring."

"That's suicidal," another voice interjects. Looking over, I see another man pull up to the bar, an empty glass in his hand as he signals for a refill. He's the physical opposite of the spacer, tall and thin and clean shaven, his two-piece uniform spotless. "Take my advice, friend, and stay out of Alliance space."

The trader gives the other man a scornful once-over, easily determining from his natty appearance that the man is no spacer. "What would you know about it?" he says with a snort.

"Only that what the Tellurians claim is going on over on their side of the border isn't so."

"How would you know that?"

"Because I was over there." The tall man points to a patch on his sleeve. "Lionel Merrins, holorecorder for GNS Reporting."

The credential is enough to catch the spacer's attention. "Okay, I'll bite. What's *really* going on over there?"

"I'm not sure—"

"Ha!"

"—but I do know it's not what they're saying. For instance, that little blow-up at Tiersten a couple weeks ago? It was no accident."

Tiersten? What was a casual interest in the conversation ratchets up ten degrees at the mention of the colony. I inch across my stool, trying to get closer to the discussion without being noticed.

"Go on," the spacer says.

"The Tellurians are trying to claim it was a malfunction in the power relay, but my ship was right overhead in orbit when it happened, and let me tell you, that blast was not a malfunction. It was sabotage."

"Sabotage?"

"Oh, the Tellurians fed us this slagheap about a breakdown in the power grid, but we had the readings. That was a bomb, plain and simple. Of course, we couldn't report it, not with a Tellurian war cruiser breathing down our necks, but anyone could see that spaceport was blown to kingdom come. Like a little power relay could do that."

"You think the prisoners sabotaged the spaceport?

That's completely glitchy. The Tellurians already released one group of them. With negotiations proceeding, there was no reason to think they wouldn't be next."

Merrins leans in, lowering his voice slightly. "It wasn't the prisoners. It was the Tellurians."

The spacer lets out a laugh, his rapt attention dissolved. "The Tellurians? Now why would they blow their own spaceport?"

"Because these aren't your typical Tellurians, but a splinter faction. Word is the Alliance is in the middle of a civil war."

"They're not happy about the situation with New Earth," the bartender speculates.

"That's what I've heard," the newsman confirms. "After three years of stubbornly defending their half-assed claim, the Alliance government has suddenly decided to turn it over to us? It makes no sense, not with all the resources down on New Earth ripe for the plucking. All it would take is for a few of the Alliance's major commonwealths to band together, and they'd have a faction to be reckoned with."

"Do you really think they'd start a civil war over it, though?" the spacer asks doubtfully. "A war no one in the Expanse has even heard of?"

"Why not? People have gone to war for a hell of a lot less. And of course they wouldn't want us to know about it, would they? One sign of weakness, and we'd be all over them. The Alliance government would do anything to cover it up." Merrins shakes his head. "I doubted it at first too, but the things I've seen and heard over there ... Tellurian ships firing on other Tellurian ships, strange acts of sabotage, the Tellurians inviting in Celestian traders only to turn around and fire on them when they try to land or leave. Whether it's civil war or not, something is going on over there, no doubt about it." He takes a pull of his drink. "Be smart. Stay home and do a local run. The milicreds aren't worth getting mixed up in whatever's going on over there."

The spacer shakes his head. "I appreciate the warning, but a man's got to make a living."

"It's your funeral." Merrins raises his glass to the spacer, and the other man returns the gesture. The newsman leaves then and the spacer goes shortly after. I stay at my seat and ponder everything I just heard.

The explosion at Tiersten a deliberate act of sabotage? The Tellurian Alliance embroiled in some secret civil war? It all seems too farfetched to believe. The newsman was probably just putting the spacer on, having a laugh at his expense while he killed time in a bar between assignments. It certainly seems more likely than all the crazy stuff he spewed! Still, I can't help thinking about the attack on Kerr's ship and those images I saw of Tiersten. Now that I think about it, it *did* seem like an awful lot of damage for a relay malfunction.

Reluctantly, I consider Merrins' assertions. Assuming the Tellurians really are involved in a civil war, my presence here raises even more questions, top of the list being: was I sent here by the Tellurian government or this Tellurian splinter faction? I can't imagine what this supposed faction would gain from sending me. Surely their hands would be full just fighting their own people without worrying about the Celestians. Unless their purpose was to destroy the ceasefire? If they could disrupt negotiations with the Celestians, maybe it would allow them more time to get their hands on New Earth. That doesn't explain how Tiersten ties into all this though. It seems like more than simple coincidence that the site of such large sabotage happens to be the colony I—or at least the real Lia—spent time in.

I shake my head, unable to even begin to answer all the questions this new information inspires. Once again, I curse my faulty memory. I'm sick of being in the dark, of not knowing who I am or what my purpose is. *Why* can't I just remember what happened?

I pause. Maybe I can't remember what's going on, but perhaps there's another way I can find out.

17

THE MAIN RESEARCH CENTER is located in the Lower Habitat Ring. I've never been there before, my explorations so far confined to the hub and Michael's ring. Now as I stride into the center, it occurs to me that Rowan's dispensation to visit Michael only extends to the Upper Habitat Ring. I pause briefly at the door, and shrug. They didn't nab me the first time I walked into the upper ring without permission. Hopefully, they won't worry too much if I spend an afternoon in the lower ring. Still, I hurry to take a seat at the first open carrel.

The NSol, or station net, can be linked into from anywhere on the station. I access it from my chit all the time. However, to link into the Celestial Interplanetary Net, one needs equipment a little stronger than the cheap device in my hand. I queue up the viewer in front of me, frowning at the password prompt until I catch sight of a login card at the side of the screen. Username: last name, date of birth. Password: chit number.

I key in the information and watch as the CIpN slowly loads. From here, I can access information from across the Expanse, even as far out as Icarus or Nementh. Of course, a search that far out would take considerable time to yield results. The signal would have to go through any number of trans-galactic satellites to retrieve the information and then come back again. Luckily, I don't need information from backward colonies on the fringes of space.

The first thing I do once the page loads is try to pull up the TAIN—the Tellurian Alliance Informational Network. In peace time, the TAIN and the CIpN can be accessed through each other. Unsurprisingly, I get an error message when I try to access it. I'm disappointed, but only mildly so. As everyone on the station is keenly aware, a ceasefire is a far cry from peace. I'll just have to find what I'm looking for elsewhere.

I go to the Celestian newsfeeds next, focusing on the ones streaming from the planets and colonies closest to the Tellurian border. I'm not sure what I'm looking for exactly. Something to back up Merrins' claims. Strange happenings that might indicate an alliance at war with itself. For three hours I look through articles from all the top feeds, searching for anything suspicious. Nothing. Not that jumps out at me anyway.

I lean back in my chair and rub my shoulders. Either Telluria is doing a really good job of covering up its internal issues or Merrins' story was just smoke. If not for my encounter with Kerr, I would have given up long ago.

Kerr.

A thought suddenly occurs to me. I sign out of the newsfeeds and start hunting through the freighter boards. The searches take longer, the servers running the freighter pages not nearly as powerful as those running the main newsfeeds, but my persistence pays off. A pattern is emerging from the boards, from the posts put up by the hundreds of small freighters who made runs— licit or not—over the border at some time or other: a feed about a dogfight spotted between two Alliance ships on the edge of Tellurian space, a warning posted on another board about strange pirate activity in a certain quadrant, a black market request for a very illegal, very dangerous type of deton-cannon from a hauler heading into Alliance space.

"Merrins was right," I breathe aloud. "It's all here. You just have to know what to look for."

I start compiling a list of all the places with suspicious activity, carefully going through entry after entry and marking the coordinates in a simple quadsheet. I finish and hit the "display" button. A wave of dots spread across a holomap of Alliance space. I stare at them, trying to pick out anything useful from the mass. Nothing catches my eye. At least not until I think to have the computer catalog them in gradating shades of gray, with the oldest encounters being nearly black and the most recent a bright white.

There it is—a collection of dots slowly shrinking inward over the passage of time until the lightest dots cluster around just one place.

Tiersten Internment Colony.

There's no doubt about it: if there really is a civil war being waged inside the Alliance, Tiersten is at its center. Only why Tiersten? I wonder. Why a prison colony on the fringes of the Alliance? It has no population but for the prisoners and the camp garrison. Not to mention its position, which, being located about as far from New Earth as possible, seems the *least* strategic position to mount a fight for colonization rights.

I bite my lip, unable to take my eyes off all those bright white dots. It can't be a coincidence that I—that *Lia*—came from Tiersten. All this time, I assumed the Alliance government sent me to New Sol as some sort of sneak attack on one of their enemy's stations. Just another blow in their war for New Earth. Which made sense my first week here, but it's been five weeks now. If they wanted to take down New Sol, they would have done it by now, with or without me. However, this Tellurian splinter faction is a different story altogether. I stare at those white dots again. It seems very possible now that whoever sent me in, it *wasn't* the Alliance government.

Looking at the map again, I click one of the black dots. The date is from a year and half ago. So long! The ceasefire has only been in place for eight weeks. Could the Tellurian government really have been talking about sharing New Earth so long ago? I find that hard to believe. The question is: if this faction isn't fighting for New Earth, then what are they fighting for? How was it Kerr described the people who attacked her?

A desperate people fighting a war they already knew was lost.

Every hair on my arms raises as I recall her words and a shudder runs through my body. My stomach churns and for a moment I think I'll be sick. It knows. My body *knows* why I'm here. Too bad my mind doesn't.

———

I stew over the information from the research center during the ensuing week, but I don't come to any further conclusions. Although I do seem to have been sent here by a splinter faction within the Tellurian Alliance, I still don't know why. However, if they're in as dire straits as Kerr seemed to think, it would certainly explain why nobody came for me. Maybe it wasn't that they *didn't* come, but they *couldn't*.

Or maybe that's just wishful thinking. After all, the alternative is that they abandoned me here on purpose.

Still, I continue to watch the newsfeeds in the Blue Lounge every day, looking for anything out of the ordinary. Kaeti comes and watches with me sometimes. Well, perhaps *comes with me* is not so accurate as *mercilessly follows me.*

She pops up at the strangest times. In the cafeteria when I'm eating lunch, on the end of my cot when I awake, at the hygiene unit when I emerge from brushing my teeth before bed. Once I even come back from my morning jog to find her at the mouth of the SlipStream tunnel waiting for me.

"How did you get in here?" I ask, leaning against the wall to catch my breath.

"I followed you."

"Yes, but *why*?"

Kaeti shrugs and doesn't answer. I stare at her in exasperation, but her big-eyed gaze never wavers. Finally, I sigh. "I suppose it *is* nicer out here. Certainly the air is fresher." I take a deep breath, appreciating the scentless cool of the tunnel.

She cocks her head at me curiously, but doesn't say anything. Relenting, I take her hand. "Come on, we better find Lela before she notices you're gone and goes galactic."

I take Kaeti back to her caretaker, but she just shows up again a day later in the lounge, slipping into the seat beside me while I watch the feeds. I sigh and immediately link Lela. The older woman shakes her head when I tell her who's with me.

"She was supposed to be in a playgroup arranged by the officers. I didn't even realize she was gone." Lela wipes her forehead. "Do you mind? She's running me ragged."

Do I mind? I start to say yes and then stop. Kaeti's

shadowing is foreign, alien to me, who's so used to spending time alone, but it's not necessarily unwelcome. In fact, there's something companionable about her quiet presence beside me. With a shake of my head, I link off and leave Lela to some well-deserved peace. I can entertain Kaeti for a couple hours.

I take her around the hub with me, showing her all the places Michael showed me, telling her the fascinating bits of trivia he told me. She even meets Michael later that week when he comes to hang out with me. He leans down and shakes her hand, his smile in full charm mode, and then proceeds to buy us both sundaes in one of the ring restaurants. By the time Kaeti has to report back to the cargo bay, she's besotted.

I completely understand the feeling.

Ever since hearing Teal's dad refer to me as Michael's girlfriend, I haven't been able to think of anything else when I'm around him. It's strange. I only just started thinking of myself as Michael's friend, but already my thoughts are toying with the idea of being more. I find myself analyzing his every movement — his gestures, his smiles, his looks — trying to figure out where his feelings really lie. And whether I actually return them.

Two weeks ago I wouldn't have thought myself capable of anything more than friendship. Six weeks ago, I wouldn't have even thought myself capable of that. Finding out I'm Lia's clone has freed something inside of me, loosed the guilt of pretending to be someone I'm not and replaced it with the confidence of knowing what I am. No longer do I worry about keeping myself separate from Lia, about segregating her memories from my own lest I forget who I am. Instead I embrace her as myself; as the person I should have been, *would* have been, if only I'd lived another life. Lia's gone, after all, and I'm here. What's wrong with stepping into her shoes and living the life she can't?

It's just that easy, being Lia. That frighteningly easy.

Maybe it's my newfound confidence, but even my relationship with Teal has become easier. Ever since the night Michael walked out, Teal and I have been getting along surprisingly well. Instead of disapproving silence whenever I walk into the room, she actually seems glad to see me, saying hi or just giving me a friendly wave. Sometimes when Michael's busy with his schoolwork we hang out, taking quizzes from her fashion zines or just watching a teen holo together. I don't even try to question Teal's change of heart. Better not to overthink things than risk screwing them up.

Returning to the cargo bay after a quick lunch, I'm surprised to find the bay abuzz with chatter. Everyone's been on edge since the emergency drill eight days ago, but this time the talk is different. There's excitement in the voices around me. Excitement, relief, and even a tinge of apprehension. I pass close to one particularly loud group, pricking my ears to catch the edges of their discussion.

". . . heard they'll be here in two days."

"I heard three weeks."

"I'm just glad we're finally going to get out of here!"

"Is everyone going?"

"I think so. A whole convoy of ships, coming to take us home. It's about time!"

By the time I make it to my cot, I've caught the whole story, or at least as much as the refugees seem to know. A convoy of ships is coming to the station, and within days, a few weeks at most, we'll all be piled on various ships and sent home en masse. Even the Aurorans, though no one seems to know exactly where we're going.

I sink down onto my cot, a shiver going through me as I remember my meeting with Rowan. That the fate of the Aurorans still remains a tightly-lidded secret despite all of the other information that's leaked out does not bode well. Even more upsetting is the realization that in a matter of days I might lose Michael forever. Michael, Teal, Taylor. A pang goes through me at the thought of leaving them all. I already lost family once; I can't do it again!

My head jerks up. *I had family?*

Even as I try to tell myself no, a spasm of grief rockets through me. Maybe my mind can't remember, but my heart does. Is it a curse I don't remember them or a mercy?

I get up and start pacing beside my cot. I always knew my time here was limited. They couldn't keep us all on the station indefinitely. I just never realized how hard it would be to leave. Again, my thoughts go to Michael's family, and I remember Rowan's words to me. I can't ask them, I can't!

Or can I?

I shiver again, and this time realize it's not just a sense of foreboding but actual cold that's making me shake. I redirect my pacing between a couple crates and toward the wall with my locker. There's a fuzzy sweater of Teal's in there. The idea of nestling up in that blue softness suddenly seems very appealing.

Emerging on the other side of a wall of crates, I hunt along the wall for my locker. There it is, fifth from the end. I reach out my palm to scan my chit.

Hands hit my back with a vicious shove. I fly into the wall, my face whamming into the metal hard enough to make it clang, and my legs start to fold. I scrabble at the locker, my hands seeking purchase before my knees completely collapse. Something hard and metal solidifies under my fingers—the handle of the locker—and I struggle to turn and identify my attacker.

"You glitch!" a crazy voice screams. "*What* have you done?!"

Ah. I knew I hadn't seen the last of Shar.

18

I'D THOUGHT SHAR WAS angry enough at our last encounter, but this time she's absolutely livid. Her eyes are blazing, her entire body quivering with tension as though it's all she can do to keep herself from unleashing the full might of her rage at me.

A bolt of fear shoots through me. Last time I had the advantage of surprise and my own not-so-inconsiderable temper. This time, it's Shar who clearly has the edge. More than an edge. She could kill me, I suddenly realize. Right here behind these cargo containers before anyone even realizes what's happening.

I should scream, but for some reason my throat doesn't seem to work.

"What did you *do*, you little leaker?! What did you tell them?!"

I shake my head, confusion and shock keeping me frozen against the wall.

Shar grabs my collar and bangs me against the locker again. "Don't play deficient with me! I *know* it was you who must have told them. Tell me what you said!"

I have no idea what's going on, but my dormant temper is finally starting to rile, my own fury igniting at being ambushed by this lying thief. This time when she grabs me, I grab her back, fingers sinking into the front of her jumpsuit. I yank with all my strength, trying to pull her off-balance enough to make her loosen her grip. She grunts but hangs on, the two of us careening over the floor as she struggles to keep upright.

"I gave you the stupid reader back! Why'd you have to tell on me?"

"Tell who?" I scream back, finally finding my voice. "I have no idea what you're talking about!"

My shoulder glances against the wall as we whirl in another circle, and I trip, falling backward over my own feet before I even realize what's happening. We both go down in a heap, Shar on top, and in a desperate move, I reach up and grab her throat. A sizzle of white snaps and pops along my mind. Words burst into my brain.

Don't touch her, don't touch her, don't touch her!

I gasp and yank my hand away, but Shar is already scrambling off of me.

"*Who* are you?" she breathes, eyes wide in horror. *"What's that in your head?"*

I shake my head, unsure how to answer when I don't even know what she's seen. I almost don't catch her words, she mumbles them so softly: *One-fifty-nine, one-fifty-eight . . .*

My mind flies to my clock.

00:01:58

Slag! I lost time during the fight, and Shar saw. She *saw* it! Just like Rowan would have seen it had he touched me just a few minutes later in my entry interview.

"You're a *psychic*!"

Shar jerks back as if slapped. The hatred and anger are still in her eyes, but now they're clouded by something much stronger. Fear.

I don't get it. So she's a psychic. What does she have to fear from me? If anything, I'm the one who should be angry, without that half-star on her jumpsuit to tip me off.

Understanding pours through me. A psychic, spending six weeks living in a crowded cargo bay full of refugees with nothing but a couple of dirty jumpsuits to wear? On a station with a strong PsyCorp presence, no less? I don't think so. PsyCorp takes better care of its people than that.

"You're unregistered."

She flinches. "Why did you have to tell them?"

"Who?"

"PsyCorp!"

"I haven't talked to PsyCorp," I deny. "Not about you. I didn't even know you were a psychic until you jumped me like a lunatic just now."

"Oh yeah? Then why have they been watching me? Why did they link me to say they want to see me in an hour?"

"How should I know? You—" I stop, recalling my own interview with them just a few weeks ago. "Wait. Are you from Aurora?"

Shar blinks in confusion but nods. I laugh, unable to resist the irony. There I was, completely vaccing out four weeks ago because I thought PsyCorp had discovered my little secret, and now Shar is doing the exact same thing—and all for nothing! It's actually kind of funny now that it's Shar and not me.

Well, *mostly* funny, I think, irritatedly rubbing my back. It would be funnier if my face didn't hurt and my back wasn't bruised.

"What? What's so funny?" she demands, terror choking her voice with every word. "Do you *know* what's going to happen when they—"

"Power down!" I interrupt, pity finally kindling in my heart at her obvious distress. "They don't know anything. PsyCorp is doing interviews with all the Aurorans. They told me so themselves when they brought me in a couple weeks ago."

"They—they are?"

The hope in her eyes is almost worse than the hatred. It's hard to stay pissed at someone who has the expression of a kicked puppy.

"They're trying to figure out what to do with all of us," I elaborate. "They just want to know if you have friends or family you can go to."

"Oh. Not me." Shar lets out a visible sigh of relief and absently rubs her head. "I suppose you're going to move in with those friends of yours?"

I shrug uncomfortably and finally answer, "It's complicated."

We don't say anything for a minute.

"I thought you figured it out when we slapped hands before," Shar says tentatively. "There was something glitchy when we touched."

"I know."

She looks at me curiously. "What are you? You're not a psychic, I can tell, but you're sure not normal either."

"Forget it," I order her. "Just forget it! It's not anything. Not anymore. Keep your airlock sealed, and I won't tell PsyCorp about you. Deal?"

Her jaw trembles at the mention of PsyCorp, but she quickly nods. "Deal."

We don't shake hands on it, neither keen to touch the other again, but I don't think Shar will betray my secret. She's too afraid of PsyCorp to risk it. Afraid? No, terrified, more like! As I watch her go, I wonder why. She won't get in trouble for not registering. As she's a minor, it was technically her parents' responsibility, not hers. Besides, PsyCorp needs every psychic they can get, especially with the war on. They won't waste time or energy on punitive measures. Plus if Rowan's right, PsyCorp will probably be a far better option than whatever is in store for the Auroran refugees. Not that I tell her that.

No, it's in my best interests to keep my opinions to myself. Her fear of PsyCorp may be the only thing standing between me and discovery.

————

I dream again tonight—more of those fleeting sensations when you feel like you're both asleep and awake. The images make perfect sense and yet no sense at all.

The barbed wire fence stretches long and taut between the posts. On either end, a guard tower rises up into the air, manned with soldiers armed with LS-3500s. They're merely a gesture though, nothing more, and we all know it. There is no safety; not here, not anywhere.

On the post, a red light remains dull and unlit. The force fence is offline again. Just as well. No one really believed it was working anyway. Not after what happened before.

A siren screams, so shrill I can almost see it with my eyes, red and blinding. No, that's the light from the post, suddenly come to life. I run to the fence and jerk my head back and forth, frantically searching for the threat, but no one is there. No one at all.

I'm inside now. The room is small and spare, with a table and chairs, a flag, and little else.

"Are you sure you want to do this?" someone asks me.

It is a man in the tired green and grays of the Tellurian fleet. His face looks as tired as the clothes he's wearing, the smudge of dirt on his face matching the dirt on his uniform.

"What choice do I have?"

"There's always a choice. Even in the darkest hour, we still have the freedom to choose."

He's trying to be encouraging, but I can't help laughing at the blatant lie. I shake my head. "Not me."

The man nods, accepting my decision. His eyes are full of resignation. "I'm sorry. You know that, right?"

I laugh, the sound bitter and hard. "Save your apologies for your maker. You'll need them."

The scene changes again and now I'm in some kind of bunker, all gray and concrete and hard.

"Lia. Lia, sweetie, please!"

The woman presses against the glass, her eyes pleading and scared. She is beautiful, though her blonde hair is lank and greasy, and black circles ring her eyes. As I watch, her body seems to shrink in on itself until her clothes hang off her form in limp folds. A yellowish cast comes over her skin, and I know she will not last much longer.

"I don't know what they told you, but it's not true. Look in my eyes—you know me! You know what I say is true."

"I know," *I tell her, resting my hands gently on the other side of the glass from hers.* "I know."

In a way, she's right, and it's that understanding that takes my heart apart every time.

Suddenly the glass is gone, and she's right there. I reach up to touch her face, my hands trembling as I cradle her papery skin.

Fangs explode from her mouth. Her hands twist in my

hair, an unearthly howl rising from her throat, and then she lunges—

I wake up screaming.

I'm so loud that when I get my bearings back, I think I must have woken half the cargo bay. I haven't though, the majority of people still unmoving in their cots. Lots of people suffer from nightmares here; we've learned to sleep through the ruckus. A handful of people near me are awake though, a few glaring at me, but most with pity in their eyes. I nod at them as if to say, *I'm sat*, and force myself to lie down again. Only I can't stop trembling, the images painfully clear in my head rather than fading the way dreams quickly do. Suddenly the cot dips. I sit up, eyes narrowing as I make out a flash of red in the faint glow of the night lights.

"Kaeti?"

"It's okay, Lia," she whispers, her small hand touching my cheek. "I have bad dreams, too."

I'm dumbstruck. I have a nightmare, and it's Kaeti, little Kaeti, coming to comfort me? I should send her back to Lela and her cot, but I don't. I just lie back down with her curled up in my arms.

It helps.

When I wake she's gone, and I can't help wondering if Kaeti was as much a dream as everything else. I dreamed more after I slept again, but the images were faster that time, too fleeting and nonsensical to grasp. Still, they were more powerful than anything I've dreamt since coming on the station.

They're just dreams, I tell myself firmly. *Nothing more*.

But they don't feel like *just* dreams, not the next night or the night after. In fact, they don't feel like dreams *at all*.

"Ha! Beat you, Michael!" I lean back against the door to his apartment, laughing between breaths as Michael pounds up beside me.

He slumps against the door with a wheeze. "No fair! You had a head start."

I snort. "Whatever. I'm just faster than you, like I've always been. Loser buys ice cream, and *that* would be *you*," I tell him, poking my index finger into his chest for emphasis.

He grabs my arm and yanks, pulling me off balance. I shriek and clutch at his shoulders as he laughs. Even when I get the better of him, Michael always seems to find a way to turn the tables on me. It's one of things I like about him.

Hitting the door control, Michael loops an arm around my shoulders and walks me inside. "Alright, Li-Li, you'll get your ice cream. Just let me change my shirt first."

I grab a glass of water and say hi to Taylor while he disappears into the bedroom. The sound of Teal's shrieks immediately follows, and I grin. Michael is shaking his head when he comes out. "Don't go in there," he warns. "If you go in, you may never find your way out again."

Before I can ask what he means, Taylor interrupts. "Michael, you never took the trash out to the recycler."

"Aw, Gran, can't you see Lia's here? I'll do it later."

"I think Lia can wait ten minutes."

"Oh, yeah, I can wait," I agree with a mischievous smile.

Michael gives me a mock glare. "Traitor!" But he goes to do Taylor's bidding.

Taylor and I laugh together at Michael's expression,

then Taylor asks me about things down in the cargo bay. I answer and ask her how things are going at work.

"Well, the misters are still broken—I went into work this morning to find out they'd been going full blast all night. The technicians still don't seem to know what's wrong. Other than that, things have been going well. We've been looking at installing new filters in the lower ring . . ."

As I listen to her talk, I think about PsyLt. Rowan's enjoinders and the rumors in the cargo bay about the convoy. I feel so comfortable here, surrounded by Michael and his family. Suddenly asking to stay with them doesn't seem as impossible as it did before, especially now that I know I really am Lia, in a way. Maybe I can feel Michael out later on this evening, see how his family might react to my asking.

Wandering into the bedroom to wait, I immediately see what Michael meant about never finding my way out again. The room, at least Teal's side of it, is a maze of clothes. Half her closet must be spread out over the room, and in the middle of the chaos stands Teal, holding up a couple shirts in front of her as she stares in the mirror.

"Hey, Lia." She turns to me with a serious look. "So what do you think? The blue? Or the purple?"

I glance over at Teal and consider. "The blue, definitely. With that brown skirt over there and the silver belt."

"You think?" Teal gathers the outfit together as she explains that she's choosing an outfit for her date-that's-not-a-date-since-Taylor-doesn't-let-her-date date. I shake my head as she tries on the outfit, unable to decide if I'm jealous she has so many combinations of clothes to try on or relieved my limited selection makes choosing an outfit easy.

"You're lucky," Teal suddenly says, shedding the silver belt and trying on a gold one.

"What do you mean?"

"It doesn't matter what you wear. Michael would still be crazy about you no matter how you looked."

My blush is instantaneous, pink petals of embarrassment unfurling across my cheeks at the matter-of-fact observation. Teal is altogether too shrewd for my comfort sometimes. I try to keep my voice casual. "Michael and I are just friends."

Teal snorts. "Are you sure about that?"

I look away and toy with a bottle of makeup on the dresser. In truth, I'm not sure about anything. Michael and I just . . . *are*. For all my ponderings, I haven't been able to come up with a better definition than that. Maybe I don't actually need to.

Teal takes pity on me and changes the subject. "Too bad we don't have the same color palette," she says, taking the mocha foundation spritzer from my hands and picking up a tube of LongLash, "or I could give you an entire makeover while you wait. Michael wouldn't even recognize you when he got back. Hmm, maybe some mascara and a little clear lip gloss would work."

I stand still and let her apply the makeup. At her motion, I lean forward and peer in the mirror. I look the same, but *different*. More vibrant, with the strawberry gloss making my pink lips shine and the mascara making my eyes more defined. I continue to examine my new look as Teal disappears into the bathroom. Maybe it would be worth it to spend a few milicreds on some makeup of my own. I wonder what eye shadow might look good with my gray eyes.

Wait a second. *Gray* eyes?

No. No, no, no, it can't be! I don't have gray eyes, I have green eyes! Like Lia.

I fumble for my chit, fingers shaking as I bring up the digitals of me and Michael from when we were kids. I pull up the first digi and enlarge it, and then another, and another. I can't see the eye color in all of the images, but I can see it in enough of them. Without a doubt, Lia had green eyes, while mine are gray. The dull gray of a cloudy day, not even remotely mistakable for green no matter how I turn my head in the light. My heart sinks as I recognize what this must mean: I'm not Lia's clone after all.

No, I shake my head. That can't be right. We have so many similarities! It was too perfect, me being Lia's clone.

I examine the digital of Lia in the sundress again. Excepting the eyes, it looks exactly like the age-diminished digital of myself. I narrow my gaze, searching the smallest details. There, on the inside of her forearm, is a distinctive birthmark a couple shades darker than her skin. As if to prove myself wrong, I shove up my right sleeve.

The skin is perfect. White and soft without even a mole to mar it, let alone a birthmark. A lump forms in my throat. So it's really true—I'm not Lia's clone.

Deactivating my chit, I slowly lower my hand. Once again I'm back at square one, without a name or a past, just as clueless as I was before. Disappointment sings through me, and I push back the tears forming in my eyes. So what if Lia and I have a few similarities? Lots of people get motion sick or are good at math. It was stupid to think I could be Lia's clone. It was stupid to think I could be somebody.

"Hey, I'm all done. Ready to go?"

No, I'm not ready; I'm not ready to go at all. More than anything, I just want to rewind the last ten minutes, to go back to that brief time when I finally knew who I was. When I was finally someone worth being with Michael.

But as Pandora could tell you, once the box is opened it can't be closed again, no matter what ends up coming out of it.

Taking a deep breath, I give Michael a dazzling smile. "Of course."

"Cool. Let's go, Lia."

I hear her name, and inside I die a little.

19 WE GET ICE CREAM AND go to the park. Usually I enjoy spending time out in the habitat ring. Surrounded by all the marks of a real planet, it's easy to pretend Michael and I are back on Aurora together. Not today though. Today all I can think about are those ugly gray eyes looking back at me from the mirror and the missing birthmark from my forearm. All I can think about is the fact that I'm not Lia. Not one bit.

I don't know why it bothers me so much. The belief that I was Lia's clone is only a recent development; I was friends with Michael long before I thought that. Yet the disappointment of being wrong is almost crushing, like being told you won a prize only to find out later it was all a mistake, that it was someone else who earned the honor you thought was yours. Someone better than you.

The park is quiet and pleasant this time of day, the air refreshing and odorless. We walk along a path to a fountain at the center and sit on the edge to finish our ice cream. Michael is telling me a funny story about one of his classmates, but I'm finding it hard to pay attention. My thoughts are elsewhere.

". . . so there he is, standing in the middle of the classroom, *completely* soaked! Even Ms. Niles was laughing, it was so funny."

My far-off brain recognizes that this is the place where I'm supposed to respond, and I force a laugh. The sound is hollow and thin in my ears, though Michael doesn't seem to notice.

"You should have seen his face, Li-Li. I've never seen anyone look so shocked in my life."

Li-Li. Resentment flares in me at his use of the nickname. *Lia's* nickname. Getting up, I chuck my half-eaten cone into the trash, my appetite gone.

Michael frowns at me. "Is something wrong?"

"No," I lie. "What would be wrong?"

"Hey, you're the one who wanted ice cream so much, and now you just threw half of yours away."

I look away. "I guess I'm not as hungry as I thought I was."

Michael finishes the rest of his cone, and we head across the grass toward the playground. I say little, replying to his conversation with cursory answers, unable to conjure up more. Hard as I try, I can't seem to summon back the Lia who just beat Michael in a race to the apartment an hour ago. She's vanished into thin air, and in her place is this hollowed-out stranger who is only too aware that she's not who everyone thinks she is. Who is only too aware she's not the girl Michael cares for.

We sit on the swings and drift, Michael still talking and me listening. After a while, Michael offers to push me.

A playground, grass, white flowers everywhere.

"Higher, Michael! Push me higher!"

"How high, Li-Li?"

"To the sky!"

I jump off the swing, my stomach twisting at the memory. *Lia's* memory. "I don't want to swing anymore."

Michael jumps off as well. "*What* is your problem? Is it something I said?"

"Nothing's wrong—"

"Bullslag! You've been acting strange ever since we left the apartment. What's wrong? Is it something Teal said? Because if it is—"

"Teal didn't say anything." Tears are threatening now, and I wish he would stop badgering me to try to explain something I can't even explain to myself.

"Then what is it? Are you mad at me?"

"I'm not mad at you."

"No? Then what's wrong? Talk to me, Lia—"

"I'm not *Lia*!" The words come boiling out of me, frustration and hurt and guilt all entwined together in a rush. My face goes ashen as I realize just what came out of my mouth. *Oh slag! Did I really just say that?*

Michael is staring at me wide-eyed, hurt and confusion showing in his face, but not suspicion. I struggle to cover my error even as I wish with all my heart I could just admit the truth.

"Why are you even with me, Michael?" I ask. "Because I'm Lia from Aurora, and you feel obligated to spend time with me because we were best friends a long time ago?"

"It's not like that."

"No? If my name were anything other than Lia Johansen, we would never have even met. I would have been just another poor refugee stuck down on Level Eight while you went on living your life in the habitat ring with Taylor and Teal and all your friends. Admit it, Michael! The only reason you like me is because I'm Lia from Aurora. Well, I'm not *her* anymore, and you don't have to pretend I am just because you feel some sense of duty!"

My eyes are burning now, but I can't bear the thought of crying in front of him, of making even more of a fool of myself than I have already. I look at the ground, waiting for him to admit what I know is true—that it isn't me he likes, but Lia. A girl long gone, whom I can never be no matter how much I will it.

"You're right," he finally says, and my heart crumples in my chest as though it is nothing more than paper. "I went down to the cargo bay looking for my friend Lia from Aurora, and if you were someone else we never would have met.

"Look, I know you're not the same person you were on Aurora anymore," he adds, as though he's not killing me with every word he says, "but you're wrong if you think that's the only reason I like you."

I dart my eyes up, blinking back tears to dare a glance at his face. His eyes are so serious, as serious as I've ever seen Michael, and so sincere I feel my eyes filling again.

He continues. "Yes, I look at you and see Lia from Aurora all the time. Your smile, your laugh, the snarky comments you make, and that annoying way you can always beat me in a footrace. I'd be lying if I said I didn't like those things, but I'd also be lying if I said I didn't like the new, serious Lia from New Sol just as much, if not more, than the fun Lia from Aurora."

Michael shakes his head. "The old Lia? I could never have told her all that stuff about my parents. She would have teased me mercilessly about my fears of being drafted. She wouldn't have just listened, not like the new Lia did. The old Lia would have gone completely galactic when I walked out on her after that message from my dad. She would have stormed out, and I would have had to spend a week making it up to her before she was my friend again. She wouldn't have waited for me, for hours, without any idea when I would come back, just because she wanted to make sure *I* was okay. Not like you.

"She definitely wouldn't have understood how important Teal is to me, let alone figured out a way to win her over. I won't even try to guess how you managed that! Teal's hated every girlfriend I've ever had, and yet somehow in a matter of weeks you've got her asking for fashion advice and sticking up for you as fiercely as if you were one of the family."

His voice goes soft. "I don't care what your name is or where you're from. I just like you because you're you." He hesitates. "Just like I hope you like me because I'm me, and not because I'm Michael from Aurora, the only person left in the galaxy you know."

My mouth drops open, pure shock running through me at his words. It never occurred to me that funny, confident Michael might be just as uncertain about me as I am about him. It never occurred to me that he might like me just for being me, and not Lia.

I close my eyes and savor his words. *I just like you because you're you.*

When I open them again, Michael's watching me closely, insecurity written across his face, and I realize I have yet to answer his question, though it wasn't actually phrased as a question.

I walk up to him, look him in the eyes, and tell him, "I like you because you never gave up looking for me, because you include me without even stopping to wonder if you should, because you confide in me and make me want to confide in you, and yes, because I can beat you at footraces." He laughs a little. "I just like you because you're you."

I'm not sure if he hugs me or I hug him; it really

doesn't matter. All that matters is that I'm back. Not Lia's clone, not the me who was pretending so hard to be Lia, but just *me*. For the first time since coming on this station, it doesn't matter that I'm not Lia.

We hug for a long moment, and then Michael's grip finally loosens. Taking the cue, I reluctantly pull back.

Just in time for him to lean down and kiss me.

His lips only brush mine for a moment, but pure ecstasy shoots through me all the same. I tighten my arms around his neck and kiss him back, reveling in the sensations curling through every part of my body. My heart is dancing, thumping so hard I think it might jump out of my chest. Elation soars through me, rising like a bird on the wing, higher and higher—

00:01:57

My eyes shoot open, shock dumping down my spine like a bucket of icy water. I swallow my gasp and another second ticks down.

00:01:56

Panic starts to rise, and I press my lips harder to Michael's, as though the increased pressure can tamp down my fears. My clock has started multiple times since my initial malfunction, but I haven't gone off yet.

00:01:55

At the back of his neck, my hands curl into tiny fists. It *always* stops after five or ten seconds. Twenty seconds, tops. That's the most it ever dropped, and that was during my first fight with Shar.

00:01:54

Surely a little kiss doesn't rate on the same level as a knock-down, drag-out fight, no matter how great a kiss it is.

00:01:53

Still, it's kind of hard to concentrate on the task at hand with it ticking down like that. Frag it! My first kiss (as far as I know) and my stupid clock has to ruin it?!

00:01:52

Michael lifts his head and the kiss ends. I stifle my disappointment and smile back at him. No need to take out my frustration with my vaccin' head on him!

00:01:51

He leans his forehead against mine, his voice low as he whispers something to me. I miss the exact words in my distraction. My mind is starting to get that stretchy feeling, and it's making it hard for me to focus. He's saying something about how amazing that was, I think. I murmur my agreement, trying to focus on Michael even as my mental eye continues to watch my clock.

00:01:50

00:01:49

00:01:48

Okay, it's been ten seconds now, time to shut off.

00:01:47

00:01:46

00:01:45

00:01:44

00:01:43

Anytime now! A spark bursts in my right eye, then another, and I turn my head slightly, hoping that whatever they are, only I can see them. How would I ever explain to Michael why I have sparkles in my eyes? *Well, Michael, it's my heritage as a genetically engineered bomb. But don't worry, I won't blow up, really I won't!*

I sneak another peek at my clock. I've lost another five seconds. It's been twenty seconds now.

00:01:38

Twenty-one.

00:01:37

Twenty-two.

00:01:36

Stop!

00:01:35

Stop it *now*!

00:01:34

I *mean* it! Stop!

00:01:33

Oh, God, it's not stopping!

00:01:32

It's not stopping, it's not stopping, it's not stopping!

00:01:31

Three more seconds. The stretchy feeling is reeling across my mind like a sheet, the sparkles popping in both eyes now. The panic is building again, and I can't push it away this time. It's really happening! Nova, I'm going Nova!

00:01:28

Michael!
I shove myself away from him, horror bursting over me as I realize what going Nova will mean.
"Lia?"
His voice is so blissfully unaware, so innocent in its ignorance. Michael, Michael, Michael! If only you knew what a monster I am!

00:01:26

Warmth floods my forearms in a rush and my last vestige of sanity snaps. Every thought flees from my mind, overridden by one sharp, panicked impulse.

Run!

20 **I TAKE OFF AS IF** an entire cadre
of PsyCorp was after me. My legs fly
over the grass, eating up the ground
as though the beat of my legs could
overtake the tick of my clock, but that menacing instrument just keeps going.

00:01:20

00:01:19

Behind me, I hear Michael yelling my name, his feet pounding against the walk as he tries to catch up to me. I lengthen my stride, opening up the distance between us even further. Before long his voice starts to fade—no surprise there. Even without my head start, he wouldn't have been able to catch me. Good! The farther away I can get from Michael, the better.

I slow slightly as I fly out of the park, my panicked mind only now stopping to wonder where I'm going. With a sinking feeling, I realize there's nowhere *to* go. Not on this station. Despair pours through me as I think of Michael, blown to pieces by the very girl he just kissed! *Think!* Where can I possibly go that will put Michael out of my reach?

An airlock immediately comes to mind. Even if the

vacuum of space doesn't stop my clock, at least I would be off the station. Only I don't know of any airlocks in the habitat ring, and I highly doubt I could find one in the—

00:00:53

—fifty-three seconds I have left.

I jerk my head around, looking for a solution, and catch sight of the SlipStream station up ahead. Good enough! My body is already heading in that direction before I even make up my mind to go there. Those tunnels are reinforced, aren't they? Maybe they'll help shield the rest of the station from the force of my blast. If nothing else, they'll take me farther away from Michael. My chit is vibrating like mad now—no doubt Michael, wanting to know why the hell I ran off like a vaccin' banshee just moments after we kissed!

I ignore it and head into the station, pushing past the people on the platform and slipping into the walking tunnel bordering the train tracks. Even once in the passage I don't slow down, though my heart is practically beating out of my chest and my lungs are screaming with exhaustion. Instead I run harder, pumping my arms to get every last bit of speed out of myself. How much time do I have left now?

00:00:41

Forty-one seconds. Make them count.

I push every other thought out of my mind, tuck my head down, and just run.

I'm only twenty meters from the far end of the passage when my foot stomps on a loose shoelace. My ankle rolls and I go flying, smashing into the tunnel floor and sliding forward on my face. The force is enough to knock the wind out of me, and all I can do is lie there, eyes squeezed shut as I wait for the end.

It doesn't come.

After the longest wait—*surely it must have been forty-one seconds by now!*—I dare to glance at my clock.

00:00:41

If my face wasn't currently smashed into the floor, my jaw would have dropped to my feet. I was so focused on getting away from Michael that my clock stopped, and I didn't even notice! Indeed, now that I think about it, I realize my symptoms are gone, the sparkles dimmed and the stretchy feeling nearly vanished. How long, then, was I sprinting like a lunatic through the station while my clock sat still and complacent in my head?

A snort pops out of my mouth as I suddenly picture how I must have looked to all the regular station dwellers, calmly going about their business while some blonde-haired psycho sprinted past them like the Hounds of Orion were on her tail. A chuckle follows and then suddenly I'm laughing, great belly laughs oozing out of my mouth in a torrent that can't be stopped.

I heave myself over onto my side and just lie there, laughing and laughing until my sides ache and my stomach hurts, and even then I can't seem to stop, one laugh turning over into the next until finally one morphs into a sob instead, and then I'm just crying—crying and crying as if the world really did end, right here on my face in this cold tunnel, and with it, the one person left in the galaxy whose life means anything to me.

———

One minute and seventeen seconds. That's how much time I lost when Michael kissed me.

Even wrapped up in my white blanket on my cot in the cargo bay, the realization makes me shiver. To lose so much time in a single instance, without even a warning! Now even I can't deny the truth that's been staring me in the face ever since I first lost seconds on that SlipStream.

It's not a matter of *if* I'll go Nova, but *when*.

At one time, it wouldn't have mattered to me. I cared for no one on this station, and no one on this station cared for me. If anything, I would have felt impatience waiting for my time to come. Things are different now. Michael, Taylor, Teal, Kaeti. What war effort, no matter how great, could possibly be worth their lives? None that I can think of.

My chit vibrates to signal an incoming link. Michael. Again.

With a sigh, I shut it off. I *can't* talk to him. It was hard enough coming up with an explanation for my crazy behavior the first time. If I have to tell the story one more time, it will probably all fall apart like a house of holo cards.

He was waiting for me when I got back to the cargo bay. Smart Michael—he knew I'd have to come back eventually. When I saw him there, I almost turned around and ran straight out again. I would have, except that in my heart I knew Michael deserved better. Maybe I couldn't give him better, but at least I could give him an explanation. Of sorts.

"Didn't you hear me say 'Race you!' before I left?" I asked at his incredulous inquiry, trying to brazen it out as best as I could. He didn't buy it for a second though. Michael may be overly trusting, but he's not a deficient.

"Well, you see . . . It's just that . . ." I said, drawing out the words as my brain scrambled for a better lie. "The truth is I thought I saw someone."

"Someone?"

"A . . . an officer, I mean. You see, a few weeks ago PsyCorp pulled me into their offices. They were upset because they found out I'd been visiting the habitat ring even though us refugees aren't supposed to be there."

Michael's face cleared a little, but his expression still showed skepticism. "That's why you took off without saying a word, because of some officer?"

"Oh, well, I didn't tell you this, but it's the same officer that broke up this fight I was in."

"You were in a *fight*?"

"It was no big deal, just this other refugee from the bay, but the officer was really mad about us fighting. He said if he caught us again, he was going to have us brain-drained by PsyCorp. When I saw him in the park I guess I just kind of vacced out a little. I'm *really* sorry," I rushed to add. "It wasn't you, I just didn't want to get into trouble again. Plus, I knew if the officer caught me, you'd find out about the fight and everything else, and I guess I just didn't want you to know. Please forgive me, Michael."

Michael just stared at me for the longest time, and then finally shook his head. "I don't know if that's the craziest truth I've ever heard or the lamest lie, but I forgive you." He laughed. "As if I could ever stay mad at you. Just say something next time, okay?"

He leaned in to kiss me before he left, and I turned my head at the last minute to give him my cheek. He didn't say anything, but I could tell the rejection stung.

Still, I knew better than to offer him anything more. One more kiss and I probably *would* have blown the station.

A flicker of a smile passes over my lips. In a way, that's kind of a compliment, not that Michael will ever know it.

My amusement passes quickly, sobered by the depressing realization that I can *never* kiss Michael again. It's too dangerous. In fact, just being on the station is dangerous, with my clock poised to start again at any moment and me with no way to deactivate it. Once again, I bemoan the fact that my makers didn't include an instruction manual for my head, even as I acknowledge the horrible resolution I've been trying *not* to think about all night.

I have to leave. It's the only way Michael will be safe from me.

The only problem is that I have nowhere to go. The obvious solution is to simply let the military ship me off to wherever they decided to send us Aurorans. The people around me would still be in danger, but unless I go off and live on some uninhabited rock on the edge of the galaxy, that will be a risk wherever I go. At least Michael and his family would be safe, and that's what really matters to me.

I consider the solution for several minutes, and then reject it. The rumors of the convoy are just that—rumors. While I have no doubt the military will resettle us eventually, I have no idea when that will be. It could be in a week or it could be in a month. I can't afford to wait that long; it's too risky. I *have* to get off this station as soon as possible. Could I buy passage on one of the outgoing liners somewhere?

Activating my chit, I link into the NSol and check the

transit boards. Even the cheapest passage is out of my price range, and with a sigh I shut it off again. What am I going to do?

For a brief second, I consider coming clean. Lifting down to Level Eleven, walking into PsyCorp, and announcing to all and sundry that I'm not Lia Johansen at all, but a Tellurian bomb who could explode at any minute. Boy, wouldn't Rowan sure be surprised! It would almost be worth it to see the look on his face when he realized just *what* he let onto the station.

Until they brain-drained me or shoved me out an airlock or shut me up in a lab somewhere to study me, that is. If at all possible, I'd prefer to save Michael *without* getting dissected or dying.

With a sigh of frustration, I collapse back on my pillow. Waiting for the military to move is starting to look like my only real option. In the meantime, I'll just have to be super careful not to do anything that might jumpstart my clock. No taking the SlipStream, no riding the lift unless absolutely necessary, no kissing Michael. In fact, I probably shouldn't even see him again. I can link him to say goodbye.

Ha! Like Michael would let me cut all ties with him just like that. He would just keep coming back to the bay until I gave in. Besides, the idea of staying on the station and *not* seeing Michael seems like the worst sort of torture I could imagine.

My mind circles back around to the idea of getting off the station. Maybe if I talked to Rowan, he could arrange for me to get sent away sooner. It wouldn't have to be a military transport; anything would do at this point. A passenger liner, a courier ship, a cargo hauler.

An idea flashes into my brain, and I sit bolt upright

on my cot. Reactivating my chit, I pull up the NSol and link the first trans-link company I can find. A bored-looking woman comes onto the screen.

"Starcom Intergalactic, how may I assist you?"

"I'd like to make an interplanetary call, please."

"IS THAT JOB OFFER still open?"

After a ten second lag, Kerr blinks in surprise. "Well, hello to you, too," she says, and I realize I didn't even say hi first. Luckily, Kerr doesn't seem offended by my shortness. She leans back in her chair and gives me a considering look.

"So what's up, kid? Did you finally realize your life-long ambition to work on a freighter, or are you just sick of station life?"

I shrug, being a bomb poised to blow up not seeming to fall under either option. "It's time to move on," I answer at last.

"Fair enough. You know, I was about your age when I started on the freighters."

"You were?"

"Yep. I was fifteen. Bored, reckless, eager to get off the dirt-poor colony where I was born and go, well, any-where really. My milicreds ran out on this hole of a sta-tion—Kendriss Station. It was little more than a refueling stop for haulers, not like New Sol at all. It was either starve or get a job. Luckily one of the freighters passing through was short-handed enough to take on a scrub of a girl like me, and here I am, twenty-odd years later with a ship of my own and a crew of fourteen under my com-mand."

"Wow," I say, and I mean it. It sounds like Kerr didn't have much more than I do now when she started out. I wonder if that's why she offered to help me—because I remind her of herself at my age. "You must have worked really hard."

"You better believe it, kid. You will too if you're really serious about doing this. A first-run contract on a freighter is no walk on the moon. You pretty much get stuck with all the slag jobs—the hard stuff, the boring stuff, the gross stuff no one else wants to do. The pay is terrible, the hours are worse, privacy is pretty much non-existent."

"Then why do it? I mean, if you don't have to?"

"Because in all the galaxy, there's no better way to see the stars." She raises an eyebrow at me. "If that's what you want."

"It's what I want."

Well, that's not strictly true, but it's what I have to do, which seems close enough. Kerr's job offer all those weeks ago, barely marked at the time, now seems like a lifesaver. A way to get off the station and away from Michael. I do feel a pang of guilt at signing on under false pretenses, but I remind myself that this way any loss of life if—*when*—I go Nova will be minimal. A freighter crew of fifteen is nothing compared to a station or a colony of hundreds or even thousands. Whatever my original mission was, I want no part of it now. None of the people on this station deserve to die, no matter which side of the war they happen to be on.

Kerr nods and glances at her tip-pad. "All right then. I'm currently on a run out on the eastern fringes, but I should be back in your area in a four-square or so."

"Four weeks!" The words blurt out of my mouth when her answer reaches me. "That's too late!"

"Too late? Hey, if you're in some sort of trouble with station security, I can't help you."

I take one look at Kerr's hard eyes and rapidly shake my head. "No, nothing like that. It's just, there's this boy . . ." I stop, unsure how to describe the urgency of my situation without actually describing the situation.

Kerr's face remains blank as she waits for my response. Then, to my surprise, she bursts out laughing. "A boy? Ha! I should've known it was something like that. Teenagers!" When her amusement finally peters out, she goes serious once again. "Look, kid—there's no way I'm getting there any faster, but I suppose if you're that desperate to get off the station, I could hit up some of my contacts, see if anyone near New Sol is looking to hire on."

I nod swiftly in agreement.

"If I vouch for you though," she continues, "you better work your tail off. No slacking around for a two-square only to decide you miss your boyfriend and want to come back."

Now my own eyes go hard. "Once I leave, I'm not coming back. Ever."

"Okay. I'll see what I can do." With that, Kerr cuts the com.

I link off the Starcom Intergalactic site and deactivate my chit. I called Kerr; it's done. Now I just have to hope she comes through for me.

Before it's too late.

———

There's blood on my pillow when I wake the next morning. Eyes on the red stain, I lift my hand to my face. My nose bled while I was sleeping; I can feel the dried remnants crusted in my nostrils and on my cheek. I carefully blow out the thickest of the clots into a tissue and immediately regret it. Without the blockage, the sour-and-sweet smell is more piercing than ever.

I clean up in the hygiene units and then go to my locker for a change of clothes. Without thinking, I choose one of Teal's outfits, start to close up the drawer, and stop.

What am I doing?

These clothes aren't for me. They're for another Lia, the one who watched teen holos with Teal and helped Taylor in the kitchen and kissed Michael in the park. That Lia can't exist anymore. The new Lia is a freighter grunt, the sort of person suited for grungy shipsuits and frayed bandannas, not short skirts and cute tops. Dropping the clothes back into the locker, I reluctantly wriggle into one of my jumpsuits.

As soon as I put it on, I want to take it off again. It's been weeks since I wore one of my jumpsuits; I'd forgotten how unflattering the baggy garments are. The one I'm wearing is the one I malfunctioned in. I can tell because of the gray stains on the collar and chest, still indelibly etched in the fabric despite repeated washings and even Taylor's best efforts. I sigh as I imagine Michael seeing me in it, then remind myself I'm not supposed to see him anymore.

As if my thoughts have summoned him, my chit starts vibrating. I'm tempted to shut it off, but I know if I do he'll just keep linking until I finally answer. Instead I pick up, keeping it on audio-only so he can't see my attire. I keep the conversation short, evading his questions and putting him off when he talks about meeting him again. By the time he hangs up, I feel terrible. So terrible,

I'm tempted to throw off this stupid jumpsuit, put on my best outfit, and go see him. More than tempted, actually. I'm halfway out of my jumpsuit before I come to my senses.

Pulling out my original box, I start throwing things in—the clothes, the pillow and blanket, the frilly toiletries, the reader. It's time to get rid of all this stuff before it makes me completely forget who I really am. *What* I really am.

She's still asleep when I reach her cot, sprawled on her back, one arm hanging off the bed and a small pool of spittle at the corner of her mouth. I slam the box to the ground with a loud thud, taking a sort of maniacal delight when she bolts upright with a start.

"Huh? Whah?" Shar looks around dazedly, stopping when she finally notices me looming over her.

"You want my stuff?" I kick the box into the leg of her cot, and she jumps. "There! It's yours."

"What in a black hole . . . ?"

I don't stick around long enough to hear Shar's befuddled questions let alone answer them. Giving my stuff away to her was hard enough; the last thing I want to do is explain it. Besides, better to let her sweat it out, wondering if I booby-trapped the box somehow, than explain that I gave it to her because I figured she was the one person I wouldn't stoop to begging it back from. It still rankles, though, giving away my precious things to my worst enemy.

Worst enemy. A bitter laugh chuffs from my throat as I realize the truth. Shar is no longer my worst enemy, not by a long shot. No. *I* am.

The day passes slowly. Since I have to take the lift up to eat anyway, I stay in the Blue Lounge for the rest of the day. I watch the viewer until I'm completely bored out of my mind, and then I watch some more. Sitting in one place seems the safest way to spend my time. There's nothing more about Tiersten, but one of the news stations does a story about the ongoing negotiations between the Celestial Expanse and the Tellurian Alliance. Apparently the talks are going well, and the first in-person summit between the two sides is scheduled for only six days from now. The news reporter hints that the summit may even be taking place on New Earth, allowing the Celestians to finally take their first steps ever onto the planet, though of course nothing official has been declared yet.

I frown at the news. A summit meeting in only *six days*? After three years of bitter war, how could they possibly come to an agreement in just a matter of weeks? I can see how the Celestians might go for it, if they believe they'll be getting New Earth at last, but I find it hard to believe the Tellurians would give up the planet so easily. Unless they've booby-trapped it as surely as Shar believes I've rigged the box. Maybe there's a secret armada on New Earth just waiting for the Celestians to come. Or worse—a whole army of *me*s.

I envision a whole planet full of Lia Johansens, all wired to blow, and I shiver. *God, I hope that's not the case!*

It's late, almost midnight, when I return to the bay. As I approach my cot, I know immediately Michael's been here. A single red rose sits on my pillow. I pick it up and hold it to my nose, wishing I could actually smell it.

"He waited over three hours."

The elderly woman who sleeps near me is still awake, watching me from the warmth of her blankets. She props herself up on an elbow. "I told him I would pass on his gift, but he insisted on waiting. The officers finally kicked him out when they turned the lights down."

Michael waited for me? My eyes go suspiciously moist, and I rub my sleeve against my face.

"You'd better get up early tomorrow if you want to continue avoiding him," the woman adds shrewdly.

I nod, not trusting my ability to speak, and go get ready for bed. I'm just finishing in the hygiene unit when my link vibrates. Kerr.

"You're in luck," she says without preamble. "A friend of a friend has a cousin who's currently docked on New Sol. They'd only planned on stopping for a day to refuel but got delayed by last-minute repairs. The captain says they'll be shoving off in three days. There's a berth, if you want it."

"I'll take it."

Kerr raises an eyebrow. "Just like that, no questions asked? You must be desperate." I shrug, neither denying nor confirming. She nods at last. "Well, I looked over the contract on your behalf, and the pay isn't great, but it's comparable to what a first-timer of your age and experience could expect. Word among the freighter circuit is that Captain Standish is a tough master, but a fair one. Work hard and you should be fine."

I nod, touched that she would go to so much trouble on my behalf. "Thanks, Captain Kerr."

"What's with all this captain stuff? On the day you come work for me, you can call me captain. Until then, it's just Marissa."

"Thanks, Marissa," I agree, even as I inwardly swear never to work for her. The last thing I want to do is put her in danger. Her being so far away suddenly seems like the biggest stroke of luck.

"Well, Godspeed, kid. Send me a link sometime and let me know how it all works out." Marissa goes to cut the com and stops. "Look, it's not my place to pry into your affairs, I know that, but if ever I saw someone with unfinished business, it's you. I don't know what's going on with you and this boy, and I don't want to, but finish it before you go. Break up with him, speak your piece to him, whatever it is you need to do. Because if you don't, you'll regret it for the rest of your life."

I continue to think about her words even after she links me the job details and signs off. If only I could tell Michael everything. If only there was some way to make him understand why I have to go. But how do I explain a mission I don't even understand myself? How do I explain what I am to him without losing his regard forever?

I can't.

———

The dreams come again when next I sleep. The prison camp, the doctor, the military commander, the woman with the sunken cheeks, now joined by a man who looks just as sick. Their images mix and blur in my head; their voices shout in a chaotic jumble. In my dream, I hold my hands over my ears and beg for them to stop. Anything, if they would just let me alone. The voices suddenly go dead, but for one voice, a man's voice.

We'll stop, he says, *when you go Nova.*

I can't, I whisper. *I'm afraid.*

The old man smiles gently. *You don't have to be.*

No?

No, he answers with a shake of his head. *You don't*

have to be afraid because it will be glorious. More glorious than you could possibly imagine.

Glorious.

———

I wake to find that while I was sleeping, another two seconds have slipped away.

00:00:39

22 **THE NEXT MORNING, I TAKE** my neighbor's suggestion and hie myself from the bay before they even raise the lights. It's just as well; I couldn't sleep anyway with all the dreams. They've been coming every night now, ever since Shar touched me. Even in the day, sometimes, I find my mind starting to drift, as if reaching for something. What if, just what if . . . ?

A chill comes over me, and I shake my head, breaking off the thought before it can fully form. Grabbing the lift up, I go about my morning routine of breakfast, jog, and watch the news. When the hour gets late enough, I seek out the freighter I'll be shipping out on, *Comet's Kiss*. The ship is slightly smaller than Kerr's, with a complement of nine, plus the captain and now me. Les Standish is just as Kerr said, hard but not unfair. He links me my contract, explaining the various details as I bite my lip in anxiety and try to take it all in.

"Don't 'print it if you're not sure," Standish says briskly as I hesitate, my thumb hovering just over the screen. "Once you sign, you're mine for a year. The freighter life isn't easy. I have no room for anyone who doesn't want to be here."

"I do want to be here," I protest, but my thin voice doesn't convince even me.

"Look, you don't have to sign right now. Go home,

think about it. We're leaving at oh-eight-hundred the day after tomorrow. If you want to come, be here with the contract 'printed by then. Otherwise, we'll go without you. I'm sure we could always pick up someone at one of our other stops."

I want to protest—*I'm ready to sign right now!*—but instead I find myself nodding and shaking his proffered hand. As I walk away, I castigate myself for my indecision. I know I have to go. Why couldn't I just sign that deffin' contract?

I think back to what Kerr said the night before, about making sure all my business is finished. Maybe that's my problem—I can't leave without seeing Michael one last time. For all that it would be safest to link him from space, he deserves better. He deserves to have his best friend from Aurora tell him she's leaving. In person.

The thought elates me and fills me with dread at the same time. I want so badly to see Michael again, but how do I tell him he's losing his best friend forever? It would almost be better to leave with the Auroran refugees; at least then I would have an excuse for going. Still, it should be safe enough to talk to him, I reason. I've seen Michael a million times without ever losing seconds. As long as he doesn't kiss me, I should be okay.

As long as *I* don't kiss *him*, I should be okay.

I link Michael before I can lose my nerve. He doesn't pick up, but that doesn't surprise me. He's probably in class right now. Instead, I leave a message for him to meet me on the roof of his apartment building later this afternoon. I think of the rose he left on my cot, that expensive rose, and I know he'll come.

It occurs to me that there's someone else I need to link before leaving tomorrow. I pull up the station directory, and soon after, Rowan's face comes up on my chit.

"Lia, you read my mind. You're one of the final people I was intending to meet with in the next couple days. Are you sure you're not a psychic?" he asks, and I smile wanly at the old joke only psychics ever seem to find funny. "So what's going on? Did you talk to that family you told me about?"

"No, but I got a job. I'm shipping out on a freighter the day after tomorrow. I thought you'd want to know."

"A freighter? Wow, you're the last person I would have pegged for that kind of life. Are you sure that's what you want?"

"Is my alternative any better?"

He hesitates for a second. "No," he admits. "So what happened with that friend you mentioned before?"

"It didn't work out," I reply shortly. To deflect attention away from myself, I ask, "Is it true what they're saying, that a convoy will be coming for all of the released prisoners soon?"

"It is, but keep it quiet for now, okay? An announcement will be made later today or tomorrow, but until then, we'd prefer to keep the gossip to a minimum."

"What about the Aurorans? Where are they going? Not that it matters since I already have a job," I hasten to add. "I'm just curious. I won't tell anyone."

Rowan gives me a look, and for a moment I think he can see straight through my eyes and into my soul. "I believe you." He rakes a hand through his hair. "I suppose it will be coming out soon enough. There are a couple colonies—Dayav and Mechanra. The Aurorans are going to be resettled there."

Dayav and Mechanra. The names don't sound familiar. A bad feeling starts pooling in my stomach. "Just how old are these colonies?"

"Dayav is two years old. Mechanra, a little less. They're twin planets orbiting the same star."

Two years! That's barely enough time to even get the terraforming process started. The only people on a colony that young are the terraform workers themselves, the people who treat the soil and water with the compounds that will begin the planet's transformation. Sending the refugees there is in effect sentencing them all to a lifetime of hard labor. No wonder Rowan urged me to cultivate my relationship with Michael's family.

"It's not what I would have chosen, believe me, Lia, but it wasn't up to me. It wasn't up to PsyCorp. The Celestian government saw a chance to kill two birds with one stone—solve the refugee problem and staff the new colonies—and they took it. Why pay good creds to support a bunch of refugees when they could put them all to work instead? At least, I'm sure that's how they see it."

For all that the reasoning makes a certain amount of sense, it's still horrid. All those unsuspecting people in the bay . . . How betrayed they'll feel when they learn their fate! My heart skips a beat when I think of Kaeti, and then I remember what Rowan told me previously, that minors under sixteen wouldn't be affected.

"What about the children?"

"Families with two parents will go to the colonies. Orphaned children will be sent to settled worlds and put into foster care. Single-parent families are being decided on a case-by-case basis."

So Kaeti will go into foster care somewhere. I suppose it was always bound to happen with her parents both gone. I feel bad for Lela, though, who will be losing her "children" for a life of hard labor on a new colony. Shar, too, won't escape the sentence. She's at least sixteen, I'm sure of it. I should feel smug and self-satisfied at my enemy's fate, but somehow I don't. Instead, I find myself hoping she'll get over whatever hang-up she has about her psychic abilities and just fess up to PsyCorp. Well, just so long as she waits until after I'm gone to do it. Can't have her ratting on me to the brain-drainers with whatever she *thinks* she knows about me!

Rowan enjoins me to secrecy once more, and I agree not to say anything. As I link off, I wonder briefly why he trusted me with the news, but I don't have to ponder it for long. After all, if anyone could understand how hard it is to keep a terrible secret shut up inside, it's me.

———

When I step out onto the roof of his building, Michael is already waiting for me, standing by the ledge, looking out over the ring. He doesn't turn at the scrape of the door, though I know he must have heard it. I lean on the ledge beside him.

"Hi."

"Hi," he says back. Michael turns to look at me fully, and my hands self-consciously go to my jumpsuit. He's not looking at my clothes though; he's looking at the rose tucked carefully in my hair. For a brief instant, I think he's going to reach out and touch its soft petals. Then the moment passes.

I pause, uncertain how to start. "Thank you for the flower. It's beautiful."

Michael nods but doesn't say anything. His characteristic smile is missing today, replaced by this grave, oh-so-grave face, as if he already knows what I'm here to say. It's tripping me up, making the impossible words I have to say even more impossible.

I inwardly laugh. *Who am I kidding?* The words would have been impossible no matter what face Michael showed me. Well, I came here to say something. Best to just say it. "I'm leaving, Michael."

Whatever he expected me to say, it wasn't that. He blinks, head shaking slightly as he takes in my words. "What do you mean? Where are you going?"

I take a breath. "I've taken a job on a freighter. I ship out the day after tomorrow."

"I don't understand."

"I helped out one of the freighter captains a four-square ago. She offered me a job—"

"You've known you were leaving for a *month*, and you never told me?"

"No, no, it's nothing like that," I hasten to explain. "I only found out about the job yesterday. The captain has a friend who had an opening."

"So you took it? Just like that?" Michael shakes his head again, and it's clear he's having trouble processing it all. Not that I blame him. If he came here and told me he'd enlisted in the navy and was leaving in two days, I would be just as overloaded. "I don't understand. Why do you want to leave?"

"It's not that I *want* to leave—"

"Then don't go!"

"It's not that simple." I try another tack. "Look, we both always knew my time on this station was temporary. I don't live here like you, Michael. I'm a refugee, a former prisoner from an internment camp. It was only a matter of time before I had to go."

"That's why you're going? The authorities are kicking you out?"

"Well . . ."

"Then it's no problem!" His trademark smile is suddenly back, so bright it could run a million solar collectors, and my heart stutters under its power. "You can stay with us. Gran loves you; she would say yes in a heartbeat."

"It would never work. The apartment is already small for the three of you. Where would I even sleep?"

"You can have my bed, and I'll sleep on the couch. Trust me—Teal would far rather share a room with you than me."

His answer is so quick, I know he's thought about it before. It's like a kick in the heart, to know I could stay if only I asked. Something starts crumbling inside of me, and I know that if I don't end this and get out of here soon, I never will.

"Michael—"

"It'll be perfect. You can finish school with me, and then once we graduate—"

"Michael."

"—we can do anything we want. Stay and work on the station, join a colony, even take a freighter job if that's what you really want. It'll be you and me, Lia, just like it was befo—"

"No, Michael, it *won't*!"

He blinks as my vehement words finally get through to him. "Why not?"

"Because I'm not Lia."

"This again? I thought we talked about—"

I grab him by the shoulders, cutting him off mid-sentence. "No, you don't understand, Michael. I'm not speaking metaphorically. There *was* a Lia Johansen who lived on Tiersten Internment Colony. I just don't happen to be her."

I might have hauled back and struck him, he looks so stunned. He doesn't speak for a full ten seconds, but just stares at me with this uncomprehending expression on his face. Should I have held back the truth? Gone to the grave with my secret? It's what I'd planned to do, but he was so sincere, so earnest as he invited me to stay that I suddenly couldn't *not* tell him the truth. Well, in for a penny, in for a pound. I try to explain: "My name isn't Lia Johansen. I'm not Auroran; I'm not even Celestian."

"I don't understand. Your name was on the screen."

"That's because I told the station officials that's who I was when they checked me in. Since the Auroran database doesn't exist anymore, they had no way to disprove my story."

Michael stares over my shoulder, eyes fixed on something in the distance, and I can practically see the wheels turning in his head as he tries to make sense of things. "No, that can't be right. If you're not Lia, then how did you know all those things about me? About us? Like how I lined my cap with alumna-seal because I was convinced Mr. Russell was an alien, or how Lia always said 'To the sky' when I pushed her on the swings. How did you know Teal's name or even my name, for that matter?"

"They gave me some of Lia's memories before I came, to get me past PsyCorp. That's how I knew."

"They?"

"I can't tell you who."

"Can't tell me who? What, like you're some kind of spy working for a secret Tellurian agency?"

I nod my head. *Yes, Michael. Better for you to think I'm a spy than a bomb.*

"So an unnamed secret agency used Lia's identity and memories to get you onto New Sol so you could spy for them."

"Something like that."

"Then these peace talks they've been talking about on the viewer all this time are just a smokescreen while the Tellurians plan their next attack. Is that what you're saying?"

"Yeah, I think so."

He cocks his head and meets my eye. "So what's your real name, then?"

I hesitate a moment, then admit, "I don't know."

"You don't know?"

"I don't remember. Not my name, my past, my parents, not even my mission! Something went wrong with my memory, and all I know is that I shouldn't be here. I'm dangerous, Michael. To you, to Teal, to Taylor, everyone. I have to go before I hurt someone I care about . . ."

My words trail off. Michael is laughing. In little chuckles at first, and then larger hoots, and then finally great big belly laughs. He's actually crying a little bit, he's laughing so hard, a tear hovering in the corner of his eye. I stand there, stunned as he laughs his head off at my deepest, darkest secret. Of all the reactions I'd imagined, this was the last one I'd expected.

After a minute, he finally calms down. He wipes his eyes with the back of his hand and shakes his head. "Geez, Lia, you sure had me going for a minute. Going off on a freighter, being a Tellurian spy . . . I don't know how you always come up with this stuff."

In answer, I activate my chit and silently pull up my freighter contract.

"It's true then? You're really leaving?" Michael asks, the smile dying on his face as he takes in the contract.

"It's true."

He takes a breath, and then another, and another, almost as if he's girding himself up for something. At last he says, "It's the kiss, isn't it? That's why you're going away."

"The kiss?"

"I should have known after the way you lit out of there."

"No, it wasn't that. I explained—"

"Come on, Lia! Do I look like a complete deficient? Do you really think I believed that complete pile of slag you tried to feed me about avoiding some officer? At the time, I thought you were just trying to spare my feelings, that you didn't know how to tell me you just wanted to be friends. In fact, that's what I thought you were coming here to tell me."

He whirls away and paces a couple steps, then comes back, his mouth pressed in a thin line. "You know, if you didn't want to be with me, you could have just said so. You didn't have to sign on to some freighter and make up some stupid story about being a spy. We're not kids anymore, Lia. Grow up!"

"But—"

"You want to go? Fine, go!"

"Michael, it's not like that!" I grab his arm as he turns to leave, and the rose falls out of my hair. He angrily shakes off my grip.

"No? Then what's it like?"

My mouth flaps a couple times, no ready answer coming to my lips. I tried to tell him the truth and he didn't believe me. What lie would convince him of something the truth could not?

"Yeah, that's what I thought," he says bitterly when I don't reply.

This time when he wheels around, I don't try to stop him. I just watch as he storms across the roof and through the door back into the building. He doesn't look back once. The rose lies on the concrete beside my foot, its petals crushed and defeated.

I press my hand to my chest. Everything inside of me is cracking now, fissures rippling out from my chest as if all my innards were spun from glass. Maybe I don't know my name, or what I am, or if I have a soul, but I am sure of one thing. I do have a heart.

23 I THUMB MY CONTRACT as soon as I get back to the bay. I feel completely numb inside, as though the thing crushed underfoot wasn't merely a flower, but my own heart. Marissa was wrong; tying up my loose ends was the *worst* thing I could have done. It would have been far better to take off without a word and only send Michael a message once I was safely away. Anything would have been better than enduring that painful face-to-face confrontation.

Slipping into the shadowed nook between a couple crates, I lean my forehead against one of the lockers. The metal is cool under my hands, soothing against my pulsing head. What did I expect would happen? For Michael to slap me on the back and congratulate me on my new job? No, I wasn't naïve enough to expect that, but a hug, an "I'll miss you," maybe a "link me?" Yes, I had expected those. I had gone looking for a real goodbye and instead all I'd done was hurt the person I cared about most in the world.

A soft moan slips from my mouth. More than anything, I wish I could go back and find some way to show him what I am. To prove that everything I told him is true, and that it's not really him I'm trying to escape but myself. It's a foolish fantasy; even if he would listen, I have no way to prove any of this. All I can do now is forge ahead and try to ignore the horrible, gaping hollow inside of me.

Even though *Comet's Kiss* isn't flying out until the day after tomorrow, I start making preparations to leave. It doesn't take long. Now that I gave away all the things I got from Michael's family, my pile of possessions is pathetically small, even for a freighter hand. Well, I do have the milicreds I made doing various odd jobs on the station. There's no reason I can't add a little to the pile.

I don't buy much. Some clothes—pants, shirts, and tanks like I've seen other spacers wear, in tones of brown, black, and olive green; a couple game holos for my off-duty hours, though I know those hours are likely to be few; a tool belt with a knife, laser cutter, multi-tool, measuring sensor, and a few other tools of the trade; and a duffle to put it all in. Everything is used, but I don't mind. I couldn't afford it all if it were new anyway.

As I reenter the bay after my shopping trip, I glance at the timescreen on the wall, wondering if it's late enough to go to bed. Drowning myself in sleep seems like a good option at this time. To my surprise, a familiar figure stands just to the left of the screen.

"Teal?"

She turns, the searching look fading from her face as soon as she sees me, to be replaced by a set expression. Contrition washes over me as I realize I never said goodbye to her, or Taylor for that matter. I was so focused on my meeting with Michael I completely forgot. Not that I would have been able to go in and face them after what happened. I smile, thankful I'll at least have the chance to say farewell to Teal.

"Teal," I say again as she reaches me, "I'm so glad—"

Smack!

My head slues back under the force of her slap, the

crack loud enough to make several heads in the vicinity turn our way. I drop my duffle and grab my cheek.

"How *could* you?! How could you do that to Michael? After all he's done for you!"

"I'm sorry, I—"

"I knew you were bad news from the moment he came home and said *Lia* was back!" Teal sneers. "I knew you'd end up being just another disappointment, another person he would end up losing. As if he hasn't lost enough people already. He already lost you once, and everyone else on Aurora. Our parents, his friends on Stella and all the other stations we lived on. Why did you have to come back and just mess him up all over again?"

"What, you think I did this on purpose?" I ask, spurred to my own defense in spite of myself.

"You tell me! You're the one who glommed onto Michael—"

"*He's* the one who came and found me."

"—insinuated yourself into his life, acted like his best friend—"

"I *am* his best friend!"

"Then why are you running out on him? Why are you leaving him?"

"I'm not leaving *Michael*," I protest. "I'm leaving *for* Michael."

"What in a black hole is *that* supposed to mean?"

I take a breath and stop. "I can't explain," I say weakly, wishing more than anything I could. "All I can say is that I have to do this. I have to go—for Michael's sake, for yours, for Taylor's—"

"Don't! Don't even try to pretend you care about all of us or that you're doing this for *our* sakes. Whatever you told Michael up there on the roof, it's pretty obvious it wasn't for *him*." Teal shakes her head, anger seeping from every pore as she mutters to herself. "I thought you were different. That you really cared about Michael. Waiting around all evening just to make sure he was sat ... How could I have been so deficient as to be taken in by *you*?"

"You weren't taken in about anything! I *do* care about Michael, and I have since ... I don't even know when! Don't you get it? Michael's all I have. My parents, my past, everything is *gone*. Without him, I'm nothing." I pause. The contempt in Teal's eyes has dimmed, uncertainty mingling with her scorn, and I grasp for the opening, small as it seems. "Believe me, if I could find a way to stay, I would."

She stares at me for a long moment, clearly undecided, and then her eyes fall on the duffle bag at my feet. Her eyes harden. "Obviously you didn't try hard enough."

She brushes past me with a hard swipe of her shoulder. I stumble, regain my footing, and call, "Teal!"

She doesn't turn around.

I start to follow her, and then think better of it. What did she say, after all, that wasn't true? Oh, she was wrong about my intentions—hurting Michael was the last thing I ever wanted to do—but that doesn't change the end result. She's right. I came back into his life, his best friend Lia from Aurora, only to walk out again without even the grace of a real explanation. Or at least a believable one. No wonder Teal blew a circuit.

A slight smile curls my mouth as I think of thirteen-year-old Teal defending her older brother so fiercely. After all this time, I finally understand why she disliked me so much. It wasn't that she was afraid I'd come between her and Michael; she was afraid I'd hurt him. And she was right.

Shouldering my duffle, I make my way back to my corner. I feel sick to my stomach as I remember how upset Michael got when his dad canceled on him. Why did I think he would react any better to my leaving? At least he still has Teal, I console myself as I set my duffle down under my cot. Sharp, tough-as-nails Teal, always keeping herself just the smallest bit protected from the world, and her brother too, inasmuch as she can. That's what's so great about Michael, I realize. While Teal has become jaded by her losses, Michael is still open to the world around him. Big-hearted, honest, ready to ward off life's perils with a grin and a joke, to find a friend where others would only see a stranger.

The way he found me.

A bit of liquid trickles over my lip, and I reach up to touch my face. Did Teal's slap open up a cut I missed? But it's only my nose, bleeding again. I wipe the blood off with my hand and check the timescreen: 1958. Thirty-six hours until the *Kiss* shoves off. My lips twitch as I remember my last thirty-six-hour countdown. That countdown was to my death; this one is to my new life. So why do I find this one so much more terrifying?

Maybe because, unlike before, this time I have so much more to lose.

Settling down on my cot, I close my eyes and begin the wait.

————

Stars twinkle around us in all directions as we stand together in the observation deck below Level Thirteen.

"How did you ever find this place?" Michael asks, pressing up against the glass to gaze in wonder at the velvet cloak enshrouding us.

I shrug. "Oh, I have my ways."

"Well, it's amazing! You're amazing." He turns to me and our eyes meet. His enraptured gaze is for me alone now, and I can barely breathe through the rushing of my pulse. Michael reaches out a hand and cups my cheek. "You have the most beautiful eyes," he says, and even before he leans in, I know he's going to kiss me.

It's perfect. The pressure of his lips and the soft touch of his hand on my face. I reach for him, wanting more ...

A tear falls on my cheek. Confused, I pull away and swipe at the moisture.

It's gray. Gray and thick and metallic.

Fluid suddenly fills my eyes, streaming out of the corners and from beneath the lids. I glance up at Michael in shock. "Michael, help me!" I plead, but he only jerks away in disgust.

More fluid washes over my eyes and everything goes gray.

We're on Level Five now. My eyes are clear and my face clean. Around us, station personnel walk by in every direction, all going about their normal duties.

"Are you going to go Nova now?" Michael asks me.

I gasp. "How do you know about that?"

He points to my face in answer. This time it's blood that spills down my face, pouring from my nose and dripping on my jumpsuit. I clap my hand to my nose, but I can't stem the tide.

"It's time to fulfill your mission," he says.

"I can't. Even if I wanted to, I don't know how. My clock is broken; I don't know how to fix it."

He just looks at me. "Obviously you didn't try hard enough."

Suddenly we're surrounded on all sides. Teal is there, and Taylor and Rowan. The doctor, the military com-

mander, Lela with Kaeti, the sickly man and woman, and others. So many others, crammed into the shadows on all sides, pushing up around me.

"Obviously you didn't try hard enough," Teal echoes.

"Obviously you *didn't try hard enough," the military commander says.*

"Obviously you didn't *try hard enough," the sickly woman adds.*

"Try hard enough."

"Try hard enough."

"I did *try," I protest, throwing out my hands to ward them off. "I tried!"*

Another figure steps out of the shadows. Shar. She stares at me for a long time. "Obviously you didn't try hard enough," she whispers. Slowly, deliberately, she reaches out and touches my forehead. White spots burst in front of my eyes and everything falls away. Everything but for a child's voice, singsong and high, echoing through my mind.

"Cross your heart and hope to die, stick a needle in your eye."

━━━━━

I pace around the walks of the hub, too tired to jog anymore, but unable to stop and sit still. The words from my dream, *Teal's* words, have been racing around my brain since the moment I awoke this morning.

Obviously you didn't try hard enough.

Could it really be true? Is there really no solution to my predicament or is it just that I was afraid of what the solution might mean? In my heart, I fear it might be the latter. For what if the solution means blowing up this station? What if the solution means killing my best friend? It's easier to run, to remain ignorant of my past. To go far away and forget that I was sent here for a reason.

Easier, yes, but is it a choice I can live with? After what happened with Michael and Teal, I'm starting to think it isn't. Unlocking my past could doom my future, but there's also a chance it could save it. If nothing else, I need to know that at least I did everything I could to find out. I need to know the consequences of my decisions before blindly choosing. Otherwise, Teal's right. I didn't try hard enough. Isn't Michael—everyone, really—worth trying for?

My feet make the decision before my mind does, for I'm halfway to the lift before I even know I'm going there. My heart is thrumming in my chest as I rise the one level to Eight and make my way back to the bay. Maybe she won't be there; maybe I won't be able to find her anywhere.

No such luck. Shar's sprawled on her cot perusing, of all things, *my* old reader. She sits up when she sees me coming. Her spine is stiff and her eyes wary. I can't blame her. One day we're fighting and the next I'm giving her gifts for no apparent reason. If I were Shar, I'd suspect I was bat-slag crazy, too.

I stop at the end of her cot. "Hey."

"Hey," she answers slowly.

Still in the dirty tank and baggy gray shorts she sleeps in, Shar hardly looks like the sort of person anyone would go to for help. However, I'm not seeing her as she is now. I'm seeing the girl whose last touch inspired a series of nightly dreams about my past. I'm seeing the girl from my dreams who touched my head after saying I didn't try hard enough. I'm seeing the unregistered psychic who might just possibly be able to tell me what I need to know.

"I need your help."

The wary look in her eyes intensifies. "With what?"

"I need you to tell me who I am."

**24** **MY WORDS CLINCH IT.** She really does think I'm bat-slag crazy now. "Look, I don't know what kind of joke you're trying to play, Johansen—"

"It's no joke," I interrupt. "I need you to use your psychic abilities on me."

That gets her attention. She jumps to her feet and grabs me by the collar. "Are you *lunar*?" she hisses. "Anyone could hear you. *Seal it!* Just seal it! Or are you here to bust me?"

"What people hear—what *PsyCorp* hears—is entirely up to you." My eyes flick to the hands that still hold me.

Shar's eyes narrow as she grasps the threat. Her nostrils flare in anger, hands fisting tighter over my collar, but her eyes . . . In her eyes is *fear*. Pure, gut-wrenching, ice-in-your-veins fear. Hatred wars with terror, and for a moment, I'm sure she'll refuse me. Call my bluff and tell me to go frag off. Then with a growl, she releases me. She paces back and forth in front of her cot for a minute. When she finally looks back at me, the fear is gone, her eyes now guarded and hard. "So say I help you. What exactly do you want me to do?"

"I have some memories—blocked memories about my past. I need you to try and access them."

"What sort of memories?"

"How would I know?" I ask evasively. "They're blocked. I can't reach them."

"If they're blocked, it's probably for a reason. It would be better not to know."

"I *have* to know."

Shar frowns. "Why don't you just go to PsyCorp then? They're trained for this sort of thing. I'm sure that creepy psylieutenant whatever-his-name-is would be happy to help you uncover whatever horrible mystery lurks in your past." When I don't answer, realization slowly dawns across her face. "You have a good idea what it is, and you don't want them to know, do you? So frag-nosed little Lia Johansen has something to hide, too. Well, isn't that something."

I have her now. She just can't resist the urge to get some dirt on me. It's not ideal—what if she runs straight to PsyCorp with whatever she finds out?—but I have to hope that her own fear of discovery is enough to keep her away from them.

"So do we have a deal?" I ask.

"Fine." Shar spits on her hand and extends it. Her hand trembles, and she yanks it back, folding her arms across her chest and tucking her hands safely out of sight. Her eyes dare me to say something. I don't take the dare. Instead, I spit on my own hand and hold it out. "Deal?"

After a short pause, she relinquishes her hand long enough to slap mine. "Deal."

White flashes in my head at the contact, and we both jump back. No need to start anything before we absolutely have to.

———

"Are you sure you still want to do this?"

Tamping down my nerves, I nod. "Yes."

I'm sitting cross-legged on the floor of the tunnel across from Shar. Though I can hear the faint rumble of the SlipStream through the wall, on this side it's quiet enough to hear a chit drop. Silent, deserted, private — it's the perfect place for what we're about to do. Save for Michael, I've never seen anyone else in here, and it's unlikely he'll venture out to the hub anytime soon after what happened between us.

A pang flits through me at the thought of Michael. I push it away and extend my hands. "Well?"

Shar fidgets in her spot, scratching her arm and picking at a non-existent bit of lint on her T-shirt. If I didn't know better, I would think she was nervous. Afraid, even. About what, I have no idea. After all, I promised not to rat her out to PsyCorp if she helped me.

"You realize this could be dangerous," she says, her voice smaller than I've ever heard it before. "I'm not t-trained for this; I'm not really trained at all. Anything could go wrong."

Seizures, brain damage, death. It's one of the reasons all psychics are required to register with PsyCorp — to ensure they receive the training they need to keep from accidentally harming anyone. Letting Shar into my mind is a risk, but it's one I'll have to take. Assuming Shar doesn't get cold feet and back out on me, that is. Her anxiety is almost palpable now. Funny, she doesn't strike me as the type to balk at breaking a few rules.

"What's wrong?" I scoff. "You scared?"

"Maybe I am!"

"I don't know why. If something happens, it's going to be to me, not you."

"Yeah, well I'm going to be the one who has to explain your dead body to PsyCorp," she retorts. She takes a long breath, visibly pulling herself together, and adds, "Do you know what kind of penalty unlicensed psychic activity carries?"

"Then don't frag up."

Hatred flares in her eyes and her gaze hardens. "Fine," she agrees sarcastically, "but if you die, I'm throwing your corpse out the nearest airlock."

I actually smile faintly at that. *This* is the Shar I know—the belligerent, sarcastic girl who hates everything and everyone. Better her than the nervous, self-conscious Shar who momentarily reared her head.

I hold out my hands to her. "Agreed."

This time she takes them.

A flash of white bursts in my head at her touch. Fear pulses through my chest and every nerve ending in my body screams for me to pull away, but I only squeeze her hands tighter. Then I feel it. A presence, something foreign and unfamiliar, sliding into my mind.

I force down the instinct to fight, to repel the presence with all my strength, and instead try to accept the invasion. It's not easy. Though it doesn't hurt, it feels strange and uncomfortable and inappropriate. Like having a stranger touch you in your most private places. I squeeze my eyes shut, as though not being able to see Shar will help. It doesn't. Opening my eyes again, I gasp. I can still see Shar sitting in front of me, legs folded and elbows resting on her knees, but now I can also see myself, wide-eyed and slightly trembling. It's like I'm seeing from both our eyes at the same time, one image superimposed over the other.

"C-can you see it too?" I ask.

"Yeah."

I remind myself to breathe, and watch as my chest swells and subsides. "Is this supposed to happen?"

"I-I'm not sure. Maybe it would be easier if we close our eyes."

I watch myself nod, and then shut my eyes again. It does help not to see the double images anymore. After a minute, I start to relax a little. Though Shar's presence feels alien and far, far too intimate, it doesn't feel threatening. I sit back and wait for her to do her thing. And wait. And wait.

"Um, Shar? What now?"

"I don't know! I told you I wasn't t-trained in this. I thought maybe it would be obvious once I went in, but it's all so big." She takes a breath, and I can hear how shaky it is. No, more than that—I can *feel* how shaky it is. Wisps of fear leak in around the edges of my mind, and my heart picks up tempo the smallest bit.

"Big?"

"Vast, like an ocean rippling with currents in every direction. I just, I don't know where to go." Panic limns her voice, and the fear suddenly sharpens, high-pitched and unallayed. Her hands tighten on mine, bone-crushingly hard, and I can't help letting out a squeal.

I try to yank my hands away. "Shar? Shar! Let go, you're hurting me!"

She doesn't seem to hear me. Desperate, I dig my fingernails into the back of her hands. *That* gets her attention. She lets out a yelp, arms jerking in surprise, but it seems to do the trick, as both the grip and the fear suddenly ease. "Thanks. I needed that," she says quietly. She takes a deep breath. "Maybe you could try thinking about something. Something specific."

Okay, that seems easy enough. Eyes still closed, I let the first thing I can think of pop into my head.

"Cereal, with a banana sliced on top," Shar says.

"It's what I had for breakfast this morning."

Shar directs me to recall something else, and I do, bringing to mind our first fight in the cargo bay, when I jumped her for stealing my reader. She lets out a snort of amusement. "I sure didn't expect that." More emotion blooms in my brain—a feeling of surprised respect, I realize after a minute. Shar's emotion, not mine.

We try a few more memories, all of which Shar picks up with ease. It's almost kind of fun, like a game, with me trying to come up with progressively harder images while she tries to guess them. Shar mentally rolls her eyes at my thought, clearly much calmer now than when we started, and nods. "Okay, I think I've got it. Try to access one of your blocked memories now."

My previous anxiety comes racing back, but I do as she says. I start with the transport, thinking about my last moments before disembarking on the station, then slowly work my way back. It's not particularly interesting—sleeping, eating, and staring out the window mostly—though Shar does get a kick out of seeing me half-electrocuted by the malfunctioning door control. At last I get back to my very first memory, that of being in the spaceport getting ready to board. Taking a deep breath, I try and push myself back even further. Where was I before that?

My name is Lia Johansen, and I was a prisoner of war.

"Whoa!" Shar's nails bite into my hand as her fingers clench.

I yank my mind away from the memory back into the safe realms of the present. "What is it?"

"I don't know, I need to see it again. Go back. Do it once more."

My heart is racing now, fear starting to rise up now that we're so near my past, but I obey, pushing my mind back to my very first memory and then beyond. It reels out again, that catchphrase that has haunted me as far back as I can remember.

My name is Lia Johansen, and I was a prisoner of war.

"My name is Lia Johansen, and I was a prisoner of war," Shar repeats aloud as I pull myself back to the present. "It's like the pathway to your memory has been rewritten."

I frown. "What do you mean?"

"Well, think of your mind like a gigantic city, with each memory being a different house or building within the city. Every memory has a different set of directions you have to take to reach it. Normally when you can't remember something, it's because you no longer know the directions to get there. Only in your case, it's like there's this roadblock, a detour, forcing you to go down another road, back to—"

"My name is Lia Johansen, and I was a prisoner of war."

"Exactly. Whatever's blocking your memory, it's not natural, that's for sure."

"Can you break through it?"

Shar hesitates, and again I feel that spike of fear. "I don't know. Maybe. This time when you hit the road-block, I want you to try again. I want you to keep trying and trying until you get through."

My palms are sweating—or maybe it's Shar's palms that are sweating, who can tell?—but I nod and take my-self back into the past. *Where* was I before?

My name is Lia Johansen, and I was a prisoner of war.
I break off and try again. Where was I . . . ?

My name is Lia Johansen, and I was a prisoner of war.
Again.

My name is Lia Johansen, and I was a prisoner of war.
Again.

My name is Lia Johansen, and I was a prisoner of war.
Again.

My name is Lia Johansen, and and and and and and and and and and—

My head jerks back as something explodes in my brain. Spots of color burst across my vision, images reeling across my mind in a cacophony of senses—sight and sound and touch and smell.

Then everything goes haywire.

25 *and and and and and and and
and and and and and and and and
and and and and and and and and
and and*

Error: Failure to execute Sequence 34912048
Re-sequencing initiated

*My name is Lia Johansen and and and and and and and
and and*

Error: Failure to execute Sequence 34912048
Re-sequencing initiated

*My name name is is is Lia Johansen-sen-sen-sen-sen-
sen-sen-sen-sen-sen*

Error: Failure to execute Sequence 34912048
Re-sequencing initiated

*My my my my name name name name name name is is
is Lia-a-a-a-a-a-a-a-a-a-a-a-a-a-a*

Error: Failure to execute Sequence 34912048
Re-sequencing initiated

*M-m-m-m-m-m-m-my n-n-n-a-a-a-me is-is-is-is-is L-l-
l-l-l-l-l-l-l-l-l-l-l-l-l-l*

Error: Failure to execute Sequence 34912048
Re-sequencing initiated

*M-m-m-m-m-m-m-m-m-m-m-m-m-m-m-m-m-m-m-m-my
my m-m-m-m-m-m-m-m-my m-m-m-m-m-m-m*

Error: Failure to execute Sequence 34912048
Re-sequencing initiated
Error: failure to re-sequence

Re-sequencing initiated
Error: failure to re-sequence
Initiating reset to Basic Mode One
Error: failure to reset

Initiating reset to Basic Mode One
Error: failure to reset

Initiating Emergency Wipe
Wiping initiated
Wiping . . .
Wiping . . .
*Wiping . . .

******

Initiating Hard Reset
Resetting . . .
Resetting . . .
*Resetting . . .

My name is Lia Johansen, and I was a prisoner of war

26

"... TAKEN WHEN AURORA Colony fell, I lived in an internment camp for two years along with ten thousand other civilian blah blah blahs." I roll my eyes at Doc Niven. "Come on, do I really have to do this again? I know it, I swear."

The doc just raises an expectant eyebrow. With a sigh, I start again.

"My name is Lia Johansen, and I was a prisoner of war. Taken when Aurora Colony fell, I lived in an internment camp for two years along with ten thousand other civilian colonists. My parents died in front of me from starvation and sickness. Oh, and I wept for them. There, see?"

"Good," Niven says. "Now remember, this will be your core memory once we activate the biochip. You'll probably be able to access a scattering of other memories from your past, but the biochip will block anything recent."

"What will happen if I try to access anything off-limits?"

"The biochip will automatically reroute your mind back to your cover story."

Doc Niven grabs the tool he used to insert the chip and puts it in the sterilizer. I can't help raising a hand to my eyes as I remember how he inserted the biochip behind my left eye, the clock behind my right. He used a local anesthetic, so it didn't hurt, but the way he popped out each eyeball and put it back in will probably haunt me for the rest of my life. At least, it would if I remembered it for the rest of my life. Once the biochip is activated, I won't remember any of this.

I shiver at the thought. Somehow out of everything that's going to happen, it's losing my memory that scares me the most. Not going Nova, not dying, but forgetting who I am. Forgetting why I'm doing this.

"We won't actually activate it unless it's really necessary, right?" I ask the doc, though I already know what he'll say.

"Wherever we end up deploying you, it will most likely be necessary. The enemy knows of our resistance; they're watching for us to make a move. They'll have their psychics out in force, looking for anything out of the ordinary. We can't chance them finding out what you are before you can complete your mission. Suppressing your memories is the only way we can make sure they won't discover your mission if they force you to undergo a psychic check."

I sigh and look down at my hands. "I know."

Water runs in the sink. "How's your nose? Does it still hurt?"

Still looking down, I shake my head. "No, it doesn't hurt, but I can't smell anything anymore."

"That's normal."

"I can't taste anything, either."

A towel swishes through the air. "I'm not surprised. A large part of taste is smell. It's not uncommon for people losing their sense of smell to lose all or some of their

abilities to taste as well. It may pass, or it may be permanent. Even if it comes back, your sense of taste will
probably be weak. I'm sorry."

"It doesn't matter."

I hear his footsteps come back and then his large
hands take mine and squeeze. He gently turns my arms
over and runs a finger over each forearm. "They've
healed well. No one should be able to tell what's underneath the skin."

Raising my head, I look at the doc. The skin of his
face is sagging, and his hair has gone almost completely
white. The look in his eyes is ineffably sad. He manages
a small smile when he sees me watching him.

"So many expectations, and on such young shoulders!
You've lived so much life in your two years here. We have
no right to ask more of you, but we do anyway. Not for
our sakes, but for humanity's sake, for the Celestians'
sake. You may be their only hope. And they don't even
know it."

I look away. "What if something goes wrong?"

"Then all you can do is die knowing you did your
best. We all did our best. If there truly is a higher power
up there, may He look down and protect us all."

"That's *it*? Trust to a higher power?"

The doc chuckles at my incredulity. "Well, I could go
into a long lecture on the workings of the clock and biochip if you want, but you won't remember it anyway."
Niven releases my hands and chucks me lightly on the
chin. "Have faith that it will all work out, and it will."

My thoughts turn to my parents. "I'm not sure I have
any faith left."

As if reading my mind, the doc asks, "Have you vis-
ited them lately?" I shrug, and he shakes his head, chid-

ing me. "Go see your parents. They don't have much longer. You'll regret it if you don't."

I give him a look. "*They* don't have much longer, or *I* don't?"

"Unfortunately, both."

———

My parents are in a building on the other side of the compound. I wander slowly across the deserted grounds. The place is far from impressive—a few buildings, a ruined lookout tower, and a force fence stuck on a plot of dull dirt adorned with clumps of yellowed grass.

When Tiersten Colony was first settled, this place was constructed as one of a few dozen weather-control stations to guard against the lightning storms and dust devils. Continued terraforming over the years eliminated the worst of the storms and made most of the control stations unnecessary. Ironically, this one was abandoned altogether a couple hundred years ago when the tower took a stray lightning strike. Now it's the final retreat of our resistance cell, for however long we can hold out. Once this place falls, there is nowhere else to go.

Not that I'll still be here by the time that happens.

I look around me and grimace for about the thousandth time since coming here. It's an ugly place—both the weather station and the land around it—all brown and yellow and brown. I heard a scientist once say that we could terraform Tiersten for a million years and it would never look any better than this. Tiersten is just one of those planets. Probably why the Tellurians ended up turning it into a penal planet instead of a real colony. Internment camps full of Celestian POWs, broken

weather stations, and one misbegotten resistance cell—
that's all that can be found here now.

A movement on the far side of the tower snags my
attention. I squint, catching a glimpse of dark hair and
olive skin. Storm, just a few years younger than me and
the only other child left in the resistance. Not that Storm
is his real name. No one knows his name, for he never
speaks. The kids at the internment camp all said he was
brain-damaged. They all said he had been struck by
lightning. Stormbrain, they called him, Lightning Rod. I
asked him once if what they said about the lightning was
true. He just looked at me with those strange brown
eyes of his—intelligent eyes that seemed to belie the rumors.

"I drowned once," I'd finally offered when he didn't
answer. "Back on Aurora, when I was really little. They
say I actually died for a minute, before the rescue workers brought me back."

He only shook his head at me, though what he was
saying "no" to, I had no idea. But the terrible scars on his
right hand, burned into the fleshy ball of his thumb and
radiating up through his palm into his fingers, told me
something had happened to him.

Someone calls my name and I turn. Captain Jao, the
commander of our dying resistance, is hailing me from
the back corner of the fence. I stiffen momentarily; then,
with a final glance at Storm, I reroute my steps. One
can't ignore the resistance commander, no matter how
much one might want to. He nods at my perfunctory
greeting. His sleeves are rolled up, and he's tinkering
with the control box on the corner post.

"How is the work on the force fence coming?" I ask,
noting the red light on the post is unlit.

"I'm trying a new frequency, but I'm not optimistic,"

he admits, adjusting one of the nodes. "For all our hopes, the force fence certainly didn't protect us at the internment camp. The most it will probably do is warn us the enemy's here, and by the time that happens . . ."

"It will be too late," I finish. It's exactly what happened at the main internment camp where we were previously headquartered. By the time we knew they were there, the enemy was already in the camp. No one within half a mile of the main fence escaped—not the thousands of Celestian POWs nor the resistance members hiding in plain sight among them. Only a handful of us managed to flee through the back. A resistance cell of over a thousand reduced to thirty-eight in the span of an hour.

No, I correct myself as I think of my parents. Thirty-six.

"There's a scientist on Aganir who's supposedly had more success using the fence to keep them out. No one else has had any luck replicating his success, though. Maybe we should have settled the resistance on Aganir instead of Tiersten. Not that I'd want to live there—nasty place, it's like breathing underwater in a garbage dump." Jao flips a switch and the red light goes on. "There! That'll have to do. Days like this, I really miss your mother. She was a genius with this sort of thing. Well, even if we had her help, it would still only be a matter of time."

I shy away from the mention of my mom and concentrate on his last comment. "Surely the resistance lives in other places besides Tiersten and Aganir."

Jao shrugs and shuts the control panel. "Scattered pockets here and there, maybe, and we still have a few ships out there that remain ours. They'll do their best to slow the advance of the invasion, to try and hold the quarantine and keep anyone from leaving Tellurian space. If they can find a way to violate the ceasefire and sabotage any peace talks with the Celestians they will, but . . ." He spreads his hands in a gesture of helplessness.

He doesn't have to finish. I know as well as Jao that Tiersten was the main home of the resistance, and with the internment camp fallen, it's only a matter of days, weeks at most, before the last of the resistance falls. Jao doesn't have to tell me that. Despite the fact that I'm only a teenager, the captain has never tried to sugarcoat the truth for me. It's one of the things I like about him.

Used to like about him. It's one of the things I *used* to like about him, when I still liked him. Today, though, with my stomach roiling in dread at seeing my parents, I can't help wishing he'd lied just a little.

"That's actually what I wanted to speak with you about," Jao continues. "The ceasefire has been made official."

I swear softly. "When?"

"We picked it up on the coms this morning."

"It won't be long before the enemy tries to push into the Celestial Expanse, then."

"No." He takes a breath. "It gets worse. The first official act by the 'Tellurians' now that the ceasefire is official will be the return of five hundred 'prisoners of war' from Tiersten Internment Colony. A gesture of *goodwill*, you see." Jao's lips twist at the irony.

My heart sinks as I realize what's coming. "Can't we find some way to tell the Celestians? To warn them about the invasion?"

"The Celestians will never believe us. You know that. How many times have we tried to tell them over the past two years? How do you make someone believe in something you can't see, hear, touch, smell?"

"But the psychics could show them the enemy. If we sent in a member of TelPsy—"

"We sent in a list of psychics as long as my arm! Dozens of good people, to planets and stations across the Celestial Expanse, all sent to spread the word in the only way we could." Jao's voice lowers. "And do you know how many came back? Do you know how many were ever heard from again?"

I lower my head, already knowing the answer. "None."

Jao sighs. "And the few times we managed to bring a Celestian official here, someone important, they disappeared off the face of the galaxy before they ever made it home again. The enemy was always one step ahead of us."

"You think they've already infiltrated the Celestial Expanse."

"Yes, but not in force, not beyond the point of no return. They're going to use the internees to start their real invasion. How many prisoners of war are on Tiersten alone? Thirty thousand? Forty? That doesn't even count the internees on the main prison worlds. We can't let those prisoners reach New Sol. We can't let the ceasefire hold."

"I'm going to be on that initial list of five hundred prisoners being sent into the Expanse, aren't I?"

"We always knew that you would be our last resort. One final hope when all else failed." Jao looks away. "With our inside knowledge of the main internment camp, it shouldn't be that hard to get you in. A little hacking into their records, and no one will even know you're not supposed to be there."

I briefly close my eyes. I always knew I would be deployed at some point, that I would be responsible for the deaths of hundreds, maybe even thousands of people.

It's just they weren't supposed to be people I *knew*. Tiersten prisoners I'd lived with and worked with, hung out with and hoped with. Maybe they've been suborned by the enemy, but how can I complete my mission knowing that I'll be ending any hope of freeing them one day?

"Is this going to be a problem?"

My eyes open. "No."

"Because if it is, Doc can probably—"

"I said it's *fine*," I answer a little too sharply. I strive for a more reasonable tone. "You know this is likely to be a trap, right? Sending out the five hundred prisoners from Tiersten? The enemy is trying to draw us out."

Jao nods. "I know, but I think if we manage things right, we'll slip right past their trap. Your biochip will have to be activated. Otherwise, if they have any of our weaker psychics under their control, a casual touch could expose you. Once you've left, we'll sabotage the Tiersten spaceport by blowing out the main power relay. This should prevent any more prisoners from being shipped out."

"Sabotage the spaceport? An undertaking of that sort would take every last person we have! Even if you succeed, it's unlikely anyone will survive."

Captain Jao doesn't answer. Not that he has to. We both know it's better to go out on our terms than the enemy's. I'll be making my own last stand even as Jao and his people make theirs. After that, the Celestians will be on their own. We just have to hope that what we've done will be enough.

I meet Jao's eyes and finally nod. As I'm walking away, his voice calls out to me one last time. "Lia!"

I stop, though I don't turn.

"You know I wouldn't send you if I had any other choice, don't you? That if there were any other way, I would take it." Defeat colors his every syllable, and if I hadn't believed it before, I would have known it now.

The resistance is dead.

"Yes," I whisper, so softly I know he'll never hear me. "I know."

———

A soldier greets me at the entrance to the control station. The basement in the station is a relic from the past, a leftover from when the dust devils had free rein over Tiersten. Now, it's used as a holding area for two very special prisoners. My parents.

Cool air enfolds me as I make my way down the stairs into the basement. Something clanks in the far recesses of the sub-floor, and my heart jumps. I do not want to be here. I do not want to see them. I almost turn around and leave, but I force myself to continue. Doc's right. I should see them once more before I go. I owe it to them.

I owe it to myself, to remember why I'm doing what I'm doing.

The guards sit at a table playing electronic ping pong. I purposely avoid looking at the screens monitoring my parents and instead watch the guards swing their tip-pads at the holographic ball. How long has it been since I played a real game? Any sort of game? With someone my own age? Not since the internment camp anyway.

"Here to see your parents?" Cavendish asks, hitting pause on the game as she gets up.

I nod, and she gives my shoulder a pat. A burst of comforting sympathy rushes through me. I pull away and give her a look. "Shouldn't you be saving your powers for something important?"

She gives me a wry grin. "Who's more important than

you? Come on. You'll feel better once you get this over with."

She takes me down the hall to a door, and I stare through the small window that looks into the room. A bed, a couple of chairs, a table, a few books. We took very little with us when we fled the internment camp, most of it practical stuff like food and weapons, but when it comes to the few niceties we have, almost all of them ended up here—that scented soap of Cavendish's, Niven's grandmother's chenille throw, even Jao's stash of chocolate-covered pretzels. Not that anyone begrudges my parents the little extras. You can't begrudge people you pity.

Cavendish keys in the codes to take down the force fence and unlock the room. For a long moment, I don't move, fear freezing me in place.

"Do you want me to come in with you?"

Her words tear me out of my trance. I do, and yet I don't. At last I shake my head. "No, I can do it."

"Okay then. We'll be keeping an eye on the monitors just in case." She taps the chit under her ear. "Link me when you're done."

I nod. Then, taking a deep breath, I open the door and go in.

It's the smell that hits me first. Sharp and sour, like an astringent, but with a pale, sweetish after-odor. I gasp. It's the first time I've smelled anything in two weeks. I knew, theoretically, of course, that I would smell something when I came into this room. I just didn't expect them to smell like *this*.

"Hi Starshine."

I tense at the sound of his voice, and slowly turn. "Daddy."

He's sitting in a chair not immediately visible from the window. Revulsion flies through me at the sight of him, and I fight the urge to recoil. He looks worse than last time, far worse. His gray eyes are completely sunken in, his cheekbones practically slicing the air through the slack skin of his face. The yellowish cast over his skin, as though he is suffering from jaundice, is new, and his body, already thin the last time I saw him, is positively skeletal now. I can barely see in his shrunken form the man who raised me. He looks as though he's being slowly eaten away from the inside out.

Which is, of course, exactly what's happening.

"It's good to see you again."

I nod and glance away, unable to return the sentiment. My eyes fall on my mother where she lies on the bed, asleep. She doesn't look nearly as bad as my father, thin but not skeletal, eyes ringed with dark circles but not sunken. Her skin is still the pale, creamy white she passed down to me. In sleep, she looks normal, as though she's simply overworked and exhausted, and not . . .

"How's Mom?" I ask.

"Hanging in there," Dad answers after a second. "I've given up trying to explain things to her. Without psychic abilities of her own, she's unable to fight the reality distortions being forced on her. Her perceptions are just too skewed at this point to accept the truth. Maybe it's for the best. She'll live a lot longer if she doesn't try to fight it."

Not like him, though Dad doesn't say it out loud.

I swallow hard, wishing for about the millionth time that my parents were whole and healthy, and we were somewhere far away from here, somewhere they could never reach us. I push away the thought, knowing it for the futile thing it is. "None of us may live much longer."

"The force fence?"

"A warning, nothing more. Jao said if we still had Mom, things might be different, but not now."

"No, now she would just sabotage the work without even knowing why, and do a damn good job of it too. Remember the roamers?"

I laugh softly. "That's Mom—best mechanic in the galaxy."

She was infected on our flight from the internment camp, she and one other from our party, though of course no one knew it at the time. On the run, with the enemy bearing down on us, Dad and Cavendish didn't have a chance to check everyone. It was only when we were finally able to stop for a short break later and caught Mom tearing out the intelli-wires from the roamers that we knew.

She'd been taken by the enemy.

Mom managed to disable three roamers before we caught her, though we'd been stopped less than ten minutes. Dad liked to joke that it was some kind of record. That's Dad—always able to find something to laugh about even in the darkest situation. Or maybe it's just his way of showing that no matter what happens, he'll always love us. He'll always be proud of us.

It was only as they were subduing my mother that the other one showed itself. Corporal Sanderson had time to get off one shot before a rifle blast took him down. It was an accident; Jao didn't mean to kill him, just disable him. No matter his intentions, the alien, suddenly unbonded with its host's death, fled for the nearest possible replacement. My dad.

That's how, in just a matter of minutes, I lost both parents. Infected by the same filth that had taken down the entire Tellurian Alliance in only three years.

"So how are you doing?" Dad asks quietly, and I realize my jaw is clenched tightly enough to make my teeth ache. Pain chokes me at the question.

My parents are dying a slow, horrible death, the resistance is nearly crushed, and in a week I'll be going Nova on five hundred of my former friends and compatriots. I'm dying inside. My spirit withering up and drying, its edges curling up like a browning leaf at the end of autumn making its final fall. How am I doing? I can barely walk and talk and breathe, the pain is so great.

"I ... Daddy, I ..." I suddenly can't talk, can't breathe past the horrible pressure smothering my chest. I slump forward, bracing my hands on my knees as I gasp for air that doesn't want to be breathed. Every inhalation now is a fight, my body both fighting breath and fighting to breathe at the same time. I should com Cavendish, but I can't seem to do anything.

Cold hands cover mine and suddenly a rush of love bursts through my chest. It spreads under my skin and fills my veins, and then I can breathe again, my lungs unlocking and air flowing in.

It's okay, Starshine. It's okay. Our time together has been so short, but I still love you more than anything in all the galaxy. You're my girl, my light in the dark, my starry, starry night. You are strong. My beautiful, strong girl.

My father's voice fills my mind, gentle and loving, and I mentally gravitate toward the voice, wanting to be near him, just him, with every fiber of my being. I slide though the psychic connection before he realizes what I'm doing, wanting to burrow myself in his mind like I used to burrow myself in his hugs.

Wait, sweetie—

Something grabs me, impaling me on its claws and

yanking me in deep. Slimy and acrid and pulsing, it wraps around me, smothering me, choking me, consuming me alive. The cord connecting my spirit to my body starts to thin, and I scream, fighting against it with all my will. But the dark thing is stronger. It bites down on me with a thousand mouths. Pain shrieks through my mind as I feel myself being eaten alive.

A light bursts around me and the thing falls back. Its grip loosens, and in that brief moment, hands grab me and shove. I snap back like a slingshot, and suddenly I'm back in my own mind.

Eyes jolting open, I frantically backpedal, falling over my feet as I try to get as far away from my father as I can. My butt hits the floor, but I continue to scoot back, away from his stricken face until my back hits the door.

"Starshine, I—"

"Stay back! Stay away from me!" I push myself against the door, helpless to do anything but watch as Dad raises his hands and slowly backs away. His knees shake as he collapses back in the chair. Then he does something I've never seen him do before in my life.

He puts his head in his hands and cries. "I'm sorry, baby, I'm so, so sorry."

Over and over, he just keeps saying it, until I start crying too, not out of fear and hurt, but shame. Shame that for even one short moment I couldn't distinguish my dad from the dark thing that lives inside him now, eating him alive one second at a time.

This is the reason I have to do what I'm going to do. This is the reason I have to go Nova. Because if my going Nova will prevent even one kid from losing their parents the way I have, it'll be worth it. No matter what the cost.

After a while, I realize Cavendish is linking me, asking in frantic tones if I'm all right and telling me she's coming in.

"No, it's okay," I reassure her. "I'm okay." I'm not going to flee this time.

Cavendish clearly doesn't believe me, but she does back off at my word, though she stays poised at the outer door, ready to let me out the minute I call.

After a while, my dad wipes his face and lifts his head. He looks so exhausted, as though he just ran an ultra-marathon on a brutally hot day. No wonder he deteriorated so quickly these past few months. How could he not, fighting that *thing* inside him every second of every day!

"Is that what it feels like then? That horrible, slimy thing wrapped around you all the time?"

He shrugs. "You get used to its presence after a while. It doesn't speak, not in words, but it pushes perceptions into your mind. False understandings that distort reality, making you believe that what's true isn't, and things that aren't real are, all meant to influence the way you act. Eventually you learn how to fight it, to push it back." Dad glances back at the bed where Mom is still sleeping. A wisp of a smile touches his mouth, and I know what he's thinking: Mom always could sleep through anything. He turns back to me. "If it's any consolation, I don't think your mother can feel hers at all. Most of the infected can't."

I nod. It's how they were able to sweep through Telluria so easily. Their bodies, incorporeal and beyond our range of sound and vision, simply invaded us one after another and no one even knew they were there. Except the psychics. It was the Tellurian Psychics, TelPsy, that finally discovered what was going on. They're the ones who formed the resistance; they're the ones that started teaching the rest of us to fight.

My knees wobble a little as I get to my feet, and I reach for the table to steady myself. My hand knocks into the lamp, and it falls before I can catch it, shattering on the floor with a loud crash. The figure in the bed stirs and sits up.

"Arron?" my mom says, squinting a little as she rubs sleep from her eyes. "What's going on?" A smile lights up her face as she glances over and sees me. She climbs out of bed, stretching as she comes near. She gives her husband a playful slap on the shoulder. "Arron! Why didn't you tell me our daughter had come to visit?"

Dad looks down. "We were just having a little father–daughter talk before you got up."

"A talk? Judging from the casualties, it must have been some conversation," she says, spying the broken lamp. She peers at me more closely, no doubt seeing the tear tracks on my cheeks, and her face creases with concern. She looks at Dad again, and her expression suddenly clears. "He wasn't telling you that story about aliens from New Earth taking over the galaxy, was he?" She laughs. "Your dad was just pulling your leg, silly. You know that, right? Everything's fine, I promise. Come here, sweetheart." She opens her arms to me.

I stare at her, my beautiful, brilliant, amazing mother. My mother, who sabotaged three roamers during our escape, all the while thinking she was fixing them. My mother, who thinks her husband is suffering from cancer. My mother, who used to beg me to let her out of this cell, because in her mind she's been wrongly imprisoned for some minor transgression. My beautiful, brilliant,

amazing mother, whose open arms are the most won-
derful and terrifying thing in the entire world.

And that's when I finally flee.

———

Consciousness comes back in a rush. I jerk upright from
my spot on the floor and almost bang into Shar where
she crouches above me.

"What the h—" she starts to say.

"They're here!"

"*What?* Who's here?" Shar glances frantically down
the length of the tunnel in either direction. "I don't see
anyone. Where are they?"

"Everywhere," I whisper, horror dawning as I finally
understand why I'm here. Why I can't simply turn my
back and walk away. "They're everywhere."

27 **ALL THE PIECES** are starting to fall into place now. My broken memory, why no one ever came after me when I failed to go Nova, the information I uncovered on the nets about Tiersten, and my suspicions that a splinter faction exists within the Tellurian Alliance. Even that godawful smell that's been getting worse with each passing day. While our two sides have been fighting it out in some petty war, an alien species has taken out half the human race without a single shot fired.

And now that they've burned through the Tellurian Alliance, they're coming for the rest of us.

It seems crazy, unthinkable even, but I know it's true. Those visions I had weren't like my earlier dreams, a meld of truth and fantasy. They were actual memories. The scene in the clinic, the conversation with Jao, the meeting with my adoptive parents—they're all real.

Painfully, frighteningly *real*.

Beside me, Shar is looking at me like I've completely lost it, her eyes wide and her body instinctively pulling back from me. No, it's more than that, I realize upon closer look. Her hands are trembling and the skin around her mouth is white.

"It's okay," I tell her. "I'm sat."

"Sat?!" she bursts out. "You were *dead*!"

I blink. "Dead?"

"Yes, dead! As in, not breathing. No heartbeat. That sort of dead!"

It's obvious now that Shar is close to hysteria, her earlier joke about disposing of my body out an airlock notwithstanding, and I hasten to reassure her again.

"It's okay, I'm not dead. Just tell me what happened."

"When? Before or after you started seizing?" Shar asks, a small bit of sarcasm creeping back into her voice now that her initial fear has started to subside.

"Both."

Shar's eyes widen at my matter-of-fact tone, but she answers. "One minute I'm trying to bust a path through the memory block, and the next I'm being blown out of your mind." She involuntarily reaches up to rub her head. "I blacked out for a minute, I think, but when I came to you were writhing on the floor, stuttering nonsense syllables. I was about to link a medic when you suddenly stopped. I was relieved at first, but then you didn't open your eyes or move, and I realized you weren't breathing."

"How long?"

"I don't know. It felt like forever, but in reality I think it was only a minute or two. I was about to start chest compressions when you suddenly rose from the dead."

Two minutes? That's all it took to experience all that? It felt so physical, like I was reliving the memories in real time. It seems amazing that I experienced it all in such a short span. Not that it matters. All that matters is that I know why I was sent here now. The question is: what am I going to do now that I know?

"So you want to tell me what's going on? Who's here, and *what happened*?"

Shar. That's right, I'd forgotten about her for the

moment. I don't answer immediately, chewing on my lip as I think about what she told me. She was blown out of my mind; she has no idea what I remembered. She has no idea what I am or where I came from. Perhaps it's better for her not to know.

"Don't you dare, Johansen!"

I lift my head. "What?"

"I know that look. You're thinking you're not going to tell me, or you're going to make up some bullslag lie. Well, I already know more than enough to get you in trouble. One anonymous link from me and PsyCorp will lock you up and throw away the key."

"Then why don't you call them?" I challenge, my temper rising at being threatened. Shar squirms a bit, not answering, and I laugh. She knows as well as I do that turning me in to PsyCorp would be the same as turning herself in. There's no way they wouldn't find out about her once they started mind-scanning me. My laughter doesn't last long, though, tempered by the sudden realization that I actually *want* to tell her. It's too big, this secret. It's not meant to be kept, but shared. The Tellurians fell because nobody knew, not enough of them anyway, and not in time. For the Celestians to have a fighting chance, they *have* to know.

Something tickles my brain at the thought, and I snatch for it, sensing it's something important, but the memory flees before I quite catch it. I frown but let it go. It'll come back; I'm sure of it. Whatever Shar did, it opened a hole in the memory block, and like water seeping through a leak in a dam, the memories will trickle back a little at a time until the sheer force of my past breaks it down entirely. I just have to be patient.

"Fine! Don't tell me. But then I won't tell you what I *did* see when I was in your head."

Shar starts to get up, and I grab her sleeve. "Wait." Something in her voice tells me she really did see something important in my mind, and that she's not just making it up as a ploy to get my attention. I need to know what it is. But can I trust her?

I open my nostrils wide and breathe in. Lean closer and sniff a few more times. Nothing. The air is completely odorless, with no sign of the telltale sour-and-sweet. Amusement bubbles up in me as I think of the good doc's handiwork. They couldn't figure out a way to see the aliens or hear them or touch them, but they found a way to smell them out. It would almost be funny if the situation weren't so deadly serious. As it is, I'm grateful for this small tool of detection, even if it does mean I no longer get to enjoy the taste of ice cream.

Ice cream. I got the wrong kind when I went to the park with Michael. I got Asteroid Chunk Chocolate when I should have gotten Rum Raisin. That's my favorite.

I shake off the memory and focus on the situation. Shar. Letting go of her sleeve, I offer my hand. "You want to know? Then come see. Just remember, there'll be no going back once you know."

Shar hesitates. "You could just tell me what's going on. I don't need to see it."

"Yes, you do. Your choice. Are you in or out?"

Just like before, she can't resist the challenge. She takes my hand.

I show her everything. My mission to go Nova, my meltdown in the hygiene unit shortly after arriving, the subsequent loss of seconds culminating in my run for Michael's life. I show her the conversation I overheard in the bar and my subsequent findings in the research center. Lastly, I take her into the past. To Doc Niven, to

Jao, to my parents. By the time we finish, I'm exhausted and sweating. Shar is completely white-faced.

I drop her hand. "So now you know."

Shar doesn't say anything, not to me anyway. She's mumbling nonsense under her breath, her head shaking slightly, her lips trembling. I'm starting to think it was a mistake to tell her when she lifts her head and catches my eye.

"Am . . . am I . . . ?"

Understanding dawns. "No! No, you're not. I can smell them, you see. I wouldn't have told you if you were infected. Besides, with your psychic abilities, I think you would be able to sense it if one bonded with you."

"Is that why they didn't infect me? Because of my abilities?"

I shrug. "Maybe. A strong enough psychic could fight their influence, could tell someone. Perhaps they didn't want to risk it."

Shar shudders. "What *are* they?" she asks, her voice barely more than a whisper.

"We usually just referred to them as the enemy, but we had many names for them. Soul-Suckers, Mind Stealers, the Dark Shadows." The names tumble out of my mouth without me even having to think about it. My voice drops as the phrase comes back unbidden, "*In Spectris Intra.* The Spectres Within."

"Where do they come from?"

I pause, the answer to this one not so automatic. I think back to my memory, to my mother's question: *He wasn't telling you that silly story about aliens from New Earth taking over the galaxy, was he?*

"New Earth. They came from New Earth."

As soon as I utter the words, I know they're true. It's why they found no sentient life there, though the planet was ideal for it; the Spectres would have eaten through any sentient life centuries ago. It's how the Tellurians were infected. All it took was one survey team. They thought they were exploring the greatest treasure of the century, and all along they were bringing back the very plague that would destroy humankind.

"New Earth? It can't be! That's what we've been fighting for all this time," Shar slowly finishes.

"That's what the Celestians have been fighting for all along. The Tellurians, at least the ones I knew, weren't fighting for a planet. They were fighting for the human race."

I know that now. Everything the resistance did was to keep the war going, to keep the Celestians from touching down on New Earth, and to prevent the passage of Spectres across the border. The war was the resistance's way of quarantining the Alliance from the Expanse. At least it was until the Spectres became so concentrated among the Alliance's population that even the resistance couldn't stop the peace efforts. They couldn't stop the ceasefire.

My, aren't I a fount of information now? The grim thought pops up from nowhere. All this time I've been desperate to know why I'm here, and now that I do, I almost wish I could go back to ignorance. No, not quite. If there's one thing I'm glad of, it's that at least I know I was given to loving people and raised as their own. What was it Niven said? I'd only been alive for two years? So it's just as I always thought—I'm a genetically engineered bomb who was born and then rapidly aged to maturity. Waiting in the wings until finally the time came to slap Lia's name on me and send me off to die. Maybe I was even engineered from the DNA of my adoptive parents, my embryo implanted and carried to term by my mom herself. I remember my dad's gray eyes and my mom's blonde hair, so like my own, and a pang of longing sweeps through me.

It's okay, Starshine, I hear my dad's voice in my head. *It's okay. Our time together has been so short, but I still love you more than anything in all the galaxy.*

I feel a sudden stab in my chest. Just because we only had two years together doesn't make me love them any less. My dad was right. Our time together *was* too short. Far too short!

My parents' faces flash in my mind and suddenly all of my pain, all of my sorrow, all of my grief, locked away inside all these weeks while I wandered on this station without past or memory, well up in my chest at once. I gasp, all breath reft from me in a single instant. I clench my jaw, lips trembling as I struggle to push back the wall of pain, but one tear squeezes out of my eye before I can stop it, a single drop rolling down my cheek in a streak of gray.

As if reading my thoughts—and maybe she actually is—Shar suddenly says, "I'm sorry. About your parents, I mean."

I'm sorry, too, I say. Or at least, that's what I would have said, if only my words weren't held hostage by the noiseless sobs suddenly quaking in my chest.

No! I've already wept for my parents a hundred times. I can't cry for them anymore, I won't! Not this time.

So I don't, dashing away every tear that runs down my face, while inside I force my sobs to swallow themselves up one by one, silenced and put away before they can ever reach the surface.

After a long time, Shar suddenly says, "All right, you told me. It's only fair I tell you: there was something else in your head besides the memory block. I saw it right before I was blown out of your mind, just after I punched a hole in the block."

I blink. "What, you mean like a second memory block?" I'd assumed Shar's half-assed job of breaking the block was the reason I could only remember some things and not others, but a second block could explain it, too.

Shar shakes her head. "I don't think so. This was different. Not a block, but a plant. I think someone implanted false memories in your head."

I let out a wistful sigh, immediately realizing what she saw. Lia's memories, implanted in me so that I might successfully pass as her long enough to fulfill the mission. I suddenly wonder what happened to her, if the real Lia is still alive and well, or dead and buried under the ground. I think back to my time on Tiersten, but if I ever knew her fate, I don't know it now.

I shake my head. I suppose this is one mystery I'll never know the answer to.

———

The stench hits me as soon as we step out of the tunnel and back into the hub—a sour-and-sweet reek so intense it's enough to make my nostrils burn. I automatically pinch my nose in the hopes of heading off another nosebleed.

"What is it?" Shar asks in alarm.

"They've multiplied."

The words slip out without conscious thought, my brain putting the pieces together without my having to think about it. The smell was present but faint when we arrived on the station, and mostly confined to the cargo bay where the refugees lived. Now it's a burning odor pervading every section of the hub, even going so far as to spill over into sections of the ring. I look around, imagining their invisible bodies packed wall-to-wall, and I shiver. How many are there now? Thousands, tens of thousands? It's a good thing Shar and I did our experiment in the tunnel. In here, I would never have been able to distinguish if she were infected. The smell is too powerful.

Shar glances around fearfully, her eyes searching for an enemy that can't be seen. "How do you know?"

"It's what they do," I say, the answer trickling from its long-time bondage in my mind. "They exist in a dormant state until a compatible host comes along—hundreds of years, we think, if necessary. Once they find a host, they bond with it, feeding off it like a parasite until they're ready to divide."

"Then what?"

"The new Spectre goes off to find its own host, while the old one stays bonded in the current one and starts the process all over again. They'll keep multiplying until the host is completely used up, spreading their progeny across every populated zone they can reach. Once the host dies, they're released from their bond to find a new host and start again. If no host is available, they'll go dormant until one comes along."

"What do they want?"

I look at Shar. "To spread. To eat, to multiply, and to spread."

We reach the lift and step onto a platform going down. Beside me, Shar looks like she's two steps away from completely overloading. I suppose I should feel the same way, but all I feel is a grim determination. Maybe I only consciously remembered all this an hour ago, but inside I knew it all along. Just like I knew when I saw the spaceport blow at Tiersten that the resistance was dead.

A hard fist squeezes my heart as I remember those images of Tiersten. Doc, Cavendish, Jao. They're all dead now, or worse. Regret pours through me as I remember my last meeting with Jao right before I left.

"I'm sorry," he said, his eyes full of resignation. "You know that, right?"

I remember laughing, the sound bitter and hard. "What for? Sending me off to blow up five hundred innocents or infecting my dad?"

"Both. Everything."

My smile could have cut glass. "Save your apologies for your maker. You'll need them."

How I hated him then! Now, shame fills me as I finally see the man in the memory for what he was. *Jao, you deserved better from me. Why is it only now that you're gone that I can finally forgive you?*

Again those images of Tiersten, blackened and burned, dance in my head. Jao promised to take out the spaceport before any more infected refugees could be shipped off planet. He kept his word. Now I have to find a way to keep mine.

We can hear the clamor from the cargo bay as Shar and I step off the lift onto Eight. Exchanging a confused glance, we enter to find the entire bay in an uproar. It doesn't take long to find out why.

The announcement has been made; the convoy will be here in three days to take everyone home.

I creep around the edges of the bay, Shar at my side, watching the celebrations of the ex-prisoners with growing horror. Even leaving out the Aurorans, there must be at least four hundred former prisoners from over twenty assorted worlds here. I imagine the convoy, ship after ship crammed to the brim, not only with infected prisoners, but hundreds upon thousands of unbonded Spectres just waiting for hosts.

My skin goes cold. If the prisoners are allowed to get on that convoy and leave, there's no place in the Expanse the Spectres can't go.

"*Johansen*," I hear Shar whisper, and I know she sees it too. I can hear it in her voice. "What are you going to do?"

I shake my head. "I don't know."

Only I do know, at least in general, if not specifically. Because there's no way I can let any of these people get off this station. Now I just have three days to figure out how to stop them.

28 **I HOVER NEAR THE WALL** just inside docking ring 7D. I'm wearing my new clothes—a pair of brown trousers, tank top, and a loose olive-green shirt, open with the sleeves rolled up. The clothes feel strange, but nice. They're the first clothes I've picked out for myself in years. Not the Tiersten garb, or the fleet-issued jumpsuits, or even Teal's idea of high fashion. Just me.

Around me, people rush by carrying crates and bins as they lade the final pieces of cargo for the upcoming run. I hum quietly to myself as I watch them. *Hmm, Hm hm, hm Hm, Hm hm.* It takes me a second to recognize the melody.

Cross my heart and hope to die.

I shake my head. Where did *that* come from? It's been weeks since I had that creepy dream of the school playground.

Glancing at the timescreen, I note the hour: 0745. Captain Standish should be here any minute now.

As if my very thoughts conjured him, the captain strides into the docking ring just seconds later. He breezes past without even noticing me, and I have to run a few steps to catch up with him.

"Captain Standish!"

He turns, spots me, and stops. "So you made it after all," he says, faintly surprised. His sharp eyes take me in from head to toe. "Or maybe not?" he adds, eyes zeroing in on my empty hands.

"I want to thank you very much for the opportunity, but I can't come with you."

"No, you can't, can you?"

I hesitate, thrown by the comment, then nod. "It turns out I still have a few things to do here."

"Fair enough. Good luck to you. Give Kerr my best the next time you see her."

"I will."

He strides off without a backward glance, his life continuing on, his world completely unshaken. I briefly wonder if he's been infected. For all I know, Spectres have been hitching rides off the station for weeks now, either by possessing the crews or just slipping onto their ships unseen. Possible, but I don't think so. The smell wouldn't be nearly so piercing if the Spectres had been leaving as quickly as they'd been multiplying. Besides, most of the haulers stopping here are small potatoes. Independents with limited space and uncertain destinations, just as likely to be heading into Tellurian space as they are deeper into the Celestial Expanse. It's the convoy that's the real score. With such a diverse group of refugees to repatriate, the convoy would be the perfect delivery system for an alien race looking to spread itself throughout the Expanse.

Which brings me back to my problem: keeping those refugees from boarding that convoy.

Pledging to keep everyone on the station and figuring out a plan to do it are two entirely different matters, I've realized. I'm not an officer, or a station resident, or even a legal adult. How a single teenager is supposed to stop an entire alien race from taking over the galaxy is beyond me. Well, no, that's not entirely true. I know how I was *supposed* to stop them.

I was supposed to go Nova. To blow up the station and kill them all in one fell swoop. The problem is that even if I could bring myself to do it, I don't know how. My clock is still stuck at thirty-nine seconds, and with the convoy coming in just two days, time is running out. What am I supposed to do? Make out with Michael in the hopes my clock will start again? Against my will, an ironic smile twitches my lips. It would be a nice way to go, at least. Not that Michael would ever kiss me again after what happened between us.

I shake my head. Every plan I've come up with so far seems doomed to failure. Shar's suggestion to simply tell the authorities won't work. Even if I could find someone who's not infected, what would they do? The Spectres are non-corporeal; they can't be killed. At least, not by any means we found. We could send the convoy away— quarantine the station—except the minute we do it the Spectres will know we're on to them. They'd infect every person in this station, and the quarantine would be lifted as if it never happened. Having the station quarantined by an outside party might work, though everyone on the station would still be lost. However, that would suppose I could get a message to the right people in time, *and* that they'd believe me. Not likely; not when an in-person psychic connection is needed to prove my story. I'm starting to remember why Jao and the others thought my going Nova was the only solution. There's a reason my purpose is to destroy, even if that ability is yet untested.

My purpose.

For a split second, I get the strangest sense, like I'm missing something important, some key piece of the puzzle. Then the feeling evaporates.

I stifle a curse. For all that I understand now, so many things still elude me, locked away in my head even as other things tumble free without thought. It will all come back eventually, I know. The question is: will it be in time?

Shaking my head, I make for the lift station. It's almost eight now; time to stop standing around. I'll get some breakfast and then head to the Blue Lounge to think. Maybe something will come to me. I still have two days after all. Surely that'll be enough time to come up with *something*—

Whumpf! A small, redheaded bundle suddenly emerges from the crowd and throws herself at me. I stagger back under Kaeti's weight.

"Did you hear, Lia? We're going home!"

It takes me two tries to speak. "Yeah, I heard. Did they, uh, did they say where you're going?"

"No, but Lela says we'll be going somewhere nice. Somewhere I'll have a real bed and everything."

So they didn't tell the Aurorans about Dayav and Mechanra. Probably figured the prisoners would riot if they knew the truth. I would almost feel sorry for them, if I didn't know their lives were already as good as over. According to Jao's sources, every single member of the original survey team to step onto New Earth is dead— consumed alive by the Spectres within. What's more, Jao's intelligence indicated hundreds more were dropping by the day. Three years seemed to be about as long as the average human host could last. I shudder as I think how quickly the human race could fall if the Spectres get a foothold in the Expanse.

"What about you, Lia? Aren't you excited?"

I try to smile. It's hard, though, when I imagine the dark thing that surely must be residing within this little girl. They say infected children last a third of the time infected adults do. A lump forms in my throat, and I have to clear my throat twice before I can answer. "Sure I am."

"Will you come celebrate with us later tonight? Lela's letting us all have cake."

"I'll try, Kaeti."

"Promise?"

I take a breath and finally nod. "Promise."

"Cross your heart?"

Something flares in my brain, and my mouth drops open. "What did you say?"

"Cross your heart?"

And hope to die. Stick a needle in your eye.

Memory comes back in a blinding flash, and suddenly I know the answer to one of the biggest questions plaguing me since that night I malfunctioned in the hygiene unit.

I know how to reset my clock.

───────

Gray eyes stare back at me from the mirror in the hygiene unit. Squaring my shoulders, I raise the needle up before my face. It's not really a needle, but a piece of wire I found in a supply shop on Level Nine. Extra long, hair thin, and extremely sharp.

And I'm about to stick it in my eye.

Cross your heart and hope to die, stick a needle in your eye. After all this time, I finally understand that strange dream. My subconscious was trying to tell me something I couldn't remember, my past leaking back to me in the only way it could. I just didn't understand because, like my other dreams, it was a mix of reality and fantasy that my conscious mind couldn't piece together. Not until now.

My thoughts flip back to this lecture Doc once gave me, previously lost but now clear as a pane of hammered glass. I asked him what would happen if there was a problem with my clock. He said he would simply pop out my eyeball and restart it, but in a pinch, he could use a long flexi-needle to reset it without removing my eye. I begged him to explain, and the details were gross enough to keep me hanging on his every word. Now I'm glad of my fascination. It may be the deciding factor between successfully resetting my clock and poking my eye out.

The sharp end of the wire nears my eye, and my hand begins to shake. *Stop that!* I command myself. It's just a simple medical procedure. Worst thing that happens, I lose the sight in my right eye. I'll still have my left. People can get by with only one eye, right? I try to think of an example, but the only person that comes to mind is Blackbeard.

Somehow the thought isn't very comforting.

I squeeze my eyes shut. *Focus, Lia.* I open them. This time when I bring the wire near, I don't pull away.

With the index finger of my left hand, I gently pull at the lower lid under the corner of my eye. I feel at the gap with my middle finger, poking at the corner lightly with the tip. Nothing. I push at the upper lid, feeling above. Still nothing. Sweating a bit, I touch the wire to the corner of my eye, prodding around the tiny bud with the needle-thin end. There! Just above, I feel it. A tiny hole the size of a pinprick. A channel leading straight back to the chip, assuming Doc wasn't pulling my leg. Taking a deep breath, I slide the end of the wire in.

It slips in more easily than I expected, the fleshy tube stretching a bit to accommodate the wire. I slide it in a tad farther—*careful, careful*—and then begin pushing it down the channel with slow, but steady pressure.

If Shar poking around in my mind is the strangest mental sensation I've ever experienced, this is, without a doubt, the most bizarre physical one I've ever encountered. I can actually feel the metal flexing and bending around the curve of my eyeball the farther I push it in. The wire, which didn't seem particularly cool before I started, feels positively frigid within the heat of my eye socket. I let out a heavy exhale as the metal curls around the back of my eyeball. This isn't so bad, I tell myself. I can do this.

Then I make the mistake of glancing in the mirror.

I immediately gag at the sight of the long piece of wire hanging from my eye. Only by force of will do I keep myself from immediately throwing up the contents of my stomach. My hand starts trembling again, and I can feel the wire inside of my eye jiggle, writhing softly against the side of my eyeball. Tiny whimpers dribble out from between my clamped lips.

As much as I want to stop, somehow I manage to grit my teeth and pull myself together. I'm halfway there. I can make it the rest of the way.

The wire slides the barest fraction of a millimeter more at my urging and then stops. This is the tricky part now, when the channel makes a sharp turn to align itself with the optic nerves. From there, it should be a straight shot back to the chip. The trick is getting the wire to bend around the curve without breaking through the channel and piercing the optic nerve. I shudder as I think what could happen if I fail.

Pierce the optic nerve, and say goodbye to the vision in my right eye.

Nudging the wire forward, I immediately encounter resistance. The wire isn't turning; instead it pushes at the elastic skin of the tube. I stop before I can perforate the delicate membrane. I pull the wire back slightly and then push forward once more. Again, it won't turn. I start to pull the wire back again.

It won't go.

Uh-oh. I tug again, but still the wire won't come back. My heart almost stops. It's stuck! The end must be embedded in the wall of the channel. I suddenly imagine myself, trapped forever with this piece of wire stuck in my eye, and almost start hyperventilating here and now. Frantically, I yank at the wire again. It comes free with a slight pop. With a shudder of relief I start to pull out the wire. Enough! Nothing is worth this. Nothing! Except my parents. Michael, Shar, Jao, Cavendish, Teal, Taylor, Kaeti.

With a curse, I drive the wire forward. It reaches the end of the channel, glances off something hard, and then suddenly the metal is turning, curving through the tunnel and down along the optic nerve. I continue to impel the wire forward before I can lose my nerve, back and back, deeper and deeper into my brain.

The end of the wire hits something hard. Light flashes in my vision.

—:—:—

And just like that, I have my life back. My clock is deactivated; I'll never go Nova.

The trembling starts again, and this time it isn't from fear, but relief. I can do anything I want now! I can live a full life, without fear of going off at any minute or hurting someone I love. After all this time of being held hostage by my own brain, I can finally make my own choices.

Choices.

I let out a soft snort. The truth is I made my choice long before ever coming on this station, and no matter how much I may want to, I can't unmake it. My lips briefly tighten.

Forgive me, Michael.

Then with a silent prayer, I poke the chip a second time.

00:15:00

My whole body freezes as I wait for what feels like an eternity, but in reality is only a second. Then . . .

00:14:59

00:14:58

00:14:57

Quickly I poke the chip again, relieved when the countdown vanishes once more.

—:—:—

I have the key now; I know how to start the final countdown. There's nothing to stop me from going Nova now. But first there's something I have to do.

Michael answers the door on my third knock. His mouth drops open the moment he lays eyes on me. "Lia!" he breathes, lunging forward and wrapping his arms around me.

"Michael."

"I thought you'd gone," Michael is saying, his words half obscured in my hair. "I thought you'd gone, and I would never see you again."

"It's okay, Michael. I'm still here."

"I was so de-fish! Getting mad at you when really I was mad at myself for driving you away. I linked practically every captain on the station this morning, trying to find out what ship you were taking, but by the time I got there it was too late. The *Kiss* was already gone."

"You came looking for me?" I lean back, astonished. A smile slowly spreads across my face as I remember Standish's reaction to my resignation. No wonder he didn't seem surprised!

Michael shrugs. "Of course. You're my best friend. How could I let you leave without saying goodbye?" He blinks, his face creasing as he finally takes in the fact that I am, in fact, *here.* "What are you doing here? The *Kiss* left hours ago."

"I guess it wasn't meant to be."

"Then you're staying?"

I nod. "Yes, I'm staying." He starts to hug me again, and I gently push him away. "You're not, though. You have to go. Take Teal and Taylor and get off this station. Now. Tonight, if possible, or else tomorrow morning. It doesn't matter where you go, just take the first passage off you can get."

"Huh? What are you talking about? Why do I have to go?"

"Because," I tell him with a sad smile, "sometime in the next forty-eight hours, I'm going to blow up this station."

29

"THIS IS LUNAR!" Michael says for about the tenth time in the last half hour. He's pacing rapidly back and forth, only pausing every few seconds to throw me an *Are-you-vaccin'-me?* look.

"Yeah, I think we've already established that," Shar replies snidely. "Now are we going to do this or not?"

The three of us are assembled in Michael's room, Shar and I sitting in a semi-circle on the carpet while Michael paces. Teal and Taylor are both out, and the bedroom door is locked. Still, my palms are sweating as I contemplate what we're about to do.

I linked Shar on my way to Michael's. I knew he would need proof to pick up his entire family and take off, and I intended to give it to him.

Once Shar arrived, I talked over the plan with her in a hushed voice while Michael was in the bathroom. Un-surprisingly, she was not happy about it.

"Are you completely glitching?" she demanded, in somewhat more than a whisper. "What if you start seiz-ing again? Or actually *die* this time?"

"Then you'll have Michael to help you dispose of my body."

She gave me a black look. In response, I just held out my hand. Fear and suspicion in her eyes, she slowly took it, only to drop it almost immediately and back away.

"Your clock! What did you do?"

I let my inner eye drift to the ticking mechanism.

$$*-:-:-*$$

"I remembered how to deactivate it . . . *and* restart it," I added before she could get too excited.

"Then you're really going to do it?"

"I have to. You know the reason why, and now I need you to show Michael as well. Then both of you need to get on the nearest transport and get the hell off this station."

To make my point, I grabbed her hand and transferred all my remaining funds into her link account. Shar watched the transaction in silence. "Are you sure this is the right thing to do?"

I just laughed. "I haven't been sure of anything since I stepped foot on this station. I am sure of one thing, though: This is the Expanse's only chance."

Shar stared at me, for once her face completely unreadable, her silence stretching out so long I started to sweat. At last she nodded. "So be it."

"Just don't let Michael see my parents or what I am. I can handle his shock, but not his pity."

"Show the Spectre but not your dad? How am I supposed to do that?"

I shrugged. "Just show the part where I'm inside his mind, I guess. Leave the rest—" My voice choked and I stopped, swallowing a few times as though it could somehow negate the aching in my heart and the lump in my throat. "He doesn't need to see the rest of the stuff with my parents, okay?"

Shar nodded, understanding and pity clear in her gaze. She'd seen my parents; she understood why I couldn't bear to see them again. Not like *that*.

Now I give Shar a speaking look as if to say, *Don't forget—no bomb, no parents.* Shar gives me a look back as if to say, *I hate you. Now seal your mouth and let's get this over with.*

Ah, if only I wasn't dying in just a day and a half, I'm sure Shar and I would end up best friends for life.

"Well, Michael?" I ask him. Still muttering, he drops down to the floor between me and Shar, completing the circle. I reach out and take both of their hands.

Compared to my first experience, the link is surprisingly easy this time. The intense fear from before is muted, almost nonexistent. Either Shar feels more confident now that she knows what to do or she's figured out how to hide her feelings. It helps that I know exactly what I want to show Michael. With the memory block already partially opened, we glide easily into my memories. It's strange having not one but two presences in my mind, but I push past the oddness and concentrate on showing Michael the important stuff. More memories have trickled in since my initial link with Shar, and I try to go back to the beginning as far as I can, showing memories of my time with Jao, Cavendish, and the other members of the Tiersten resistance. Our flight from Tiersten when the Spectres invaded is just beginning when from far away I hear a door slam open. A voice intrudes on the memory.

"You know you're not supposed to lock the door, Michael, and if you do, you should at least use a password that's more than three letters. Michael? Hello? Anyone home? What are you do-ing?*"*

A fourth presence suddenly enters the link. Shar starts to pull her hand away from mine to break the link, but I tighten my grip. Let Teal see! She has as much right to know as Michael.

The scene at Tiersten ends as we make our escape, and I move on to the memory chip, my false identity, and my meeting with Jao. Now all I have left to show is what we're fighting.

Even knowing what's coming doesn't prepare me for that first flash of terror as the Spectre grabs me. Instinctively, I try to flee the memory, but it's too late. The experience is too powerful, rolling over me like a tidal wave, and all I can do is clutch the hands in mine tighter as I relive the horrible sensation of being eaten by the Spectre in my father's body.

Fear. Revulsion. Horror. The combined emotions of not one but four people explode through my mind. They rage through me like a fire, and I cry out, the sensations too huge to contain. *Stop, stop, please, let me go!*

Then it's gone, the emotions evaporating as quickly as they arose, my mind empty and alone once again. I blink my eyes open and realize I'm no longer holding Shar's hand. She yanked her hands out of the circle to shatter the link.

Silence reigns for a long moment, then everyone's voice breaks out at once.

"Oh my God, Lia! Was *that* one of them?"

"Johansen, say something! You're not going to die or vac out or anything, right?"

"It's okay, I'm fine. I'm fine."

"What the Hell was that?!"

Teal's panicked shriek is enough to shut the rest of us up. Her body is visibly trembling, her hand resting on Michael's shoulder. She must have tried to shake him earlier to get his attention, and that was when she accidentally entered the link. Shar and I exchange a look.

"You'd better sit down."

Explaining is not easy or quick, but I manage it eventually. Teal is pretty overloaded, unsurprising considering her last minute addition, and even Michael seems pretty shaken up. I don't blame them. Still, I manage to explain the situation well enough with a little help from Shar, who sits next to me rubbing her head and refusing to look at anyone. The only thing I don't tell them is that *I'm* the bomb. Better for them to think I'm some junior demolitions expert than know the truth.

Michael shakes his head, rubs his face, and then shakes his head again. I'm pretty sure this is the first time I've ever seen him utterly speechless. I wait with bated breath for him to speak.

"So it's all true—what you told me before, about being a Tellurian agent sent here on a mission. You're really *not* Lia."

"I'm sorry, Michael. I wish I was, but I'm not. They just gave me her identity so I could get on the transport with the other prisoners. I don't know what happened to the real Lia. Maybe she's still on Tiersten."

Or maybe she's dead.

Michael bows his head. He doesn't need me to say it. After a moment, he continues. "Then you're really going to blow up the station to keep these aliens, these Spectres, from spreading?" When I nod, he asks. "If they're incorporeal, how do you know a bomb would work?"

Well, technically I don't. I'm a prototype, the first of my kind. However, even if I don't manage to destroy the Spectres, I should still be able to accomplish my primary mission. I blink. Primary mission? Oh, keeping the Spectres from spreading, I suppose. "I'm—it's a special kind of bomb."

"Is everyone infected by these things?" Michael asks, glancing around the room fearfully, as though the Spectres might be floating around him at this very moment.

"No, so far it seems to be just the ex-prisoners, and a few officers as well," I add, remembering the officer I encountered on Level Two my very first day on the station. "You, Teal, Taylor, Shar—all of you are okay. That's why you have to get off the station, now, before it blows."

"But you can't!" Michael bursts out. "You can't just blow up the station. Think of all the innocent lives you'd be taking. Maybe the infected ones can't be saved, but the rest . . ."

I shake my head sadly. "Oh, Michael, don't you understand? Every single person on this station is already lost."

I watch his face fall as the implication sinks in. Even if we stand by and let the infected refugees go, all the Spectres won't simply get on those transports and leave us in peace. The majority will go, using the convoy to spread through the Expanse in every direction, but some will stay. Enough will stay.

I'd lay odds that within an hour after that convoy pulls away carrying its terrible cargo, there won't be a single free person left on this station. I know because that's the Spectres' MO. They bide their time, waiting and breeding, until they've finally bred enough new Spectres to take every human at once. Then they attack. It's exactly what happened on Lunar Base 3 and Argos Station. It's exactly what happened at Tiersten Internment Colony. They came, they multiplied, and when the time was right, they struck en masse. Now the same thing will happen on New Sol. I can only assume the reason we aren't all slaves yet is the convoy. Compared to a fleet of ships ready to ferry them throughout the Expanse, what's one small space station like New Sol to the Spectres? No doubt they're waiting for the convoy to arrive to make their move. With the convoy due to arrive soon, it's only a matter of time. Hours, if I'm right.

The others look grim as I tell them about it. Even Michael's objections are silenced by this horrible piece of information.

"So why didn't you just blow up the transport on your way here?"

Teal's level tone cuts through the silence with ease. I glance at her in surprise. "The transport?" I ask. "Well, I didn't take out the transport because . . ."

The transport! I suddenly remember the nagging feeling I had when I first disembarked, like there was something I hadn't done, and understanding bursts through my brain. I was never supposed to blow up the station. I was supposed to go Nova on the transport!

It was my clock; that's what threw me off. It didn't start until right after I arrived on the station. I'd thought it started too early, activating right at the most danger-ous moment, when Rowan was checking me in. Only it didn't start too early; it started too *late.* The memory is coming back to me now, filtering back through the hole in my mind.

"It's all timed out now. Your clock will activate ap-proximately thirty-eight hours before your arrival. Once it starts, your real memories will come back. At that point, it's imperative you don't have contact with any possible psychics. In fact, it's best to avoid having contact with anyone at all, if you can help it. The transport should drop from the jump path approximately three hours be-fore arrival. You'll have roughly one hour to get to a con-sole and transmit the contents of the data chip—you know where it will be hidden—to the station before you go Nova."

It makes so much more sense. Why blow up a station

full of innocents when you could just blow up a transport full of enemies? Well, the refugees themselves are innocents, but they're already lost anyway. So what went wrong? Why didn't my clock start up?

I think back to my trip on the transport. Nothing really jumps out at me, only ... *the door control*. It malfunctioned a week into the trip and gave me an electrical shock. I blacked out and felt dizzy for two days afterward. What if the shock damaged the chips in my head? It would explain why my clock didn't activate on time and why it didn't count down correctly once it did. It would even explain why all my memories didn't come back the way they were supposed to once the clock started. All this trouble because of some stupid door control? I bet the doc never imagined *that* possible contingency.

I want to put my head in my hands and moan, only now understanding the full extent of my failure. By going Nova on the transport, I could have taken out the Spectres and derailed the peace talks all in one shot. Now because of my failure, New Sol is lost and the Celestian delegation is only days away from setting foot on New Earth.

Looking Teal in the eye, I sadly shake my head. "Because I screwed up. And now everyone on this station, and maybe even the entire Expanse, will pay for it."

———

Sitting in the tunnel next to the SlipStream, I stare at the wall as my thoughts chase round and round in circles. Destroy the station, don't destroy the station. Kill thousands of innocents, don't kill thousands of innocents.

Go Nova, don't go Nova.

I know what I have to do, and yet my heart feels sick

with grief. Must I really destroy a station full of people with hardly a second thought? My head says yes, but I can't help wondering how much good will come of it in the end. I'm just one girl and this is just one station. Even if I stop the Spectres here, they'll just find some other way in. Jao suspected they'd already started infiltrating the Celestial Expanse. For all we know, half the Expanse is already infected.

My thoughts flash back to the resistance, and I shake my head. For every one thing I know, it feels like there are two pieces of information I don't know. Am I merely a last-ditch effort to save a race that's already doomed? Or some small part in a much bigger plan, too small to see beyond the boundaries of my own insignificant place in it? If only I knew. If only there was another way.

Michael's voice still echoes in my head: *All those innocent people.*

Well, at least if I go Nova I won't have to live with my guilty conscience afterward.

After admitting my failure, I'd waited for the blame. For the others to round on me in anger for ever setting foot on this station and screwing up their lives. But it never came. Instead, Michael started speaking with Teal in a low voice about where they might obtain passage off the station, and what to tell Taylor, and whether they could warn anyone else. He asked Shar for her link number, explaining at her confused expression that it was so he could link her with the details for their passage.

I smile slightly as I remember the look of surprised wonder on Shar's face. Had she really expected us to just leave her, a refugee with no creds and no connections, alone to find some way off the station in just thirty-some hours? Yes, I realized looking at her face. That was Shar. She looked after herself and didn't ask anyone for help. But that's the thing about Michael. With him, you never need to ask.

My smile falters as I imagine his expression when he learns I'm not coming with them. Even as he'd spoken of passage I knew I should tell him, but I just didn't have the heart to do it. How could I explain that I'm not some junior secret agent with mad demolition skills, but a bomb? And not just a genetically engineered bomb forced into this mission by my very birth, but a volunteer as well?

"That's very generous," Jao says, *taking my release form and wadding it up in a ball, "but I can't let you volunteer for this assignment."* He tosses the form in the garbage can next to his desk.

"Why not?" I demand, pulling it out and un-wadding it. *"Because I'm still a kid?"*

"Well, yes," Jao says frankly, *"and because this whole plan was a mistake from the get-go. The Nova technology is untested; we don't even know if it'll work. We'll find another way. Besides, your parents would die if I let you do this."*

"They're dying anyway!"

A pause. "I'm sorry. It was poor choice of words. I didn't mean—"

"No, it was the perfect choice of words. Don't you see? That's why I have to go. I can't just sit here and watch them die."

"I know it's hard—"

"No, you don't!" I cry. From across the room, faces turn our way. I lower my voice. *"You* don't *know."*

"We're going to figure out a way to save them, I promise. The daily inoculations Doc's giving your parents to keep their Spectres from multiplying seem to be working. Cavendish tells me none of the usual signs are there."

"What does it matter? You still can't cure them."

"No, but it's only a matter of time before we figure it out."

"We don't have time! You know it as well as I do. We have to move soon, and I am our best hope of succeeding."

"Oh, really?"

"Yes, precisely because of my age. They're on the lookout for Tellurian resistance fighters. Tellurian adult resistance fighters. I'm a kid and a prisoner. I'm the last person they'd suspect."

"It would depend on where we inserted you," Jao objects, but I can tell he's weakening. For all his doubts, I am our best option, and he knows it.

Jao hesitates, not unaffected by my words. I drive the final stake home.

"You infected my dad. You owe *me."*

The memories have been coming back more rapidly now. Sometimes in bits and pieces, other times in whole chunks. I now know my favorite color (blue), my favorite food (lasagna), and my favorite sport (track), not that the last one was too hard to guess. All these things that I would have given anything to know just one week ago now seem so utterly pointless. I still don't know the one thing I desperately want to know though. Who I am.

Maybe I was originally engineered to be a weapon, but clearly I became more than that in my couple short years. I had parents who loved me, friends in the resistance, and even more than that, I had free will. I became an individual who could and did make her own choices. Surely I must have had a name, an identity of my own. Something they called me before turning me into Lia. I suppose it really doesn't matter anymore.

Still, it would have been nice to know my name—and my adoptive parents' names—before I died.

Pacing back and forth, I stop and lean against the tunnel wall, listening to the rush of the SlipStream as it makes its way back and forth. It's early evening; I should go to the cafeteria and get dinner. I've hardly eaten anything all day. None of us really had any sort of appetite after the link. Even now I'm not really hungry. Still, it would be something to do, something besides pacing and thinking. I could even eat my favorite food now that I remember it. Not that I could taste it.

I don't go, though. I just can't seem to comprehend eating when my whole world is about to end. Literally.

"Michael said you might be here."

I turn at the familiar voice. It's Teal. "What are you doing here?" I ask, faintly surprised to see her here. Except for her question about the transport, she was strangely silent during my entire explanation a couple hours ago. I wonder what she thinks of everything. Even now, her expression gives nothing away, her eyes guarded and dark.

"I came for the truth."

"You were in my mind; you saw it."

Teal shakes her head. "Not what you told us. What you *didn't* tell us."

I freeze. "I don't know what you mean."

"You're a good liar, Lia—or whoever you are—but not good enough. There's something you're not telling us, and I want to know what it is."

Damn! I should have known that while she was sitting there silently, Teal was examining my every gesture, every word, every explanation, looking for the chink in my story. Well, she found it, though she doesn't know what it is. Clever Teal! I hesitate, unsure how to answer.

"I'm not leaving until you tell me, so unless you want Michael on the station when the bomb goes off . . ." Teal trails off, not having to finish the sentence. She knows I know there's no way Michael would leave without her. At last, I sigh. Maybe it will be better this way.

"I can't come with you all," I finally admit. "I can't leave the station."

Teal blinks. Whatever secret she was expecting, it wasn't that. "Why not?"

I hesitate. "Because there is no bomb—"

"What?"

"I *am* the bomb."

Teal's mouth drops open. For a long time she just stares at me, utterly speechless. Then something sparks in her eyes, some piece of emotion formerly missing from her guarded expression, and I know she believes me. *"How?"*

"It doesn't matter. All that matters is that I volunteered for this mission, and I'm going to finish it."

"That's why you were going to leave before," Teal says slowly, her brain kicking in now that the initial shock is past. "That's what you meant when you said you weren't leaving Michael, but *for* Michael."

I nod. "My countdown clock malfunctioned. I've been living on borrowed time since I got here. I knew it was only a matter of time before I went Nova—blew up—and took everyone on the station with me. I couldn't let that happen to Michael. I didn't remember why I was here or what I was supposed to do then. It was only when I finally remembered . . ." I shrug helplessly. "I'm sorry. I'm *so* sorry! I'm *so, so sorry!*"

I'm not even sure what I'm apologizing for exactly— abandoning Michael? Lying about it? Even volunteering for this terrible mission in the first place? All I know is that I've never felt so much regret in my life. It pours out of my heart and fills up my veins until all I can do is apologize, over and over, as though only words can temper the outrush of grief.

I collapse on the floor, hands over my face, and at last the apologies peter out. Shoes scrape over metal, and I feel Teal drop to the floor next to me.

"I'm sorry, too," she says softly.

I glance over, confused, and she waves a hand roughly by the area of her cheek. It occurs to me that she's apologizing for the sound slap she delivered me in the cargo bay. I flap my jaw a couple times, bowled over by the utter absurdity of her apologizing for something so small and stupid in the face of much more terrible regrets. So bowled over that I start laughing. Teal's giggles join mine a second later as she gets it, and for a long time we just sit there and laugh our heads off. It's only when tears threaten that we force ourselves to stop. We sit together against the wall, trying to catch our breath.

After a while Teal whispers, "Michael will be so devastated."

"You can't tell Michael!" I say, alarm shooting through me at the idea.

Teal sits bolt upright. "Are you kidding me? *Of course* I can't tell Michael! He would *completely* vac out if he knew, do something totally deficient trying to save you and then ruin everything. We can't let that happen," she adds softly.

She raises her serious face to me, her eyes infinitely older than thirteen at this moment, and I suddenly realize that more than Michael, more than Shar even, she understands *exactly* what's at stake. For a brief moment, I don't feel quite so alone anymore.

We sit together awhile longer, shoulders brushing

and hands touching, neither wanting to leave this moment. Not with the future we have before us. Out of the blue, she suddenly speaks.

"If only there was some way to separate ourselves from them. Get all of them in one place and all of us in another."

I blink, momentarily thrown by the change of subject. Opening my mouth, I start to tell her it's impossible, then stop. Most of the Spectres have been staying in the hub, the infected prisoners confined there by station rule and the unattached Spectres seeming to prefer congregating there with their kin.

"Well, most of them are in the hub," I say slowly.

"Most?"

"I have smelled them in the rings. Not nearly so many though, and only off and on."

Teal looks at me sharply. "Are they in there today?"

I think back and nod. "Yes, I'm certain I smelled them outside the SlipStream station." I stare at the tunnel wall, eyes unfocused as I think back to all the times I smelled them. Why did I smell them some days and not others? Was it simply dumb luck or was there a reason for their presence, or lack thereof? Something Jao said to me comes back.

There's a scientist on Aganir who's supposedly had more success using the fence to keep the Spectres out. No one else has had any luck replicating his success, though. Maybe we should have settled the resistance on Aganir instead of Tiersten. Not that I'd want to live there—nasty place, it's like breathing underwater in a garbage dump.

Breathing underwater in a garbage dump.

A light suddenly goes on in my mind. What if they had it wrong? What if it wasn't the fence at all?

"Teal, are the misters working today?"

She frowns. "I'm not sure. Gran would know. Why?" At my exhortation, she links Taylor. Excitement builds in me as I hear the answer.

"Unfortunately, they shut off again yesterday morning," Taylor tells us. "The repair team only got them working again an hour ago. They tell us it's a valve problem—apparently the main valve hasn't been opening and closing properly, resulting in too little mist sometimes and too much at others. Why? Is this more research for your project, Teal?"

"Uh, yeah. Thanks, Gran." Teal links off, bringing her sharp gaze to bear on me.

"It's the misters!" I exclaim before she has a chance to ask. "There's something in the nutrient mist they don't like. Maybe it's not enough to kill them, but it certainly seems to put them off."

"I thought they didn't breathe."

"They don't, but that doesn't mean they aren't still sensitive to the air around them, the way we're sensitive to air temperature or smells. Maybe the nutrient mist just smells bad to them. Or feels bad to them, whatever their equivalent of smell is."

I tell Teal about Aganir, and she nods. "Then if we could get the nutrient mist going full blast again . . ."

"We might be able to force them out of the rings!" I finish. We grin at each other, ecstatic at the possibilities. Then reality sets back in and my smile drops from my face.

"It won't work. Even if we could get them out of the rings, it wouldn't matter. The bomb is too powerful. I'll take out the entire station when I go regardless of where I am. I'm sorry."

"Maybe not." Teal thinks for a second. "In fact, maybe you don't need to go Nova at all."

Not go Nova? My mouth drops open at the thought. Could it be that after steeling myself up to accept my fate there's a way to avoid it after all? "Tell me."

Teal leans in, and in quick, terse words, explains her plan.

30

SKULKING JUST OUTSIDE the Enviro Center, I check the time on my chit for about the hundredth time and try not to look suspicious.

That's not the easiest of assignments. Located at the edge of the Upper Habitat Ring on the topmost tier of farms, the area around the Enviro Center is not exactly a usual haunt for most of the station's teens, especially now. It's almost twenty hundred hours, and Teal has been inside the center for forty-five minutes already. I check the time again and frown. The center will be closing soon; where *is* Teal? Surely she should be done by now.

Of course, maybe it's just taking longer than we supposed. After all, it's not like either of us has much experience sabotaging the station ventilation system.

Pacing the small square of decking between the beds of crops on either side of the center, I look out over the ring. It's a unique perspective—the long tiers of farms in the foreground curving down to the city below, its buildings tiny and square in the distance. Up here, at least, there's no smell of Spectres in the air, though I did catch scents of them in the lower section of the ring on my way here. Not nearly as prevalent as in the hub, but still enough to make me shudder now that I know what the odor means. I just hope Teal and I aren't wrong in our theory.

We managed to wrangle the mister logs from Taylor under the guise of needing the information for Teal's school project. The logs showed the output from the misters for the past three months. It wasn't easy to recall all the times I did or didn't smell Spectres in the rings, but I could remember a few for sure, if only because I had the smell linked to a specific event in my head. When compared to the mister logs, my memories did seem to corroborate our theory. While Spectres were present during normal mist flow or complete shut-offs, they seemed to clear out whenever the misters ran full blast. With our theory confirmed inasmuch as we were able, we set about putting Teal's plan into motion. Now if only she would hurry up and finish.

I'm making my twentieth pass across the tier when my chit vibrates. I answer the link, grateful for the distraction. "Hey, Michael."

"Good news, Lia. I've tested it, and we're a go."

"Then it worked?"

"Yup, the screen turned on the moment I scanned it."

"You actually scanned it?" I ask, alarmed that he might have accidentally given away our plan.

"Well, how else could I determine if it would work? Don't worry—you have to punch in the code before it will go off. I doubt anyone noticed the scan."

I nod and sign off. Assuming Teal's work goes as planned, we're nearly set for tomorrow. I just wish my own mission had gone as well. It's something I'd remembered earlier, but then forgot in the stir of realizing I'd missed blowing the transport: *"You'll have roughly one hour to get to a console and transmit the contents of the data chip—you know where it will be hidden—to the station before you go Nova."*

A data chip, with all of the information we'd managed to glean about the Spectres. I can remember it now. Everything except where it's hidden, that is. I'd gone through my stuff earlier looking for it. Locker, blanket, clothes—everything I'd had on the transport. I even ripped apart the seams of my jumpsuits looking for it, but to no avail. Either I lost the data chip on the transport, or it's really well hidden.

"Can you locate the information if we link minds again?" I asked Shar after my fruitless search. "Dig in my mind until you find what happened to the data chip?"

Shar gave me a dark look and flopped back down on her cot. "Not unless you want to risk dying again. Remember what happened the last time I tried to force memories from you?"

Seizing, heart stopping . . . yeah, it's pretty hard to forget that. Plus, what if the poking around harmed my biochip or clock? They were already damaged from my electric shock on the transport, and they'd been running much longer than planned. What if Shar's digging caused them to malfunction again? Or worse—go off?

"You're right," I told Shar with a nod of my head. "We'll just have to hope it turns up before tomorrow. So you're in, right?"

Shar hesitated. "Yeah, whatever."

The answer wasn't as rousing as I'd hoped for. "We need you, Shar. You know we can't pull this off without you," I added, a note of warning in my voice.

"Look, I said I was in, okay?" Shar said in a cranky voice. Sitting up, she swung her legs off the cot and stood. "I'm going to the cafeteria. You want anything?"

Mutely shaking my head, I watched her go. While her answers weren't exactly encouraging, she had been in my head and seen what I'd seen. She knew how important the plan was; she wouldn't let us down.

I stop my pacing and glance over at the door to the Enviro Center. Still closed, still no sign of Teal. As I deliberate whether I should go inside after her, a group of workers from one of the farms passes by. I duck my head, but they don't pay me much attention. *That's right*, I exhort them in my head, *just walk right on by. Nothing going on here. You know, except station sabotage, an alien invasion, and potentially the end of the human race.*

I smile to myself, wondering how I can be so upbeat at a time like this. Maybe it's because after those horrible months hiding out on Tiersten, with my parents dying and the resistance failing, I can finally feel some hope. Maybe I've lost my parents, but I have other family now— Michael's family. I have a plan that will allow me *not* to go Nova and a chance at a new life, just like Michael talked about.

For a moment, I briefly wonder if Niven and Jao and the rest of the resistance would approve. After all, they gave their lives to take down the Tiersten spaceport. Would they be angry if I don't do the same? I don't think so, I decide after a minute. They gave their lives because they had to; they'd be happy to know I don't need to.

I'm just getting ready to go into the Enviro Center after Teal when I see a figure coming up the steps from below. From the uniform, I can tell it's an officer, and I immediately take a couple nervous steps back before reminding myself I'm not *technically* doing anything wrong.

No, that would be Teal.

The figure reaches my tier and stops a few feet away from me. "PsyLt. Rowan," I blurt out, surprised to see him, of all people, on the agricultural level. "What are you doing here?"

"I need to speak with one of the farming managers about his report." Rowan's lips twist wryly. "What, you think I spend all my days on Level Eleven brain-draining people?"

Well, actually . . .

Rowan must see the answer on my face, for he laughs. "It may surprise you, but most of my duties on the station don't have much to do with being a psychic at all. So what are you doing here, Lia?"

I start to babble out the story Teal and I concocted to get her into the center—that she'd lost an earring earlier this week while visiting with Taylor to work on her school project and had come back to look for it—when Rowan interrupts me to clarify. "I mean on the station. Didn't your freighter shove off this morning? *Comet's Kiss*, wasn't it?"

Oh. The freighter. I'd forgotten about that. "I decided not to go, after all. The friend I told you about? Michael? He said it would be okay for me to stay with them. In fact, it's his sister I'm waiting for."

I feel a little guilty lying to Rowan after all the kindness he's shown me, but I tell myself it's not really a lie. Michael *did* once say his gran would let me stay with them, and I *am* waiting for Teal. For the first time, I wonder what I'll do after this whole plan is over. Having originally assumed I would go Nova, housing had been the least of my concerns. Well, I'll figure that out later.

". . . if you could have Michael's guardian come to the PsyCorp office sometime tomorrow," Rowan is saying. "There's some paperwork she'll need to fill out to make everything official."

"Of course. I'll tell her tonight."

Rowan just stares at me for a long moment, an unreadable look in his eyes. "I'm really glad this all worked out for you, Lia. Ever since I first saw you in the cargo bay—"

"What?" I ask when he stops abruptly.

"It's nothing. You just look a lot like someone I know."

"Who?"

He laughs. "My little sister, if you can believe it. You're a dead ringer for her at that age. I know you're not her, but I can't help thinking of her every time I see you."

His sister! I remember Rowan's gentleness at our first meeting, the way he tried to warn me about the Aurorans' fate, how he confided in me about Dayav and Mechanra. Now I understand why.

"Do you see her often?" I ask curiously.

"I'm afraid not. I come from a military family. My parents, my maternal grandparents, me, my sister. She's on a posting far away. I haven't seen her in three years."

"Oh. Well, maybe you can visit her the next time you have leave."

Rowan gets a strange look in his eyes, as though he would object to my suggestion and then suddenly realizes he doesn't have to. He gives me a firm nod. "Maybe I will."

The doors to the Enviro Center open and out comes Teal, followed by a few enviro workers who pause to lock the doors. She doesn't even bat an eye when she sees Rowan, coming straight up to us as though there's nothing more natural than finding me in conversation with an officer—and a PsyCorp officer, no less. I introduce her to Rowan, and the two make small talk for a minute while I marvel at her calm. Rowan mentions my staying with her family, and I tense.

"Oh yeah, I knew Lia back on Aurora. We're like sisters. It'll be much better than sharing a room with *Michael*," she says, wrinkling her nose at the unfairness of a world where she has to share a room with her brother.

Rowan laughs, and a minute later we all part company. Teal and I take the steps leading down through the tiers. Feeling awkward about my lie, I try to explain.

"About what Rowan said, about living with you guys—"

"Well, where else would you stay?" Teal interrupts. "Unless you don't want to live in that tin can we call an apartment. Tiny, cramped place. I can't wait until I'm old enough to move away from this station and get my own place."

Where else would I stay, indeed? Grinning, I savor the warm glow spreading through my chest at the idea of having a place to call my own. Soon enough, though, I refocus on the mission. According to Teal, everything went off without a hitch.

"They completely bought my story about the earring, and having seen me with Gran a couple times, they waved me right through. They didn't even have anyone shadowing me while I looked. I guess they don't consider the filtration system especially high security. Either that, or they couldn't see past my innocent face to the evil genius inside."

"Then what took you so long?"

She shrugs. "It took me a while to get an unoccupied control station; I had to wait until someone went on a maintenance check. Don't worry—it's done. I set the system to lock open all valves in both the lower and upper rings at exactly 2230."

"*All* of them?"

"Sure, no sense playing it safe, right? With the center closed for the night, it'll be morning at the earliest before anyone realizes what happened. I changed the valve system password while I was at it, so it should take them a while to get it shut off."

I nod. "I just hope it's enough time."

Teal gives me a sidelong glance. "You and me both."

———

I wake with butterflies in my belly the next morning. Today is the day. The convoy will be arriving late tonight so they can refuel and be ready to take on passengers tomorrow. If we're going to make our move, it has to be sometime within the next several hours. My stomach clenches at the thought, though whether it is from fear or excitement, I'm not entirely sure. Probably both.

As soon as I finish my morning routine, I link Michael and ask him to meet me at the SlipStream station on the ring side. Time to see if my theory and Teal's sabotage have panned out. The first thing I do when I step out of the station is take a deep breath.

"Well?" Michael asks me impatiently.

I grin. "So far so good."

"What now?"

"Time to walk around and see if the rest of the place smells this good."

We spend the morning together, just Michael and me, sometimes walking, sometimes biking to cover more ground. Technically, I don't need him to come with me, since only I can smell them, but I want his company. After all that's passed, I finally have the chance to tell him everything I never could before. About the resistance and my time on Tiersten. About Cavendish and Jao and Niven, and how they must have died taking out the spaceport. Even about how my parents were infected on our flight from the main camp. The words pour out, one after another, and through it all, Michael just listens, occasionally asking questions when my story doesn't quite fit together.

"So if you were just another prisoner at the colony, how did you end up in the resistance?"

I hesitate, unsure how to answer without revealing that I wasn't imprisoned on Tiersten, but created there. "Well, the resistance chose Tiersten to base their operations for a couple reasons. First, because it was about as far from New Earth as they could get."

"And second?"

"Because with the only people coming in being war prisoners from the Celestial Expanse, they knew the population would be uninfected, and thus a good place to recruit from. Not like the rest of the Alliance. They chose my parents because my dad is—was—a psychic."

I tell him how I first learned about the Spectres, much the way he had, by linking with a Tellurian psychic and seeing all she knew.

Michael whistled. "They had to recruit *everyone* into the resistance individually, using only psychic links?"

"They had no other way—still don't. The Spectres can't be seen, heard, touched. We have no hard evidence of their existence to show anyone. Even my smell technology is a prototype. Only the psychics can sense them once they've bonded with a human, and only if they know what they're looking for. It's what made it so hard to fight them, and so difficult to organize a resistance."

"I'll bet. I mean, you couldn't even com someone safely with the information, not without any way to verify they're not infected."

"Or if their superior or their coworker is infected. We think it's why our previous attempts to warn the Celestians always failed. Even when we sent people in person, they had a way of disappearing."

"Well, I'll tell them," Michael says. "When this whole thing is over, I'll help you tell the entire galaxy."

My heart lurches as the declaration. *Oh, Michael!* I struggle to keep a huge grin from bursting across my face. "Promise?"

"Cross my heart and hope to die."

Stick a needle in your eye! I think wryly.

———

By early evening, we've finished our tour of the rings and have ended up on Michael's roof. Though the rings are too big to go over every nook and cranny in a day, we've covered enough for me to know that Teal's sabotage was a success. The Spectres have cleared out of the rings, at least as far as I can tell. I did have a false alarm down in the lower ring when I caught the scent of an infected officer. Luckily, he got on a SlipStream bound for the hub shortly after we started discreetly following him. I can only hope there aren't other infected people I may have missed.

"Lia?" Michael asks as we lean on the roof ledge and watch the people below. The nutrient spray is drifting around us, thick enough to feel after more than twelve hours at maximum capacity. Teal did her work well.

"Hmm?"

"I just wanted you to know that what I said before is still true. In the park, when I said it didn't matter what your name was? I still mean that. I know you're not Lia—*my* Lia from Aurora, at least—but you're still Lia from New Sol. I just wanted you to know that."

I look up in surprise, my heart fluttering at the words, otherwise implied but never spoken until now. This time, I'm the one who kisses him. Wrapping my arms around his neck, I pull his face down to mine and let every thought fly out of my head, lost to everything but the tingles running down my spine and the shivers caressing my skin everywhere we touch. When we finally pull away, Michael closes one hand around my wrist. I glance down at it, then raise a questioning gaze to his.

He shrugs sheepishly. "Just in case you get the urge for some exercise."

I laugh and kiss him again, enfolded within the cool of the mist and the warmth of his arms, and realize I've never felt more alive in my entire life.

31 **WE MEET TEAL** in the cargo bay by my cot. She spent the day lying low, tucking herself in out-of-the-way places in case anyone suspected her involvement in the mister sabotage. Now all we have to do is wait for Shar. Teal saw her in one of the docking rings just a couple hours ago, so we know she's around. I check the time and roll my eyes. No doubt Shar's purposely delaying just to prove she doesn't take orders from me.

A wisp of fear flutters over me for a brief second as I contemplate the possibility that someone figured out what we were up to, and she got hauled in by station security. Or PsyCorp, or even worse—someone infected and acting under the influence of a Spectre. After a second, I shake my head. How could anyone possibly know what we're planning? No, I'm just being paranoid.

Since we have to wait for Shar anyway, I use the time to go through my things again. Sleeping roll, headrest, jumpsuit number one, jumpsuit number two ... Tossing the second suit down on the cot, I huff in disgust.

"Still no data chip?" Teal asks, correctly guessing what I'm doing.

I shake my head. "I must have lost it on the transport. It's the only answer. I knew there was something I was forgetting when I got off. It must have been the chip."

"It's okay, Lia. We'll manage without it."

"No, it's not!" I tell Teal. "Everything we know is on that data chip. Without it, the Celestians will have to start at square one."

"Hey, easy there, Starshine," Michael says. "Everything's going to be sat."

Starshine.

My heart drops into my stomach at the word. "What did you call me?"

"Oh, um nothing. It was just something Lia's dad used to call her. I'm sorry, it just slipped out. I know you're not Lia."

My name is Lia Johansen . . .

A wave of memories shoots through my brain, a thousand bits from a thousand different moments, flashing by in a dizzying array.

Michael frowns. "You don't still get motion sick, do you?"

"I don't know how you do it. Even when we were kids you were doing all the advanced math lessons."

Michael may have been good at sports, but he was never much of a runner. No, that was always me. Me.

I am not Lia and never was her, though I borrowed her mind for a short time. And yet for a minute, it was as though this dead girl took possession of my mind. Infused me with her thoughts and personality and made me act as she would act, speak as she would speak, move as she would move.

"Yes, I look at you and see Lia from Aurora all the time. Your smile, your laugh, the snarky comments you make and that annoying way you can always beat me in a footrace."

I pull up one of the digitals Michael uploaded for me from when we were kids. The two girls look exactly alike.

Exactly alike.

I'm Lia's clone. I have her DNA, her natural talents, her personality. I'm not such a fraud, after all!

"They're on the lookout for Tellurian resistance fighters. Tellurian *adult* resistance fighters. I'm a kid and a prisoner."

A prisoner.

Not a Tellurian.

Niven gently turns my arms over and runs a finger over each forearm. "They've healed well. No one should be able to tell what's underneath the skin."

They've healed well.

They've healed well.

They've healed well.

My eyes widen as the implications of the memories hit home. I scramble to my feet and stumble toward the hygiene units, awkwardly brushing off Michael's concerned questions. Reaching the first unit, I throw myself inside and slam the door tight behind me. Pushing up my sleeves, I run my hand over the skin of my forearm. Completely smooth and unmarred.

Can it really be? Has the truth been staring me in the face this whole time, and I just never realized it?

Someone knocks on the door, and I hear Teal's voice call through the metal. "Lia? What's going on? Are you sat?"

I ignore her and instead reach for the knife from my tool belt. Taking a deep breath, I press the blade into my upper left forearm and make a shallow slice. It is surprisingly painless. I stare at the cut.

There's no blood.

Outside, I hear Teal banging on the door, but I don't answer. Instead, I lengthen the cut, drawing the knife down the length of my forearm. Still nothing. No blood, no pain. Dropping the knife, I slip my fingers under the edge of the cut and give a hard tug. The fragile skin tears, and just like that an entire sheet of skin rips off my forearm. I gasp as I see what lies underneath.

Grabbing the knife again, I turn to my right forearm. This time there's no hesitation as I run the blade down my arm and tear off the false skin, throwing it to the floor without even a glance.

I look at the digital of Lia in the sundress again. There, on the inside of her forearm, is a distinctive birthmark a couple shades darker than her skin.

I look at my arm and my heart lets out a long-awaited sigh. There, up near my elbow, is that birthmark. A single tear—born of joy, or maybe just relief—blooms in my eye. It rolls down my cheek, and I catch it on one finger, grayish and metallic.

Gray.

Gray like that fluid, viscous and silvery, filling my eyes after I malfunctioned in the hygiene unit.

Gray, like the stains that fluid left on my jumpsuit, so potent they never came out even after multiple washings.

Gray, like my eyes. Eyes I was so sure were green until a close look in Teal's mirror told me otherwise.

I suddenly know without a doubt that they *were* green. At least, they were until the night I malfunctioned in the hygiene unit and awoke to find my eyes filled with thick, gray chemicals.

Thud! The door bursts open and footsteps hurry in. They stop just behind me. "Lia?" Teal's voice says uncertainly. I turn around, a strange smile on my face.

"Well, what do you know?" I tell her, my arms extended to show the long, silver scar running down each forearm from wrist to elbow. "I really am Lia after all."

My name really *is* Lia Johansen, and I was a prisoner of war. Taken when Aurora Colony fell, I lived in an internment camp for two years, where my family was recruited into a resistance group fighting a terrible enemy. When my parents fell to this enemy, I volunteered for the most important mission of the war. Even though it meant my death.

It's back now. My long-lost identity, the very thing I've been searching for all this time, finally returned. It seems so obvious now that I know. How could I have ever thought I was a genetically engineered bomb, with no more life than a clone bred in a laboratory? How could I ever have forgotten I was Lia?

Screaming, I sit bolt upright as the nightmare rips me from sleep. Footsteps pound through the hall, and then the door flies open. The light flips on, and Niven stands illuminated in the door. He rushes in and sits down on the side of my bed.

"It was just a dream, Lia. Just a dream. You're safe, I promise." He grabs a blanket from my cot and slips it around my shaking shoulders.

I've been sleeping in the med center ever since my surgery so Niven could be on hand in case of any unforeseen side effects. Somehow, when he spoke of side effects, I don't think he meant the constant nightmares that have plagued me ever since I found out where I would be deployed. It's ironic—before the surgery, I could sleep anytime, anywhere. Not anymore.

"Tell me again," I whisper through shaky lips. "Tell me how it will happen."

Niven considers me for a moment, and nods. "It will start with a slow, stretchy feeling in your head, like your

NOVA ────────────────── 299

mind is being thinned and tautened. Then the sparks will come, in silver and gold, dancing in your vision. Your heart will speed up and the sacs in your arms will release into your bloodstream, until finally everything goes white. Then . . . Nova." He pauses, and adds softly, on cue, "It will be glorious. More glorious than you could possibly imagine."

"Glorious." I echo, letting the word linger on my tongue. "I like that."

For a moment, I think Niven might cry, though we've exchanged these words a million times, but he doesn't, his eyes clearing as they cast over me with a searching look. "What's wrong, Lia?"

I close my eyes and finally admit what I've been afraid to tell anyone for the past week. "I'm not sure I can go through with it."

I hear a sharp intake of breath from Niven. He's appalled by my announcement, and I don't blame him. There isn't the time or equipment to start with someone new. It's me or no one.

"I'm sorry!" I burst out when he doesn't answer. "I don't know what's wrong with me. I wanted to do it. I was sure I could do it, but then you performed the surgery turning me into a bomb and the nightmares started. Nightmares filled with the ghosts of my soon-to-be victims. They blame me, in my dreams. They scream at me until they're hoarse with rage."

"There's nothing wrong with you," Niven says, his hand gently rubbing my back through the blanket. "Any of us would be terrified to be in your shoes. You've endured far more than you ever should have in the two years since you were brought to Tiersten with the other Auroran prisoners. Jao was wrong to let you do this."

"No! Jao respected me. He knew that of the three

people compatible with the Nova biotech, I was our best chance for success. In letting me volunteer, he treated me as one adult to another. I wouldn't have had it any other way."

Niven chuckles. "No, you wouldn't, would you? Well, if it's any consolation, I think you'll know few, if any, of the prisoners on the transport. I don't think the enemy would risk sending in members of the resistance in the first wave." When a minute passes and I don't answer, he adds tentatively, "I may be able to make it easier, if you want."

"How?"

"Instead of letting your full memory come back when the clock activates, I could block it out. Leave Lia Johansen locked deep inside and replace her with another template. Instead of yourself, you'll just be a bomb. A genetically engineered bomb created just for this mission, with no name, no memories other than those of some girl named Lia whom you've never met. No family, no friends, no one to grieve for."

"You can do that?"

"I believe so. If you want it."

Do I want it? I think of all the things I'll lose—not just my identity, but my parents, my friends, the resistance— every reason for doing what I'm doing. Can I really give that up? But the nightmare still lingers—not just in my mind, but in my heart—and the seed of doubt inside me grows just a little bit bigger.

I think of everyone who is counting on me. Not just the resistance, but an entire expanse of people out there.

I lift my eyes to Niven. "Do it."

I gasp as the truth hits me in a hard rush. I'd assumed the memory implant Shar saw in my head when we linked was Lia's collection of memories, implanted to get me past PsyCorp. But it wasn't the memories of being Lia that were false, but the memories of being a genetically engineered bomb! No wonder I never saw the truth! How could I, when I literally had false memories in my head telling me I was *not* Lia, but a bomb created in a laboratory with no real family or identity of my own? With all the contradictions between my various memories—real, false, and blocked—my poor brain must have been working overtime to try and make sense of everything, in any way it could. It's no surprise I got my identity wrong. I'm just lucky I didn't lose my sanity.

Oh God, this whole mission has been a nightmare, and it's all my fault! If I hadn't been such a coward, hadn't forced Niven to tamper even more with my memory, I might not have malfunctioned. If nothing else, I would have remembered who I was instead of hanging around the station for weeks and putting everyone in more danger with each passing day. Shame washes over me at the realization.

"What's your fault?" Teal asks me, and I realize I'm still standing in the hygiene unit, muttering aloud to myself like a null, my false arm skin on the floor at my feet and Teal at my side.

I shake my head and stiffen my back. "It doesn't matter anymore. All that matters is that we stick to the plan. Come on, Shar must be back by now."

I scoop up the skin from the floor and shove it in my pocket. Niven grafted it over my arms to prevent the long scars from raising any unwanted attention. Luckily, my forearms look completely normal otherwise. The scars I can explain away if need be, but sacs of explosive liquids would be beyond even Teal's ability to fast talk.

Quickly, Teal and I leave the unit and return to the bay. Michael looks up in concern. "Are you okay? You rushed out of here pretty quick."

"I'm sat, Michael, but there's something I need to tell

you." He raises his eyebrows, waiting, and I take a breath. "Michael, I really am—"

At that moment, my chit vibrates. Shar. Finally!

"Never mind, Michael. I'll tell you later when we have more time. You should head off to your place; Shar's coming."

He nods and scoots quickly out of the bay while I answer the link. Adrenaline entwined with excitement and terror shoots through me as I realize—it's time!

"Shar, where are you? We've been waiting and waiting . . ." My voice trails off as I catch sight of the background behind her. A chill goes through me. It looks suspiciously as though she's on the deck of a passenger liner. But that can't be!

"I'm on the *Eye of Zeus*. It's a ship heading for the lower colonies."

I shake my head, unable to compute. "The *Eye of Zeus*? How did you get there?"

Shar shrugs. "Same way I got on the transport from Tiersten—I snuck on."

"I don't understand . . . the plan . . . You have to get off!"

"Too late. We shoved off almost a half-hour ago."

Fury spikes through me as I finally understand what she's saying. "You're *leaving*? How *could* you? We need you!"

A muscle twitches in her cheek. "I'm sure you'll figure something out, Johansen, you being so resourceful and all."

"You lying, scheming—"

"Look who's talking!" Shar yells back. "You're the one who hid the truth about Dayav and Mechanra. What, you were so busy telling me about your precious little alien invasion that you couldn't be bothered to mention I was slated for a life of hard labor on a dirt rock?"

My jaw falls open. "How did you find out about that?"

"I was in your head, Johansen. Twice! I may be untrained, but I'm not a glitch."

"It wasn't like that; I just didn't think about it. Besides, it's not like they'd send *you* there. Not when they find out what you are."

"So that's the answer?" Shar scoffs. "I be a good girl and go work for PsyCorp? No, thank you!"

"What do you have against PsyCorp anyway?" I demand.

Shar makes a face. "Like I'd ever tell *you.*"

Yup, best friends forever, that's Shar and me.

"Look, I'm not like you, Johansen," Shar says, briefly squeezing her eyes shut and then opening them again. "All noble and courageous and trying to save the galaxy like some hero out of a holo. The only person I'm trying to save is me. Right now, that means getting as far away from here as possible. I know you can't understand—"

"No, that's the thing," I say with a sigh, remembering all the times I wished I could just grab my parents and flee, somewhere far away where the Spectres could never reach. My anger deflates at the memory. "I do understand. Only I'm not as special as you seem to think, all noble and stuff. I'm just—" I pause, trying to figure out how to put it. My dad's emaciated face flashes in my mind. "I just didn't know what I was really capable of until I had a reason to fight."

I hold her eyes through the link. "Goodbye, and good luck, Shar. Who knows? Maybe one day you'll have a reason, too."

"Goodbye, Lia." She pauses, then adds, "For what it's

worth, I think the galaxy will be a darker place without you in it."

"Don't worry, I plan to be in it for—"

The link cuts off.

"—a long time to come," I finish with a roll of my eyes.

"That bitch!" Teal swears. "I should have paid more attention to her when I saw her in the docking ring earlier."

I shake my head and reactivate my chit. "It's too late now. We'd better link Michael. Without Shar, we're going to need to rethink our plan before we d—"

Eeeeeooooooeee! Eeeeeooooooeee! Eeeeeooooooeee!

The klaxons wail out through the hub, high-pitched and shrill. I gasp and exchange a terrified glance with Teal.

Too late.

32 **SIRENS BREAK OUT** in the cargo hold, but it's nothing like the reaction the last time the klaxons went off. Everyone has been through this before; they know what to expect. Most of them probably assume it's just another drill. Nothing to get worried about. Not the people *or* the Spectres.

"What do we do now?" Teal hisses, eyes wide with alarm.

No idea. "We meet Michael like planned. We'll figure it out from there."

I don't wait around for the officers to start herding people to the shelter, but grab Teal's hand and head for the exit. In our civilian clothes, the soldiers don't even look at us twice, though they stop a refugee who tries to leave just behind us.

We make for the lift in the center of the level. The first of the ex-prisoners are already being herded out of the bays, and we have to push our way through the maze of refugees, soldiers, and civilians just to reach the end of the lift line. As I jump on the lift with Teal, I think I hear my name. I glance around, but I can't see anything through the swirling crowd. Shaking my head, I glance at the time: 1847.

Compared to Eight, Level Five is not nearly so chaotic, the permanent stationers much more efficient at reacting to the alarms. Those remaining are making quick work getting to the SlipStreams, encouraged by a bunch of soldiers making sure everyone is heading to their designated place. The soldiers take one glance at the two of us and motion us toward the SlipStreams. We nod, not needing to be told, and wheel toward the nearest entrance. As we jog down one of the concourses, my nose starts bleeding again. I raise my head and pinch my nostrils, trying to contain the bleeding, which is why I don't see the stray pastry someone dropped. My foot finds it though, slipping out from under me and sending my knees to the floor with a hard bang. The false skin flops out of my pocket.

"Lia!" Teal calls, stopping a few feet ahead when she realizes I'm no longer with her.

I grab for the false skin and begin staggering to my feet when something silver drops from the skin. Stopping, I reach for it, drawing the tiny disc, no larger than the tip of my pinky, to my face. In a flash, I realize what it is.

The data chip! The one I was originally supposed to transmit to the station before going Nova on the transport, the one with all our knowledge of the Spectres.

"Lia? What is it? Are you sat?"

Rising to my feet, I wave the chip in Teal's face. "No, I found it! The data chip! It's here."

Hope rises in me and then falls. We finally have the last piece of the puzzle. If only Shar hadn't backed out on us at the last minute.

I rejoin Teal, and the two of us breeze out of the hub and onto the SlipStream platform shortly after. Michael is already there, leaning against the wall just inside and nervously fingering his dad's old chit. He snaps upright at our arrival.

"Ready? Wait, where's Shar?"

"Not coming," I tell him at the same time Teal growls, "The bitch ran out on us."

"What?"

I shake my head and motion them toward the entrance to the tunnel on the far wall. We crowd in, the door sliding shut silently behind us, and I check my chit for the time again: 1851. Based on the amount of time that's passed, I would estimate that Michael triggered the alarm at approximately 1845. Assuming that's correct, that leaves us exactly nine minutes. Nine minutes before the SlipStreams shut down and cut off the rings from the hub.

Nine minutes to figure out what to do.

"And just what do you propose we do? Walk right up to PsyCorp and tell them *we* triggered the alarm?" Teal is saying. "I can just imagine how *that* will go. 'Oh yes, officer, we're the ones who set off the alarm, but don't worry! The hub power reactors aren't *really* going nuclear. We just set it off to stop the invisible aliens taking over the human race.'"

Michael huffs. "Well, without Shar to link with the station commander and show him what's going on, we're going to have to tell *some* psychic."

"There are only a handful of psychics on this station. We don't even know if any of them are going to *be* in the rings. They might be stationed on the hub for all we know."

"So what do you—"

"Quiet!" I yell, distracted by all their bickering. "I have to think."

I glance at my chit. 1853. Seven minutes to go.

Think, Lia. I tell myself. *What now?*

The plan seemed simple enough. Teal would sabotage

the misters the night before, clearing the rings of all the Spectres or at least most of them. Then Michael would use his dad's old chit, still programmed with its officer designation, to access one of the alarm boxes and set off the reactor overload alarm. Michael assured me that even if everything looked good in the hub's power stations, it was standard operating procedure to continue with the alarm until the power analysts could do a full system check, a process which would take five hours minimum.

Meanwhile, we would all hustle to the rings before the SlipStream stations automatically shut down, thereby locking off the rings from the hub. Once there, the plan was for Shar to link with me and the station commander, showing him the *real* reason for the alarm. The pièce de résistance would be the data chip, with all of the Tellurians' accumulated knowledge about the Spectres. Even if the convoy came early, SOP demanded that they refrain from docking with us until the alarm ended and the station commander gave the all-clear. Something he presumably wouldn't do once he knew the truth.

Unfortunately, without Shar we have no way to show the commander what we're up against. Just a data chip that he may or may not believe is a bunch of station teens' idea of a practical joke, assuming he's even willing to look at it.

"Michael's right," I finally say, the cogs in my brain turning at a hundred klicks an hour as I try to decide what to do. "We need a psychic, someone who'll be willing to listen to us. And I think I know just the person."

Firing up my chit, I put through the link. Rowan answers on the seventh tone.

"Lia, I don't know what's going on, but this isn't a

good time. In case you hadn't noticed, there's a station-wide alarm. You need to get to the shelters with the others, and I need to get to my station on the hub."

"Wait! Please," I ask him as he goes to cut the link. "I need you to meet me in the rings. Not later, now. Before the SlipStreams close down."

"Lia, I can't—"

"*Please*, Rowan! I have information about . . . about the Tellurians. It's important, it can't wait."

"If you're making this up—"

"Do you remember the first time we met? How messed up my mind was? Well, there was a reason for it. I'm like your sister—I'm a patriot. You know I'm on the level or you wouldn't have tried to protect me all those times before."

Rowan scowls at me for a minute, then shakes his head. "You remind me so much of Amaya sometimes. No wonder I find it impossible to say no to you. She's been away on Earth too long."

"Wait—she's on *Earth*?"

"Yes, she's an attaché to the embassy there."

A burst of sadness sighs through me as I realize that, just like me, he's lost someone to the Spectres, too. He just doesn't know it yet. The words slip out without my permission. "Oh, Rowan. I'm *so* sorry."

He wrinkles his forehead. "What?"

I shake my head. "Nothing. Will you come?"

Reluctantly he assents, getting my location and agreeing to grab the opposite SlipStream and meet us on the other side.

Only four minutes to go now. Michael, Teal, and I clamber out of the tunnel just in time to see the Slip-Stream pull up.

"Last one," the corporal overseeing the evacuation tells us. "You'd better get on because there won't be another one after this."

We scramble on and take a spot near the back. Michael throws himself down on one of the seats, while Teal stands, hanging on loosely to one of the seatbacks. Too nervous to sit, I pace along the aisle. Now that the plan is in motion, all my doubts are rushing in like a tidal wave pounding for shore. What if Rowan decides not to meet us after all? What if he refuses to listen, or the station commander won't listen to him? What if they don't fully understand what we're up against? What if the convoy docks with us anyway? The plan seemed like such a good idea, but the more I think about it, the more panicky I start to feel. Something is picking at the back of my mind, like a dog scratching at a door begging to be let in. Something I'm missing, that I've *been* missing this whole time.

A hand touches my shoulder. Teal. "Take an oxygen pill, Lia. It's going to be sat. You'll see."

See.

With that one word, the dam in my mind explodes, blowing apart as the final piece of the puzzle comes rushing back. I know why I was sent here. I know what my mission is.

My heart sinks at the knowledge, and the hope I carried deep inside, the hope that I might somehow find reprieve in the eleventh hour, some way to avoid my fate, flares once and goes out like a dying star going supernova before finally being reduced to a black hole.

I briefly close my eyes. Perhaps Shar was a traitor, but she saw more clearly than all of us. More clearly than even me. Did she see in my mind my final mission? Or did she just know, somehow, with that sixth sense of hers, how everything had to end?

1858. Only two minutes to go.

"Teal, I need you to do me a favor. Once you get to the other side, please get every person you can to the observation decks." I press the data chip into her hand. "Meet Rowan and give him the chip. Get him to help you, tell him I asked him to."

"The observation decks? But why? Where are you going to be?"

"I had it wrong, Teal. This whole time, I thought my purpose was to destroy, but it's not. At least, not primarily."

"Then what—?"

"It's to *reveal*."

Teal frowns, confused.

I try to explain, but my words tumble out one after another, and I can tell from her glazed eyes that she doesn't understand what I'm saying. Finally I just shake my head and say, "Don't worry—you'll understand. Just make sure to be on the observation deck, and you'll see."

"See? See *what*?"

I stare off into the distance, my eyes far away as I remember Niven's words. "Something glorious," I whisper. "More glorious than you could possibly imagine."

The SlipStream whistle sounds. Thirty seconds until the doors will shut.

My feet edge back toward the exit. In the back, Michael is standing up, his face pinched in a frown as he watches Teal and me. Suddenly a high-pitched voice calls, "Lia!"

I whirl around. "Kaeti? What are you doing here? You're supposed to be with the other refugees."

The little girl throws herself through the SlipStream doors at me. "I want to come with you."

I remember the voice I heard on the lift, of someone calling me, and realize it was Kaeti's. She must have escaped her guardians and followed me here. I want so much to keep her on this SlipStream, but I can't. She's one of the refugees; one of the infected.

Or is she? I sniff, but the bloody chunks clogging my nose are too thick to smell out a single Spectre. I flash back to the time Kaeti followed me into the tunnel, and that time Michael and I took her for ice cream in the rings. I don't remember smelling anything on her then. Is it possible the Spectres somehow missed her for some reason? Like Shar, some latent psychic abilities protected her?

No time to deliberate, I go with my gut and thrust her at Teal. "Here, take her! She's clean, I'm sure of it."

Teal automatically pushes the girl toward a seat, even as she shakes her head. "*Lia, no.*"

"I'm sorry, Teal," I whisper. "When this is all over, tell Michael . . ." I pause, unsure how to say what I want to say. Finally, "Tell Michael if I could have stayed, I would have."

Her face crumples at the words, then she throws herself at me in a hug as fierce as it is swift.

For one moment, I hug her back with every bit of strength in my body. Then pulling away, I step off the train.

Just before the doors slide shut behind me.

I turn around and look back through the windows. Michael has figured it out now; I'm not coming with them. He doesn't know my plan; he doesn't know why I'm staying in a hub full of Spectres. Not consciously, maybe. But unconsciously, he knows.

He knows I'm not coming back.

Michael's shoving through the people now, trying to get to the doors, only to be stopped by the corporal, who catches him in an armlock and won't let go.

"Lia! Lia!" he screams through the window. He struggles against the arms holding him, but he's no match for the burly soldier. "No, let me go! My friend is out there! Lia, Lia!"

"Goodbye, Michael," I whisper.

The SlipStream lets out another whistle and the train begins to roll away. Strangely enough, my last vision isn't of Michael's tormented struggles, but of Teal, standing silent and alone at the doors of the train, watching me with solemn eyes as silent tears run slowly down her cheeks.

**33** **I MAKE IT THROUGH** the doors back into the hub just before they lock the SlipStream station down. My chit is vibrating like mad.

Michael.

I can't do it. If I see him now, I'll crumble. Fold in on myself and collapse like a balloon someone has let all the air out of. Sliding the tip of my knife under the edge of the chit, I force the handle down with all my might. Fire shoots through my hand as the chit tears away from the biometal filaments embedded in my nerves. The metal piece pops out of my palm, leaving five tiny pinpricks of blood at the base of my thumb. I ignore the pain and chuck the chit as far away as possible.

Making for the nearest hygiene unit, I dig in my tool belt until my fingers come up with the thing I'm looking for. A piece of wire — extra long, hair thin, and extremely sharp.

Unlike the first time, I don't even hesitate, jamming the wire into my eye almost recklessly until the tip hits my chip.

00:15:00

I hold my breath and wait.

00:14:59

00:14:58

00:14:57

Fifteen minutes. The time feels like a lifetime and a blink of the eye all at once.

Coming out of the hygiene unit, I hear it. A great clang as the metal clamps connecting the spokes to the hub release and retract. I run to the nearest lounge and stare out the observation port. As I watch, the thrusters on the hub begin firing, pulling us up and away.

The rings quickly fall away from us. Michael was right; the thrusters are fast. After all, they were designed to move the hub away from the habitat areas in the case of a power reactor breach in the hub. Teal's idea to run a reactor breach alarm to separate the two was brilliant. Luckily, Michael held on to his dad's old chit instead of throwing it in the 'cycler like he was supposed to. There will probably still be a few infected in the rings, despite our efforts to flush them out. However, once Rowan links with Teal and Michael and sees my memories through them, he'll know what to look for. He may have to use his psychic abilities to check everyone in the rings individually, but unlike the first time he checked in a mob of infected ex-prisoners, this time he'll know what to look for. *In Spectris Intra.*

The Spectres Within.

Before I know it, the rings are out of sight, too far below us to see through the viewport no matter how much I crane my head. I sigh and slump against the viewport.

00:11:14

Eleven minutes to go. My mind feels rolled out and flat, and sparks are dancing madly in both eyes. I wonder what I should do with the last few minutes of my life. I suppose it doesn't really matter. According to Niven, the explosives are so powerful, I don't think it will matter where I am on the station when I go.

I press my face against the port again. I wish I could still see the rings. Maybe I couldn't see Michael through those distant windows, but I could pretend. Pretend that he's there in one of those observation ports, looking back at me even as I gaze at him.

An idea occurs to me. Maybe I *can* have one final look at the rings.

Quickly, I head toward the lift. The station is pretty much empty now, everyone either in the shelters or at their posts. I grab a platform going down, my heart beating a rapid tattoo as the levels pass one by one.

Six. Seven. Eight—my home for so many weeks. Nine. Ten. Eleven—PsyCorp. I once thought they were my biggest enemy, but instead they turned out to be my greatest ally. Twelve, Thirteen.

I jump off on the bottom floor. The level is deserted, and within seconds I am squeezing through the door into the storage space at the bottom of the station. I thread my way through the crates and boxes and throw open the trapdoor. Then without a second thought, I climb the ladder down through the tunnel.

My feet hit the floor of the observation deck with a thud. Glancing around, I gasp in wonder. The velvet cloak of space spreads out around me, so deep and dark it transcends the color black, and in it twinkle the blazing white lights of a million stars. It's so exquisitely beautiful it makes my breath stop. How could I have not seen it before? How could I have looked from these ports without seeing this place for what it is? A vast, blazing, wondrous piece of heaven.

I collapse on my hands and knees and look down through the clear floor. I can barely see through the gold and silver sparks in my eyes, but there are the rings just below us now. My heart is pounding so hard I feel like it will burst from my chest at any moment. Heat begins filling my forearms. I hold my breath, remembering that this is where it all went wrong the last time. If it goes wrong again ...

I feel a pinch in my arms, and suddenly the heat rushes out of them, dispersed into my bloodstream, and now I'm sure. It's done; there will be no malfunction this time. I am going Nova. I check my time.

00:01:03

00:01:02

00:01:01

I'm well past the point where my clock stopped before, and still it's going strong. Completely blind now, I can't see a thing past the mass of bright sparks in my eyes. Warmth rushes through every limb, pushed through my veins by the furious thumping of my heart, and I can imagine those chemicals coming together, only a matter of time before they reach a high enough concentration to react. No, there will be no stopping this time.

To my surprise, tears start to form in my eyes. At first just one or two, and then suddenly my eyes are filled with liquid. A sob escapes my throat. I clap my hand over my mouth, but it can't stop the sob that follows. Or the next, or the next. Realization bursts through me.

I don't want to die!

I cover my face and drop my forehead to the floor, unable to stop weeping. *Oh God, I'm so scared!*

I laugh through my tears as I remember my first countdown. How fearless I was then! Going Nova was my only purpose, and I embraced it with everything I had. Only that was the false Lia, the one with no name, no family, no friends. The real Lia is nothing like her. She's not fearless; she's not brave. She doesn't want to sacrifice her life or save the world. The real Lia is terrified. Terrified and heartsick and alone, and wanting nothing more than to cling to life with every cell in her body.

00:00:26

00:00:25

00:00:24

My body is shaking now from the effort of trying to contain the reaction inside me, and I don't even try to fight it. I'm burning up, energy pulsing off my body in waves as though I was a star itself. I can feel everything in the minutest detail—the hardness of the floor under my knees, the soft flow of the air drifting around me, the coldness of the glass against my forehead.

00:00:09

00:00:08

00:00:07

My parents. Michael, Teal, Taylor, Kaeti, Shar, Rowan, Jao, Cavendish, Niven, everyone I've ever known. They flash through my mind in a million images, sharp-edged and brilliant. Aurora, Tiersten, New Sol. Every moment of my life, happy and sad, flooding my heart until I no longer know if I'm crying from grief or joy. From hope or despair. From the exquisite beauty of it all or the terrible unfairness of it all.

00:00:01

The sparks in my eyes go out, and suddenly the purest, brightest, most brilliant white bursts into my vision. For a brief moment, everything falls away, and all I feel is . . .

Peace.

The peace of a cold mountain lake, enduring through time, clear and deep and still.

Then the final second ticks down, and everything inside of me clenches, compressed together like coal to create a diamond, tighter and tighter and tighter until finally something snaps and then . . .

Nova

UPPER HABITAT RING
– FIVE MINUTES AGO

TEAL STOOD IN THE EAST Observation Deck and watched the crowd. Stationers packed the place from stem to stern, everyone Teal could find and drag along in the short minutes she had after getting off the Slip-Stream. The last-minute announcement Rowan made, calling people to the observation decks, had brought the rest. Now they milled around as much as the space allowed, muttering to themselves and each other, wondering just what was going on. Teal could have told them. *My friend is about to die, that's what's going on.*

She could've, if she'd been able to speak around the huge lump in her throat.

Teal stared out the viewport at the hub, now a hovering shape in the distance. She wished she was anywhere but here. Knowing what was going to happen was bad enough without having to watch it. She had only come because Lia had asked it of her. She thought back to Lia's hurried explanation, trying to make sense of it once again.

"Jao—this resistance commander I knew—said something to me once. He said, 'How do you make someone believe in something you can't see or hear or touch?' Don't you understand, Teal? It's the reason the Alliance fell. The Spectres came—invisible, soundless, incorporeal—and the Tellurians never had a chance. Half the Alliance was infected before anyone even knew what was happening. Even once TelPsy knew, their resistance efforts were limited, since they could only spread the word by linking with people one by one. They needed hard proof; they needed people to see. And that's what we're going to give them."

Teal pressed the back of her hand against her mouth. She still didn't really understand. All she knew was that Lia was going to die. She was going to go Nova right in front of Teal's eyes, and she thought it was going to be glorious, of all things! Even now, Teal couldn't think of those words without choking up. *Glorious?* How could Lia say that, as though her death was nothing more than a spectacle to watch? Teal had this horrible feeling inside, like she wanted to burst into tears, only she *didn't* cry. Not ever.

Except this once.

Swiping surreptitiously at her eyes, Teal checked her watch. Less than a minute to go. Something squeezed inside her chest. She couldn't do this; she had to get out. Pushing away from the viewport, she started to head for the exit, and that's when she saw it.

A light. Shining like a beacon from the very lowest tip of the hub, white and soft and so faint that at first Teal thought she was imagining it. But no, the light was getting brighter.

Teal put her hand on the viewport, drawn against her will to the light growing steadily in the distance. Others had noticed it too, now, and they pressed around her, murmuring as they tried to figure out what it was. Brighter and brighter the light grew, its rays shining out through space like a majestic lighthouse of old, providing safe passage for those adrift at sea. Hope bloomed in Teal's chest as she watched the light. Maybe this is what Lia had meant. Maybe she wasn't really a bomb at all, but something—

The light exploded out in every direction with a boom that could shake the stars. It shot upward into the hub, blowing the lowest floor apart in a maelstrom of debris. Like some avenging angel, beautiful and deadly at once, it continued upward, taking out each level in a succession of fireworks—*Boom! Boom! Boom! Boom!*—one after another, until finally the top level burst apart in a shower of sparks.

Teal shielded her eyes against the light, so brilliant it was almost like looking into the sun. All around her, people were screaming, but she couldn't tear her eyes away from the light. And then, there, within the shards of the hub, a dark shape appeared, and then another, and another, and then the entire space where the station used to be was filled with black shapes. They roiled and frothed within the light, thousands upon thousands of them, their black bodies shimmering with color like slicks of oil, like black rainbows, exquisite and unnatural.

They were the most terrifyingly beautiful things Teal had ever seen.

A hush fell over the deck as everyone stared at the brilliance before them. Then a quiet voice breathed, "My God! What *are* they?"

"Spectres," Teal whispered. "They're called Spectres." Her voice was barely audible, and yet someone heard er. The word spread across the deck, rippled through the air until there wasn't a single tongue it didn't sit upon. Then as they all watched, the dark shapes began dissolving, dissipating into the pool of light surrounding them until the last one was gone. As if absorbing their essences into its own, the light intensified, sparkling with the glow of a million diamonds against the void of space. Then it, too, dimmed and fell away into the dark.

Teal didn't even try to wipe away the tears running freely down her face. She understood now. She understood what Lia had tried to tell her. People needed to see, to *know*. The Spectres had won by lurking in the shadows for three years, taking planets down one by one because few even knew they were there. Not anymore. The ring's instruments would have recorded everything, and just like the people on this observation deck, the rest of the Expanse would finally see. They would know what was coming for them, and they could finally fight back. The blaze of light that Lia had become signified more than simply her death. It signified hope.

Teal just wished Lia had been here to see it for herself.

Casting her gaze out through the viewport, Teal searched that vast blanket of space as though, in one of those brilliant stars, she might find Lia, smiling back at her. *You were right, Lia*, she whispered silently to the blackness. *It* was *glorious.*

It was more glorious than you could have possibly imagined.

ACKNOWLEDGMENTS

To the following people, I tender my warmest regards and sincerest gratitude:

My agent, Lindsay Ribar, and the team at Sanford J. Greenburger Associates. You were worth the wait.

My editor, Betsy Wollheim, and everyone at DAW Books. I'm honored to be a part of the DAW family.

To my writer friends, who have offered invaluable advice, support, and feedback: Joyce Alton, Donald McFatridge, Diana Robicheaux, Carla Rehse, Christine Berman, Anthony Nicholas, Michelle Hauck, and Angie Sandro.

My sister, Wendy Fortune, who is not only my number-one fan, but also came up with the awesome math problem Michael attempts to solve in chapter fifteen.

And of course, my mom and dad. Nurture or nature either way, I guess my writing talents and success are ultimately *your* fault!

Thank you all for making what was a very long and lonely road just a little less long and lonely.

Margaret Fortune

—NOVA—

978-0-7564-1081-0

"*Nova* grabbed me from the first chapter, and never let go. What a ride! Unforgettable, fast-paced and original, this book kept me guessing to the end."

—Amie Kaufman,
New York Times bestselling co-author of *These Broken Stars*

"This book definitely scratched my kick-ass teen heroine itch, and it did it in SPACE. That's a perfect combo if I've seen one."

—Book Riot

And don't miss the thrilling sequel
ARCHANGEL
coming in 2017

CJ Cherryh
The Foreigner Novels

"Serious space opera at its very best by one of the leading SF writers in the field today." —*Publishers Weekly*

"Her world building, aliens, and suspense rank among the strongest in the whole SF field. May those strengths be sustained indefinitely, or at least until the end of *Foreigner*." —*Booklist*

To Order Call: 1-800-788-6262
www.dawbooks.com

DAW 8

C.S. Friedman
The Best in Science Fiction

Julie E. Czerneda
Species Imperative

"This novel bears the hallmarks of Czerneda's earlier books: strong, complex, and appealing characters and a thoughtful, intricate plot. Czerneda creates an original and terrific alien species...and the plot is packed with vivid images and events. Czerneda is a masterful storyteller and one of the best of the recent voices in science fiction."
— *Voya*

SURVIVAL
MIGRATION
REGENERATION

The entire trilogy, now available in a single volume for the first time!

ISBN: 978-0-7564-1014-8

"A creative voice and a distinctive vision."
—*C. J. Cherryh*

To Order Call: 1-800-788-6262
www.dawbooks.com

Tanya Huff

The *Confederation* Novels

"As a heroine, Kerr shines. She is cut from the same mold
as Ellen Ripley of the Aliens films. Like her heroine,
Huff delivers the goods." —*SF Weekly*

A CONFEDERATION OF VALOR
Omnibus Edition
(*Valor's Choice, The Better Part of Valor*)
978-0-7564-1041-4

THE HEART OF VALOR
978-0-7564-0481-9

VALOR'S TRIAL
978-0-7564-0557-1

THE TRUTH OF VALOR
978-0-7564-0684-4

To Order Call: 1-800-788-6262
www.dawbooks.com

DAW 73